Frights and Fancies

By the same author

Novels

The Man from the Bomb
The Dark Man (aka And Love
  Survived)
The Brats: A Novel of the Future
The Partaker: A Novel of Fantasy
The King's Ghost (aka The
  Grange)
The Haunted Grange
The Curse of the Snake God
Kepple
The Psychic Detective
Hell Is What You Make It
World of the Impossible

Novelizations

Dominique
The Awakening

Collections

The Unbidden
Cold Terror
Terror by Night
The Elemental (aka From Beyond
  the Grave)
The Night Ghouls and Other
  Grisly Tales
The Monster Club
Tales of Fear and Fantasy
The Cradle Demon and Other
  Stories of Fantasy and Horror
The Fantastic World of Kamtellar:
  A Book of Vampires and
  Ghouls
Tales of Darkness
Tales from Beyond
Tales from the Other Side (aka
  The Other Side)
A Quiver of Ghosts

Tales from the Dark Lands
Ghosts from the Mist of Time
Tales from the Shadows
Tales from the Haunted House
Dracula's Children
The House of Dracula
Tales from the Hidden World
Shudders and Shivers
Looking for Something to Suck
  and Other Vampire Stories
  (aka the Vampire Stories of
  R. Chetwynd-Hayes)
Shocks
Phantoms and Fiends

Anthologies

Cornish Tales of Terror
Scottish Tales of Terror (as Angus
  Campbell)
Welsh Tales of Terror
The Fontana Book of Great Ghost
  Stories (Volumes 9–20)
Tales of Terror from Outer Space
The Armada Monster Book
  (Volumes 1–6)
Gaslight Tales of Terror
Doomed to the Night

Frights and Fancies

R. Chetwynd-Hayes

Edited with an Introduction by
Stephen Jones

ROBERT HALE · LONDON

ISBN 0 7090 7137 X

Robert Hale Limited
Clerkenwell House
Clerkenwell Green
London EC1R 0HT

2 4 6 8 10 9 7 5 3 1

Typeset in 11/14 pt Baskerville
by Derek Doyle & Associates, Liverpool.
Printed in Great Britain by
St Edmundsbury Press Ltd, Bury St Edmunds, Suffolk.
Bound by Woolnough Bookbinding Limited.

Contents

Foreword: The Final Curtain *Stephen Jones*   11

The Cat Room   19
The Mudadora   33
Ghoul at Large   49
The Third Eye   57
The Floaters   73
The Hoppity-Jump   81
Bongla   101
The Tele-Mon   103
Big-feet   117
Package Holdiay   131
Brownie   137
The Harpy   153
Walk in Darkness   169
The Wind-billie   177
The Slippity-Slop   193
High World   207
Homemade Monster   211
The Great Indestructible   229
The Werewolf   235
The Gale-Wuggle   249

Afterword: Time Travel and Me *R. Chetwynd-Hayes*   267

Acknowledgements

SPECIAL THANKS TO Linda Smith, Edward Miller, Val Edwards, Seamus A. Ryan, Tina Rath, Richard Dalby and Dorothy Lumley for helping make this collection possible.

'Foreword: The Final Curtain' copyright © Stephen Jones 2002 for this collection.

'The Cat Room' copyright © R. Chetwynd-Hayes 1980. Originally published in *The 12th Armada Ghost Book*. Reprinted by permission of the estate of the author and the author's agent.

'The Mudadora' copyright © R. Chetwynd-Hayes 1981. Originally published in *The 6th Armada Monster Book* (as by 'Angus Campbell'). Reprinted by permission of the estate of the author and the author's agent.

'Ghoul at Large' copyright © R. Chetwynd-Hayes 1976. Originally published in *Ghoul* No.1, 1976. Reprinted by permission of the estate of the author and the author's agent.

'The Third Eye' copyright © R. Chetwynd-Hayes 1982. Originally published in *The 14th Armada Ghost Book*. Reprinted by permission of the estate of the author and the author's agent.

'The Hoppity-Jump' copyright © R. Chetwynd-Hayes 1978. Originally published in *The 4th Armada Monster Book*. Reprinted by permission of the estate of the author and the author's agent.

'Bongla' copyright © the estate of R. Chetwynd-Hayes 2002 for this collection.

published in *The 4th Armada Monster Book* (as by 'Angus Campbell'). Reprinted by permission of the estate of the author and the author's agent.

'The Gale-Wuggle' copyright © R. Chetwynd-Hayes 1980. Originally published in *The 6th Armada Monster Book*. Reprinted by permission of the estate of the author and the author's agent.

'Afterword: Time Travel and Me' copyright © the estate of R. Chetwynd-Hayes 2002 for this collection.

Foreword

The Final Curtain

IN A FIELD THAT regularly venerates its dead, living writers are our greatest asset, and for many years one of our greatest assets was Ronald Chetwynd-Hayes. It is therefore all the more regrettable that despite being a two-time Life Achievement Award winner, he never received the commercial rewards for his work that he always dreamed of. Yet for more than forty years, Ronald steadily turned out over 200 short stories and more than a dozen novels, and at one time his collections of ghost stories and humorous horrors filled the shelves of nearly every public library in the United Kingdom.

Ronald Henry Glynn Chetwynd-Hayes was born in Isleworth, west London, on 30 May 1919. He left school in 1933 and for the next six years he worked in a series of 'dead-end jobs', mainly as a butcher's errand boy and in a hardware store. Always a fan of the movies, as a teenager he appeared as an extra in crowd scenes in British films such as *A Yank at Oxford* (1938) and *Goodbye Mr Chips* (1939), as well as several of the *Educated Evans* 'quota quickies', based on the humorous stories

11

by Edgar Wallace and featuring cheeky music-hall comedian Max Miller.

He followed his quartermaster sergeant father into the Army at the start of the Second World War, rising to the 'dizzy rank' (as he described it) of sergeant in the Middlesex Regiment. He was evacuated from Dunkirk, but returned to the beaches of France on D-Day.

Demobbed after the War, writing was the last career he envisaged. Instead he landed a job as a trainee buyer in the furniture section of Harrods, the internationally famous London department store. After four and a half years, he moved to the exclusive Peerless Built-In Furniture emporium in Berkeley Street as showroom manager. During this period he would write in the evenings, once he had finished the day's work.

After selling his first story, 'The Orator', to *The Lady* magazine in 1953, Ronald's first book was *The Man from the Bomb* (1959), a science fiction novel published by the now-legendary Badger Books, who paid the princely sum of twenty-five pounds for the rights. He had to wait until 1964 for his second book to appear. After nineteen rejections from other publishers, Sidgwick & Jackson eventually published his supernatural thriller *The Dark Man* (US title: *And Love Survived*), which the author regarded as one of his finest achievements. He was also genuinely bemused by the fact that copies of the book went on to sell through dealers for much more than the original advance he received.

One day, while looking on a bookstall, he noticed a profusion of horror titles and promptly dashed off his own collection of short stories submitting it to two publishers simultaneously. 'I thought I was clever,' he said. When both publishers accepted the collection just three days later, he chose to go with paperback imprint Tandem.

When Peerless was taken over and he was made redundant in the early 1970s, Ronald became a full-time writer and began producing a prolific number of ghost stories and gentle tales of terror, many tinged with his disarming sense of humour. These

12

have been widely anthologized, and collected in twenty-five volumes, beginning in 1974 with *The Unbidden*.

Like many others of my generation, I began reading Ron's funny and fear-filled stories in Herbert Van Thal's legendary *Pan Book of Horror Stories* and various other paperback collections and anthologies of the time.

Although less prolific as a novelist, he was always aware of how difficult it was to earn a living writing short stories. Consequently, he produced thirteen full-length works. He never planned out his novels beforehand: he would simply sit down at the typewriter, begin writing and see how they turned out.

More than half a dozen of his books featured the haunted mansion of Clavering Grange, dealing with either the building or the tainted ground upon which it stands, and spanning the centuries from Elizabethan times to the far future. He also wrote eight stories and a novel featuring Francis St Clare, 'the world's only practising psychic detective', and his attractive psychic assistant Frederica Masters. For several years the characters were regularly optioned by Hammer Films for either a movie or television series.

Ronald was also an accomplished editor, and he put together a number of exemplary anthologies, including twelve volumes of *The Fontana Book of Great Ghost Stories* (1973-80) and six volumes of *The Armada Monster Book* (1975-80), in which he often included more than one of his own stories under the pseudonyms 'Angus Campbell' or 'Henry Glynn'. He recalled that at one time, in the 1970s he simultaneously had six new books out with his name on them. In 1976 he also ghost-edited and wrote almost all of *Ghoul*, a one-shot magazine from New English Library, billed as 'a ghastly giggle'.

Ronald was also the author of two film novelizations, *Dominique* (1979) and *The Awakening* (1980, based on Bram Stoker's *The Jewel of the Seven Stars*), and his own stories were adapted for the screen in the anthology movies *From Beyond the Grave* (1973) and *The Monster Club* (1980). In the latter, based on probably his most famous and successful book, the author was portrayed by veteran Hollywood actor John Carradine. His work was also extensively adapted for radio (especially in South Africa), and his story 'Housebound' became the basis for 'Something in the Woodwork', a 1973 episode of the television series *Rod Serling's Night Gallery.*

I first began corresponding with Ronald back in 1979 when I was guest-programming a season of fantasy movies at London's National Film Theatre. We were premiering *Dominique,* and I invited him along to the screening. I did not know at the time that he was invariably reluctant to make public appearances, and as a consequence he did not turn up that evening. However, we continued to write to each other, eventually getting together and quickly becoming firm friends despite the age difference between us. We would regularly meet up whenever he did a book signing at specialist London bookstores, or when mutual friends such as authors Karl Edward Wagner and Brian Lumley were in town visiting.

Ron was always full of fascinating stories, and it was a delight to catch up with him in a pub or in one of our homes, where he would keep me entertained for hours with tales of his childhood cameos in British films of the 1930s, his early publishing career, or his meetings on the set of *The Monster Club* with such actors as Vincent Price, who portrayed a 'famished' vampire in the movie. I also managed to convince him to start attending the British Fantasy conventions, where I had the honour of interviewing him about his career in front of an appreciative audience (which could easily have exceeded the couple of hours we had to talk), and where he was rightly celebrated for his body of work.

In 1989, Ronald was presented with Life Achievement awards by both The British Fantasy Society and The Horror Writers of America for his services to the genre. The latter gave the author his only opportunity to travel across the Atlantic, an experience that made almost as much of an impression on him as the accolades of his peers.

14

When I began editing professionally in the late 1980s, it seemed only natural that I would try to include a story by him in as many of my own anthologies as I could. I am proud to have brought some of his earlier stories back into print for new generations to discover, as well as publishing much of his newer work. I also had the opportunity to compile his two previous hardcover collections, both of which sold out of their British printings in a matter of months.

In a field that created such bestselling authors as Stephen King, James Herbert and Clive Barker, Ronald Chetwynd-Hayes continually strived to match their successes, working away in relative obscurity and always concerned about where his next commission would be coming from. Although he struggled to keep his writing tuned to the tastes of the current horror readership, he freely admitted that he did not really fit in and thought that was perhaps one of the reasons why he never successfully broke into the American market. 'They tell me my books are too subtle for the American market,' he lamented.

Apart from a couple of brief forays into the limelight when his stories were adapted for movie audiences, he was read by millions but known only to a few. 'The Victorians were the great ghost story tellers,' he said. 'It was the age of ghosts, wasn't it? Gaslight, that sort of thing . . . But we haven't got it today – what with television and the electric light, the poor ghost doesn't stand a chance.'

There is something almost warmly reassuring about his fiction: it is not simply that — almost singlehandedly — he kept alive the tradition of the typically British ghost story for another generation, but when you dip into one of his collections you are transported back to a more genteel period of fantastic literature. Without doubt, it was this safe familiarity about his work that led to a string of successful hardcover collections published by William Kimber, and later by Robert Hale, aimed almost exclusively at library sales. This popularity led to him appearing regularly in the 'higher earners' section of the Public Lending Rights listings.

*

Although Ronald was always quaintly reluctant to admit his age, it was only in the mid-1990s that it became obvious that his memory was growing progressively more vague. He agreed to be one of the guests of honour at the 1997 World Fantasy Convention in London, even though his health was obviously failing at the time, and I know he enjoyed the event greatly.

Despite being allowed to live on in his own house, where he was looked after by a part-time carer, his condition slowly deteriorated and in early 2000 he was forced to move in to a full-time care home in Teddington, south-west London. Two weeks after a hospital visit for minor surgery, Ronald Chetwynd-Hayes died of bronchial pneumonia on 20 March 2001. He was aged 81.

Although I guess I had expected the news for a year or more, when I heard about his death I reacted to his passing with more emotion than I imagined, and I still miss him greatly. His correspondence and surviving manuscripts were archived in the collection of the Science Fiction Foundation held at the University of Liverpool, where the material will hopefully be made available to future researchers.

Ronald always liked to think that he was writing for posterity, although he never really believed it himself. 'I began writing supernatural fiction because it was the only genre I could break into,' he admitted. 'I could turn them out and everybody accepted them.

'I like to think I write stories for the future. There's just a chance, with hardbacks of short stories, that in a hundred years' time someone putting an anthology together will find one of my old stories on a bookstall and slip it in because there are no copyright problems. I shall never know whether it happens or not.'

Yet perhaps somewhere out there in the 'Hidden World' he wrote about so often, Britain's undisputed 'Prince of Chill' *will* know when it happens. I would certainly like to believe that wherever he is, so long as there are editors to compile volumes of supernatural fiction, and publishers to keep them in print, he knows that his work will never be forgotten.

Stephen Jones
London, England
December, 2001

The Cat Room

WHEN THE GOODRIDGE FAMILY moved into Balaclava Cottage, Sabrina lost no time in exploring the empty rooms, leaving her parents to supervize the furniture removal men, who kept enquiring: 'Where do you want this, ma'am?' and 'Where shall we put the whatnot, ma'am?'

The 'cottage' had six rooms upstairs and six down, a fact that caused Mrs Goodridge grave concern, for she had shaken her head several times and expressed doubt that she could keep such a barn of a place clean.

'My great-uncle managed all right,' Mr Goodridge pointed out, 'and he only had a charlady in three times a week.'

'Yes, and a fine old mess it was, too,' Mrs Goodridge said. 'Still, he left the place to you, and we mustn't look a gift horse in the mouth. Vanman, that sofa goes in the front parlour.'

Sabrina ran up the stairs and began opening doors, peering into bedrooms and trying to decide which one she would like for herself. The large master bedroom would obviously be used by her parents and was, in fact, already fitted with an almost new Axminster carpet, of which her mother was vastly proud. But a much smaller room, situated at the back of the house, had two deep cupboards, a fascinating little iron fireplace and faded wallpaper with a most unusual pattern. It had a yellow background and rows of black cats' heads that ran diagonally across

19

the paper, creating the impression that they had sprung out of the ceiling and were sliding down behind the wainscoting.

Sabrina had never seen wallpaper that had looked even remotely like this and decided that this room must be hers.

'What!' Mr Goodridge was trying to move a sideboard that refused to go against the dining-room wall. 'Those cat-heads will drive you crazy.'

'No, they won't. Daddy, all my life I've wanted a room with cat-heads on the wallpaper. Never – never have I wanted anything so much.'

'Well . . . you'd better ask your mother.'

Mrs Goodridge was watching the removal men with a critical eye as they carried a sofa into the sitting-room and did not view the idea with any great enthusiasm.

'But I wanted you to have the room next to ours. Frankly, that awful wallpaper gives me the shivers. I want your father to strip it off and paint the walls with a nice pink emulsion.'

'But all of my life I've wanted . . .'

'Don't be so silly.'

'*Please.* I'll clean all of the windows once a week if you'll let me have that room.'

Mrs Goodridge flinched when one of the men bumped an armchair against a door-frame.

'Oh, very well. I suppose I'll get no peace until you have your way. But don't blame me if you have horrid dreams.'

Once the 'cat room' – which was Sabrina's own name for her new retreat – was furnished, it did look rather cosy. Her brass bedstead, complete with bright yellow spread, stood against the wall facing the window; bookcases seemed to smile benignly at the wardrobe, which nestled snugly beside the old fireplace recess; and the pretty frills of her dressing-table brightened a dark corner. When the pink-shaded bedside lamp was switched on, all the cat-heads on the walls appeared to grin with unstinted appreciation.

'Not bad.' Mrs Goodridge nodded her reluctant approval. 'But

I'm still not happy about that wallpaper. The old man must have been mad.'

Mr Goodridge grinned and switched on the overhead light.

'Eccentric, maybe. But he was a clever commercial artist. Probably designed that wallpaper himself.'

'Pity he couldn't have found a more useful way of spending his time,' Mrs Goodridge observed caustically. 'Sabrina, wash your hands. Dinner will soon be ready.'

It was two weeks before Balaclava Cottage acquired that 'lived-in' atmosphere which is an absolute necessity before a house can be called a home. During that period extra furniture had to be purchased, fitted carpet laid in the hall and curtains made for most of the windows. Sabrina helped her father cut the grass, pull weeds from the sadly neglected garden and paint the front door a lovely emerald green.

Then the nights began to draw in and the moon grew until it looked like a large ripe orange.

Sabrina woke up suddenly. One moment she was in a deep, dreamless sleep – the next wide awake, every sense alert, trying to determine what it was that had disturbed her. She raised her head and looked across the room. A full moon had transformed the window curtains into a silver screen, made the darkness retreat into corners, created slabs of shadow that lay before the bookcase and wardrobe, and turned the dressing-table mirror into a vast gleaming eye. A night breeze crept in through the partly open window and stirred the curtains, making it seem as if all the cat-heads on the wallpaper were opening and closing their mouths, as though sending out silent cries.

Then Sabrina heard the sound.

A low growl. She felt an icy wave of fear creep up from her feet and create chilly butterflies in her stomach, as she sat up and fumbled for the bedside lamp switch. Light exploded and shattered the silver gloom, sent out a pink-tinted radiance that formed a rough circle round the bed and was reflected in the wardrobe mirror.

The growl was repeated, only now it came from the region of the dressing-table. Sabrina strained her eyes, anxious to discover what caused this alarming noise, but at the same time terrified of what she might see. Suddenly she became aware of two little spots of yellow light that came round from behind the dressing-table and advanced into the room. Sabrina's hand flew to her mouth and she choked back a scream as an extremely large cat emerged into the circle of pink light. She had never seen such a cat before: long black fur that stood on end, ears laid back flat on either side of the round head, an open mouth that revealed long, pointed teeth, and eyes that glittered like polished amber discs. A long tail lashed from side to side.

The cat crept slowly forward, crouched low so that its stomach brushed the carpet. It stopped on reaching a position to the left of Sabrina's bed and looked up at her with hate-filled eyes. The growl rose to a terrifying howl. Sabrina, more frightened than at any time in her life, said the first words that came into her head.

'Nice puss . . . mice . . . milk . . .'

The sound of her voice seemed partially to reassure the cat, for the pointed ears made an attempt to become upright, the tail ceased its angry lashing and the eyes blinked. Then, as though ashamed of a momentary weakness, the black cat turned, went back on to its hindquarters and jumped towards the mantelpiece.

It disappeared in mid-air.

After a few moments spent in trying to come to terms with this alarming phenomenon, Sabrina remembered her voice again – and screamed.

'That awful wallpaper!' Mrs Goodridge exclaimed for the seventh time. 'I knew it would give her nightmares, but no one paid any attention to me. It doesn't take an ounce of commonsense to know that rows of cats' heads will do something to a child's mind.'

'But, Mummy,' Sabrina insisted, 'it wasn't a dream. The black cat was really there. And it did disappear.'

Mr Goodridge of course did his best to be practical and line up a number of indisputable facts in a neat row.

'Now,' he said heartily, 'let's put on our thinking caps. First, we haven't got a cat. Secondly, all the doors were locked, and the windows – was your window open, Sabrina?'

'Only a tiny bit,' said Sabrina. 'I don't think a kitten could have got in, let alone such a monster cat. It was huge!'

'Thirdly, then,' went on Mr Goodridge, 'even if a cat did manage somehow to get in, it couldn't possibly have disappeared in mid-air. Therefore you must have had a nasty dream. I remember once dreaming about a donkey . . .'

'But it could have been a ghost-cat,' Sabrina pointed out. 'A very unhappy ghost-cat.'

Mrs Goodridge sat down and gave the impression she would faint, if given the least encouragement.

'Did you hear, Clarence? The poor child's deranged! A ghost-cat! She thinks the place is haunted!'

'A fertile imagination, my dear,' said Mr Goodridge comfortingly. 'Takes after my side of the family, I shouldn't wonder. Now, I propose that Sabrina spends the rest of the night in one of the spare rooms and we all try to get some sleep. Tomorrow we can decide what's to be done.'

'It wasn't a dream and it wasn't imagination!' Sabrina announced angrily, exasperated – not for the first time – by the gross stupidity that is so often displayed by even the nicest of adults. 'I saw a ghost-cat, and I believe there's a reason why it's haunting that room.'

Next morning, Mrs Coggins arrived. She was tall and thin and wore a faded overall and plimsolls. She nodded her head in Mrs Goodridge's direction.

'I used to come and oblige for the old gentleman, madam, and I wondered if I could come and oblige you.'

Mrs Goodridge patted her forehead with a lace handkerchief. 'Oblige? I don't understand.'

'Do for him, madam. Do the housework, like. Me charges are quite moderate, and if you asks me to have a 'ot dinner, I won't say no.'

'It might be a good idea,' Mr Goodridge suggested, 'as this house is much larger than our old one. And if this good lady could char . . .'

'Oblige,' Mrs Coggins corrected.

'Yes, quite . . . oblige for a few hours a week, it would make things easier for you.'

Mrs Goodridge waved her handkerchief as a gesture depicting temporary helplessness.

'I'm certainly fit for nothing after last night. Let her remain by all means. Can she cook?'

Mrs Coggins frowned and drew herself upright.

'The name is Coggins, madam, and I can cook. Nothing fancy, but good wholesome fare such as the old gentleman found to his liking. If you feel poorly, just go upstairs and lie down and leave everything to me. I prefers not to have any interference.'

'I'm not at all certain . . .' Mrs Goodridge began, but her husband took her firmly by one arm and propelled her towards the stairs.

'Don't worry, dear. I'm sure Mrs Coggins will manage nicely, and Sabrina can make herself useful with the washing-up and so forth.'

With some reluctance, Mrs Goodridge allowed herself to be led upstairs, and Sabrina, who suddenly realized that she now had a source of information regarding her great-great-uncle – and even, possibly, the ghost-cat as well – carried a pile of plates into the kitchen, then grabbed a wiping-up towel.

'You show willing, I'll say that for you,' Mrs Coggins remarked, rolling up her sleeves. 'Which is more than can be said for most kids these days. Mind you don't break any of your mother's china.'

For a while Sabrina busied herself with wiping plates and piling them on to the dresser. Then she asked:

'Did you work for my great-great-uncle for long?'

Mrs Coggins nodded. 'Yus, I obliged the old gentleman for nigh on ten years.'

'Was . . . was he a strange man?'

'I don't know about strange. He kept himself to himself, which I didn't hold against him.'

'Did he ever have a cat?'

'Not that I'm aware of. Of course there was that room that he'd never let me into, and I suppose he could have kept a cat in there. Certainly I once caught a glimpse of that outlandish wallpaper, and that must mean he liked 'em. Still – what's the harm? Lots of people like cats.'

'I do agree,' Sabrina hastened to reassure the old woman. 'I like them myself.'

Mrs Coggins placed a kettle on the gas stove.

'Mind you, there's them that say things went on in this house, that weren't right or proper for a honest Christian, but I never saw anything out of the way.'

Sabrina curbed a wave of excitement and waited until all of the china had been placed in the dresser before she spoke again.

'What sort of things – these things that went on?'

Mrs Coggins poured boiling water into a brown earthenware pot, then emptied it into the sink.

'Remember – always heat the pot. What sort of things? None that need concern you. Warlock, indeed!'

'What's a warlock?' Sabrina asked.

'A man witch. Stuff and nonsense! Now, let's have a nice cup of tea and don't you go asking me any more questions. I've got work to do.'

Sabrina decided that no more information could be obtained from the old woman and presently made her way to the small room that Mr Goodridge had commandeered as a study. She removed a large dictionary from the bookcase and turned the pages over until she found the word *Warlock*.

'A wizard, sorcerer, magician,' she read aloud. 'A man in league with, or under the influence of, evil spirits; male follower of the Black Art. A familiar in the shape of a black cat was said to relay orders from the devil to the warlock or witch.'

Sabrina closed the dictionary and leaned back in her father's swivel chair. The prospect that her bedroom was haunted by a ghost-cat that acted as messenger boy for the Devil was an exceedingly frightening one, but – when considered in broad daylight – rather exciting. However, if her great-great-uncle had been a warlock, she was certain the black cat had performed his Satanic duties with great reluctance and now wanted to be set free, so he could go to wherever cats go when they die. She didn't know how she knew this – it was just something she felt sure about. After some rather fearful deliberation, Sabrina came to a heart-thumping decision. She was going to have a shot at laying the ghost-cat.

At two o'clock next morning – an hour when it was reasonable to suppose her parents were fast asleep – Sabrina crept over the dark landing, opened the door of the haunted room, then, after switching on the ceiling lamp, closed the door carefully behind her. The room still looked as cosy and unhaunted as anyone could wish for, and the girl began to wonder if her terrifying experience, had, after all, been nothing more than an exceptionally vivid dream. Then she remembered the upright fur, the glaring eyes, and knew she had been fully awake, and no amount of self-deception could alter the fact. But how did one set about laying a ghost-cat?

Sabrina sat on her bed and gave the matter full consideration. Surely the first question that demanded an answer was what made the cat appear? There was certainly no sign of it at present, which suggested that either the conditions were not favourable, or the apparition only appeared at a certain time. Sabrina tried to remember everything that had happened prior to hearing that terrifying growl. She had woken up and found the room bathed in moonlight, then she had switched on the bedside lamp. But . . . but the window had been slightly open, and the breeze was disturbing the curtains . . . and all the cat-heads on the wallpaper seemed to be opening and closing their mouths. Sabrina gulped and tried very hard not to be frightened.

The wallpaper . . . the wallpaper was the key! No wonder she had thought it to be so enthralling. Moonlight . . . waving curtains . . . dancing shadows . . . all doing something horrible to the wallpaper.

'Gosh!' Sabrina whispered, astonished at a thought that had just come to her. 'Maybe there never was a real cat at all! Perhaps it's a sort of extension of my great-great-uncle.'

She sat for some time looking at the wallpaper, and now it did appear to be very sinister indeed. Every cat-head seemed to have acquired yellow, glaring eyes, each open mouth gave the impression that it might produce a growl at any moment, and all appeared to be three-dimensional – straining to get off the wallpaper. Sabrina spoke again, deriving some small comfort from the sound of her own voice.

'I don't really want to – I'll be scared silly – but I must know.'

She got up and switched off the overhead lamp, then walked over to the window and opened it a fraction. The moon – as though waiting for such a signal – obligingly slid from behind a cloud and bathed the room in silver light. Sabrina slowly turned round and took up a position against the left-hand wall. The curtains stirred and cast flimsy shadows over the wallpaper. Instantly, the cat-heads opened their mouths, while their eyes glittered like flickering stars on a frosty night.

Then, from behind the dressing-table came a distinct low growl, and the black cat crept into view, looking even larger and more ferocious than Sabrina remembered. It came forward with stomach brushing the carpet, ears laid back, fur standing on end, and stopped a few feet from the trembling girl.

The head went back, the immense eyes became pools of yellow fire, and the humped shoulders quivered as though the creature

27

was about to leap. Suddenly the door opened, and Mr Goodridge, attired in a flower-patterned dressing-gown, entered. He said: 'I thought as much . . .' then stopped, his eyes bulging when the ghost-cat spun round with one swift movement and faced the intruder. Sabrina did her best to speak calmly. 'Daddy, please turn the light on – quickly.'

'What . . . what in the name of sanity is it?'

'The ghost-cat. Please turn on the light, then I think it will jump towards the mantelpiece and disappear.'

Mr Goodridge took what seemed to be a long time fumbling for the light switch, but finally the lamp sprang into life, smothering the moonlight under a soft pink glow. Immediately the black cat turned and raced around the bed with incredible speed. When it reached the hearth-rug, it went back on its haunches, leapt towards the mantel-shelf and vanished in mid-air.

For the space of several second's neither father nor daughter spoke, then Mr Goodridge whispered: 'Thank God your mother's not awake. But I couldn't sleep, and I heard you creeping across the landing. A ghost-cat! Great heavens!'

Sabrina, whose courage had now revived, closed the window, then said: 'I think it's not only the wallpaper, but something behind the chimney breast. I mean, why else should the ghost-cat jump towards it and disappear?'

Mr Goodridge gave the fireplace an apprehensive glance.

'Don't ask me. I never reckoned on anything like this when I took the house over. What your mother will say when she finds out there really is a ghost-cat doesn't bear thinking about. Want to move, I shouldn't wonder.'

'If,' Sabrina said slyly, 'we were to clear the matter up tonight, she need never know. Let's examine that fireplace and see what we can find out.'

Her father looked anxiously around the room.

'I suppose there's no chance of that thing coming back? I don't think I could face it again.'

Sabrina crossed her fingers and gave what she hoped was the correct reply.

'No, of course not. One appearance a night is all it has – has strength for. Now, let's look at the fireplace.'

It was she who bent down and put her head into the opening and peered up the chimney. One thing was certain, a fire could never be lit in the grate, for the chimney had been bricked up, and, if the newness of the brickwork was anything to go by, quite recently, too.

She straightened up and ran an exploring hand over the chimney-breast. The surface was smooth, but when she tapped the wall there was a hollow sound in an area about one foot square, just above the shelf.

'I knew I was. right,' she informed a still very disturbed Mr Goodridge. 'There's a small cupboard built into the chimney space. If you were to get a hammer and chisel, we could have it open in no time.'

'Perhaps tomorrow morning,' her father suggested.

'When mummy will want to know what you are doing?'

'I won't be a moment. My tool kit is in one of the spare rooms.'

While she was waiting, Sabrina tore away a strip of the wallpaper.

A shudder seemed to run round the entire room, and she jumped back. Zig-zag cracks appeared on all four walls, and the cat-heads began to fade. Presently, they took on the appearance of grey splodges. From behind the chimney-breast, Sabrina heard the distinct sound of a long-drawn-out sigh.

Mr Goodridge returned, carrying a large tool bag. He stopped just inside of the door and looked around in amazement.

'What's happened to that awful wallpaper?'

Sabrina gave what she thought was a feasible answer. 'I tore some and sort of wounded the room. Well – that's the only way I can describe it. Look – there's a plain wooden panel here. All you've got to do is prise it out – then we'll see.'

The panel surrendered after Mr Goodridge had given it a few quiet taps with his hammer and chisel; it came away with a sharp, cracking sound – and revealed a dark recess. Mr Goodridge after some hesitation – slid his right hand into the recess and brought out a small object: a grotesque image of the ghost-cat, complete with black fur and glittering eyes that seemed to be alive with hate or fear. He examined it with lively interest.

'It's quite heavy. I'd say bear skin over plaster. Let's see what else there is.'

He reached into the opening again and this time produced a roll of parchment, which he carried over to the dressing-table and laid out flat. Sabrina looked over her father's shoulder and read the following script, which had been written with a broad-nibbed pen and red ink. At least, she hoped it was red ink.

Extract from
'Unnatural Enmities and Their Retainment'
by
Conrad Von Holstein

Make ye an image in the likeness of Ye Black Cat of Set *and place it in a confined space. Then prepare a room with the same likeness depicted on all walls from floor to ceiling, each likeness to be not less than one hand's breadth from the next, all the while chanting the incantations prepared by the immortal Macradotus. Thus shall ye — when the time be right — be given power such as few men enjoy, and whatsoever wordly goods ye desire shall be yours. But be warned. Should death creep upon ye unawares, and the image be not destroyed, then shall ye walk the night hours on four feet, until that thing is done which ye left undone.*

Mr Goodridge took one long look at the open recess, the cracked wallpaper that was now beginning to peel from the walls, and finally at the cat image that lay on the bed. He sighed and said:

'Well, I guess I'll do that which was left undone. This cat thing and the piece of paper are going into the boiler right now. And let's hope that's the end of the ghost-cat.'

It was. And before long the 'cat room' became the 'pink room', when Mr Goodridge gave the walls several coats of rose-coloured emulsion.

'Very nice, Clarence,' said Mrs Goodridge. 'And much more suitable than cats, Sabrina, don't you think?'

The Mudadora

*F*AR AWAY, IN THE *midst of a dense forest, a skeleton lay half buried under a pile of decaying leaves. How it came to be there, no one will ever know, but it is reasonable to suppose that some poor weary traveller, hopelessly lost in that vast labyrinth of trees, sank down and died through hunger and exhaustion.*

Every year the north wind came howling through naked branches, chasing the dead leaves, sometimes uncovering the grinning skull, at others burying it deeper, until finally, after the lapse of many centuries, all that remained was a long mound of bracken-covered compost.

Rain turned earth into mud; sunlight seeped through the forest roof and gave life to primroses and bluebells, which lived out their brief existence in the warm, humid air – then died.

But the sun gradually gave life to something else that did not die.

Deep down under the compost, mud filled the rib cage and skull, formed a thick coating over legs and arms, gained substance from tiny fibrous roots that wormed their way in through fossilised bones and – aided by the sun's warmth – slowly, but so very surely, became a reservoir of seething, primitive life.

One day a long crack went shuddering across the mound; it widened, deepened, became a shallow trench from which a colony of ants poured like terrified citizens from a doomed city. Then it erupted, became a gaping hole, and a monstrous head that glittered with a strange, green, luminous light, came up from the dank, steaming earth. For a while – like a sleeper newly awake – it remained motionless. Then there was a grotesque heaving and a mighty rending sound, as though a million tiny roots were being torn from a long-filled grave. Suddenly IT stood upright – a squat, terri-fying figure that rightfully belonged to a half-forgotten nightmare.

There was a rough semblance of legs and arms, but the hands and feet were no more than irregular blobs of congealed mud. Ragged root ends gave the impression that the creature was covered with coarse hair, while the head appeared to be crowned by a damp, matted wig.

Presently it took one faltering step forward – then another – and grad-ually advanced across the forest floor.

Over the years, this earth-born creature was sometimes seen by charcoal burners, or men whose business took them into wild and lonely places, and they, to a man, ran faster than ever before in their lives. They spoke with hushed voices of what they had seen; and many an embellished story was told round a cottage fireplace, or in the smoke-dimmed bar of a country inn. Gradually this thing of bone, mud and broken roots acquired a name.

It was THE MUDADORA . . .

'Rosevine' was not a beautiful cottage, or even a picturesque one, being merely a square building with two windows up and two down and a green door in the centre. A once white picket fence was broken by a lopsided gate, which opened on to a cracked cement path that was flanked on either side by an expanse of weed-filled garden. Beyond, like a green and black curtain, was the southernmost fringe of the forest; a great army of trees that curved round into a vast arc, as though preparing to encircle the cottage and eventually bury it under a mass of towering trunks and interwoven branches.

'Well, what do you think of our little retreat?' Mr Carstairs enquired. 'Nice and secluded, eh?' Raymond Carstairs looked first at the looming wall of trees, then wistfully back along the dusty road that led to the distant village.

'Yes, Grandfather,' he said. 'It's certainly secluded.'

'Just the place for a boy to spend a long summer holiday,' his grandmother declared. 'I can't think how you can stand living in a town with all that noise and smoke.'

'No smoke here,' Mr Carstairs said, picking up Raymond's case and leading the way into the cottage. 'And not much noise either. Only good country sounds, like bird song and the wind whistling through the trees.'

Once in the house, Raymond examined the heavy oak sideboard, the well-worn padded chairs and whitewashed walls, with critical interest. He decided the cottage was not only secluded, but primitive as well, and thought wistfully of his parents' comfortable house back in Wolverhampton. Mr Carstairs waited until his wife had retired to the kitchen, then motioned the boy to a chair.

'Now, I understand from your father that you've an important examination to pass next term and he thinks that this is an ideal place for concentration. No distractions and so forth. So I hope you'll work hard, but find time for long walks which will benefit your body and mind.'

Raymond thought his grandfather was a bit of a windbag, but nevertheless meant well. So he said politely: 'It is very kind of you and Grandma to have me. I will try not to be a nuisance.'

Mr Carstairs shook his head in protest.

'You'll never be a nuisance. Quite the contrary. But there is one thing I'd better mention. Don't go wandering off into the forest after sunset. Apart from getting lost, there's always the chance of some wild animal on the prowl after dark.'

Raymond experienced the first flicker of interest since he had arrived at Rosevine Cottage. 'Wild, animal! Here in England?'

The old man shrugged. 'I'm not saying there is, but I've heard strange sounds coming from the forest some nights. A sort of coughing bark and once a terrible scream. Don't forget it's less than a hundred years since the last wolf was killed in these parts.'

Raymond shot an excited glance out of the window and saw the giant trees nodding their green heads. 'Gosh, a wolf? Do you suppose there are still some left?'

Mr Carstairs rose from his chair. 'Most unlikely, but there's certainly something out there, although exactly, what, I would not care to say. Now, I expect your grandmother has dinner ready. A nice hotpot.'

*

Raymond undressed by moonlight. This was made possible by the uncurtained window and a full moon, which flooded the room with silver light and would have enabled him to read a book had he been so inclined. It also turned the unkempt back garden and adjacent forest trees into a glorious wonderland where shimmering leaves and shadow-shrouded trunks seemed to rear up from a delicate green sea.

Raymond climbed into bed, pulled the bedclothes up to his chin and pondered on the possibility of getting some sleep. Apart from the brightly-lit room, a series of disturbing sounds did little to enhance the prospect of a restful night. An owl insisted on sending out a mournful hooting noise at irregular intervals; then there was an occasional, peculiar, whirring cry that may have proclaimed the hunting activities of a nightjar, plus the eerie howl of a wild cat.

Once, Raymond sat up in bed as a black fluttering shadow passed over the right-hand wall, and it was some time before he realized it had been caused by a bat flying past his window. He muttered: 'If this is the peaceful countryside, give me Wolverhampton,' and buried his head under the bedclothes.

He eventually fell asleep; sank down into a dimly-lit dream valley, where black shapeless figures perched on mountain slopes and howled, hooted and screamed a frightful chorus. Then there was one scream that was much louder than the others, an awful shriek of mortal terror. Raymond struggled up from his cocoon of sheets and blankets, sat upright, and stared with dilated eyes at the gleaming window.

The scream rang out again. High-pitched, drawn-out – it came from somewhere just below the window; probably in the garden or on the edge of the forest. Although Raymond was not at all keen to see what was making such a dreadful sound, curiosity made him climb out of bed and walk very slowly towards the window.

The moon had moved a little to the east, but it still highlighted the garden and the encroaching forest. At first, Raymond saw nothing unusual; the summer grass trembling beneath the wind's gentle caress, the softly murmuring trees, the tumultous shadows – the swift passing of a night bird. Then a small shape scurried out from the forest and came to an abrupt halt just below his window.

It was a hare. The long ears stood erect, the grey and white body was so still it might have been carved from stone, and the eyes glittered in the moonlight like fire-flecked rubies. For a while it seemed as if the night was holding its breath. Then, from the dense shadow cast by a giant oak tree, came the sound of – and this was the only description that Raymond could bring to mind – a bubbling cough. He flattened his nose against the window-pane and, by straining his eyes, could just make out a black shape that was barely discernible against the massive tree trunk. The hare turned very slowly and began to crawl back across the garden, moving in a straight line towards that hulking dark mass. It screamed twice more, and Raymond, who could not bear to see animals suffer, pulled up the lower sash of his window and shouted: 'Run . . . run . . . run!'

The sound of his voice must have broken the spell, for the hare stopped, jerked its head round, then streaked obliquely over the garden and disappeared into the forest. But Raymond felt a thrill of apprehension run down his spine when he became aware of unseen eyes watching him from the dense shadow under the oak tree; the black bulk had not moved, but it did seem as if a head was raised as though it were examining a rash intruder who had cheated a hungry hunter of its chosen prey.

The bedroom door opened and Mr Carstairs entered the room. He was wearing a thick dressing-gown and tasselled night-cap and looked suddenly very old and frightened.

'What's the matter, my boy?' he asked. 'I heard you call out.'

Raymond spoke over one shoulder. 'There's something under a tree. I can't see it very clearly.'

His grandfather shuffled with marked reluctance towards the window, then narrowed his eyes and peered down into the moon-lit garden.

'I can't see anything. Are you sure you actually saw something?'

'Absolutely positive,' Raymond replied with a certain amount of impatience. 'Look – over there – under that tree . . .'

He stopped and narrowed *his* eyes, for at that moment a small cloud passed over the moon and it became exceedingly difficult to see if, in fact, there was anything unusual under the trees. Mr Carstairs drew him gently from the window, then led him towards the bed.

'Sit down, my boy, and listen to me. In a lonely place like this it is so easy to be misled by imagination. Maybe I should not have mentioned that I heard strange sounds coming from the forest . . .'

'A bubbling cough,' Raymond interrupted: 'I heard it myself.'

'No doubt you did. And I am certain there is a natural explanation for it. Possibly some wild animal, or maybe a poor mad creature that lives out a precarious existence in the forest. But you must not worry about what you hear, or imagine you see. Just go to sleep and dream of beings that walk upright under the noonday sun.'

'But the moonlight,' Raymond protested. 'It's so difficult to sleep.'

Mr Carstairs stared at the naked window, then shook his head in self-reproach. 'Of course, how careless of me! I will drape a blanket over the pelmet board, and tomorrow I'll get your grandmother to dig out some nice thick curtains.'

The old man took a folded blanket from a drawer in the dressing-table and, assisted by Raymond, hung it over the window. Then he lit a candle, and suddenly the room was an amber-tinted refuge; a haven where sleep was a soft-footed friend, and one need not think about a black motionless something that stood under an oak tree and made a hare scream with terror.

Mr Carstairs smiled down at his grandson.

'Good night,' he said softly. 'Sleep well.'

Raymond was awakened by bird song.

He jumped out of bed, pulled the blanket from the window

and looked out upon a world that was bathed in sunlight. Gone were the nasty shadows, the eerie, shuddering movement that is peculiar to even the most beautiful moonlit scene. Neither was there the slightes suggestion of a black shape under the oak tree.

Now the forest appeared to be celebrating the birth of a new day. Branches trembled as though with gentle merriment, leaves applauded the antics of a passing breeze, dandelions nodded their golden heads, and two white butterflies chased each other with thoughtless abandon round a clump of harebells.

Raymond washed and dressed, then ran downstairs, there to be welcomed by the smell of frying eggs and bacon, and the sight of his grandmother's beaming face as she spread a snow-white cloth over the table.

'Did you sleep well?' she asked.

'Yes . . . yes, very well, thank you.'

'I was sure you would. Nothing like the peace and quiet of the countryside to make you sleep. Now, sit you down, while I call your grandfather. He's messing about in that shed of his.'

But on this particular morning, Mr Carstairs required no prompting, for he came in through the open kitchen doorway and, after sniffing in a most appreciative manner, exlaimed: 'That smells good, Martha! I'm that hungry, I could eat a bull – horns and all.'

The day started well.

Once breakfast was over and Raymond had helped to wash up and put all the crockery away in the oak dresser, Mr Carstairs looked out of the window and said: 'Now I know you must get down to your studies, lad, but what do you say to a nice walk first? Aye? Just to set you up for the day?'

Raymond agreed that this would be very nice, so they both set out, equipped with stout walking sticks and a parcel of ham sand-wiches, for Mrs Carstairs maintained they were bound to get hungry and lunch was hours away. Pine needles crunched under their feet; interlocked branches overhead created the impression that the forest was one vast cathedral, where the wind did duty as an organ, and a congregation of birds sang a never-ending song of praise. Sometimes a squirrel sped across the forest floor, then raced halfway up a tree unk, where it paused and watched the passers-by with bright, inquisitive eyes.

'I like to think,' Mr Carstairs said, 'that the forest is a neat store-house of primitive life. Birds, animals, insects, every kind of plant imaginable – heavens above knows what is taking place in those trees or under this carpet of dead leaves.'

Raymond had not forgotten what *had* taken place the night before.

'You don't suppose we'll meet – whatever it was that made that awful noise last night?'

Mr Carstairs struck at a pine-cone with his walking-stick.

'No – otherwise I would never have brought you out here this morning. The forest during the dark hours is a different place to the one we see now. It is then that the night citizens come out. The fox, screech-owl, nightjar and other creatures that do not love the sunlight. There's a man I would like you to meet. He's a strange body and lives all alone in a small cottage that has been the property of his family for generations.'

Some half an hour later found them entering a long, wide dell, where a tiny, stone-walled cottage stood in the centre of a circular clearing. It was only one storey high, with a solitary window and a stout oak door, and appeared – so Raymond thought – to be the kind of place that might well house a warlock or witch. Then he saw round stacks of wood which gave out perpetual plumes of smoke, and assumed that the occupant of this woodland cottage was a charcoal-burner.

Suddenly the door opened and a little, bowed-shouldered man ambled out on to the doorstep and welcomed Mr Carstairs with a gap-toothed grin.

'Good morning to yer, Squire. See's you've brought a young 'un with yer.'

'Morning Jasper. This is my grandson, Raymond,' Mr Carstairs said. 'He's down here for the summer holidays. Thought he might like to see how a real woodsman lives.'

The little man pulled his leather jerkin tighter about his muscular body, then stepped to one side.

'Well, if you'd care to step inside, I'll make a cup of summat 'ot. The sun ain't 'ad time to warm the glades as yet, and there be a nip in the air.'

Raymond discovered that the cottage only had one room, but this was a delightful place which had not been spoilt by broom, brush or duster. The stone floor was covered with dead leaves, a pile of old rags lay in one corner, and bunches of dried herbs hung from the rafters. A table, a narrow bed and a plain wooden chair, were the only furniture worth mentioning, but a magnificent collection of stuffed birds, squirrels, badgers and one evil-looking snake, more than compensated for this lack of comfort.

Jasper brushed dust from the chair with the sleeve of his jerkin, waited politely for Mr Carstairs to seat himself, then motioned Raymond to the bed.

'Sit you down there, young 'un. That's right. Now I'll brew some 'erb tea. Put 'airs on yer chest, it will.'

He placed a soot-coated pot on the antiquated stove, then gave three earthenware mugs a perfunctory rub with a filthy piece of rag.

'You keeping well, Jasper?' Mr Carstairs asked.

The little man tipped some greenish substance from a tin into a teapot. 'Mustn't grumble. Few twinges when the north wind comes a-blowing along the glades.'

Raymond cleared his throat. 'Do you really live here all by yourself?'

Jasper chuckled. 'Can't think of a better person to be with, young 'un. Meself don't open the door after sunset, or forget to put up the winter shutter. All being said and done, meself is a pretty reliable chap.'

He poured boiling water into the teapot, then nodded with evident satisfaction while Raymond asked a very mportant question.

'Why . . . why wouldn't you want the door opened after sunset?'

41

Jasper chuckled again, then poured dark green liquid from the teapot into the three mugs. 'Why wouldn't I want the door opened after sunset? he says! Listen to me young 'un. There's things that walk the forest glades at night that would make yer 'air stand on end. Many's a time I've seen chaps in lincoln green a-prancing about in moonlight, and it ain't bothered me none when I could look right through 'em. Then there's the Gale-Wuggle that sort of sinks down through the trees and crouches out there, a-glaring at me winder and daring me to go out. But I be too fly for that. Aye.'

Raymond said: 'Gosh!' and sipped the hot, mint-flavoured liquid from his mug. Jasper sank down beside him and poked a dirty forefinger into his stomach.

'But there be some things it bain't be good to look upon. Tell me, young 'un. You ever 'eard tell of the Mudadora?'

Raymond shook his head. 'No. Never.'

'Aye, it not be much of a ed-u-ca-tion they be giving at them fancy schools. A mighty greet thing, it be. Made from long-dead bones and mud and roots, with green, a-terribly gleaming eyes, and it be powerful hungry. Aye, that it be.'

Mr Carstairs rose hurriedly from his chair. 'I think we had better be pressing on, Jasper . . .'

The little man turned abruptly in his direction. 'Like all the rest, yer are. Not wanting to know what gives a bubbling cry in the night. If it 'adn't be for me putting a bit of summat out for it to eat – a couple of ripe rabbits, an 'aunch of dripping venison – it would 'ave been peering in through yer winder long since.'

'Yes – well . . .' Mr Carstairs put his mug down on to the table. 'I'm sure we're grateful to you, Jasper. But we really mustn't take up any more of your valuable time. Come along, Raymond.'

Raymond was not at all sorry to vacate his seat on the bed, and adroitly avoided Jasper's clutching hand that endeavoured to hold him back as they went through the open doorway. The little man shouted after them: 'You ought to listen. Game be getting pretty scarce these days, and it be coming out some dark night . . .'

Mr Carstairs grabbed Raymond's arm and pulled him towards the narrow, homeward path.

'Thank you very much, Jasper. We'll call again.'

Raymond had not realised that his grandfather could walk so fast, for he all but ran along the path and did not stop until the cottage was hidden by a large clump of trees.

'Really,' he said rather breathlessly. 'I had not realised the poor fellow was quite like that. Living all alone out here has driven him potty. No other word for it – potty.'

'Then you don't think there's such a creature as the – the Mudadora?'

His grandfather tried to laugh, but did not quite make it.

'Of course not. Pure superstition. Mind you, I'm not saying there isn't something very strange that wanders around here at night. But – what was it? – mud an bones? No – it can't be.'

But Raymond noticed that the old man said very little for the rest of their homeward journey and steadfastly refused to answer any further questions on the subject.

The day passed, and night once again stretched out its arms over forest and countryside. Raymond saw arrow-shaped formations of birds winging their way across the sky, as he sat by his bedroom window, vainly trying to study, and seemed to remember that this was said to be an omen of a pending storm. Then his grandfather entered the room carrying a lighted oil lamp, and it was time to draw the recently hung curtains; once again creating an amber-tinted haven that was far removed from the sighing forest and the deepening gloom.

'Supper will be ready in no time at all,' Mr Carstairs promised. 'How are you progressing with your holiday task?'

'So and so.' Raymond was unwilling to admit he had hardly done anything at all. 'I've sort of got to grips with it.'

'Good boy. By the way, I'm pleased you didn't mention Jasper's nonsense to your grandmother. Lately she's inclined to be a bit nervous after nightfall. And I don't want her made worse by talk of this Muddy . . . Mud . . .'

43

'Mudadora,' Raymond prompted.

'Ah, yes, indeed. So long as we're shut up nice and snug in here, there's no need to worry about such things – is there?'

Suddenly Raymond realised that his grandfather was frightened. Although he was prepared to laugh at Jasper's warning, dismiss it as the ravings of a near madman, nevertheless he knew there was something – perhaps a dreadful something – walking the forest glades at night. A creature that might even now, be lurking a few metres beyond the back garden.

'Of course, there's nothing to worry us,' he said cheerfully. 'No wild animal could get in here.'

'That's right, my boy. Haven't I always said it was some kind of wild beast that makes those horrible noises?'

But that evening, after supper had been eaten and the dishes washed and stacked away, Raymond watched his grandfather start at the slightest sound and glance anxiously at the window, as though he expected a monstrous head to push its way through the curtains, Then it was time to go to bed, and they all trooped upstairs, each carrying a lighted candle, and Mr Carstairs said – much too heartily: 'The moon won't keep you awake tonight. Eh, my boy?'

Raymond agreed it most certainly would not, even while he pondered on a daring – not to mention blood-chilling – idea.

Once in his room, he lay fully dressed on the bed and whispered: 'I won't do it. I can't.' But curiosity – which is reputed to kill cats – made him change his mind every other minute. Was there really such a creature as the Mudadora? If so, what did it look like?

There was, of course, only one way to find out.

'I'd be mad to go out there all by myself,' Raymond told himself over and over again. But suppose he were to creep from the house soon – now, for example – and hide himself behind a bush, then the creature need never know he was there, and curiosity could be satisfied without undue risk.

Without actually realising what he was doing, Raymond slid off the bed and walked on tiptoe towards the door.

Intermittent clouds drifted across the moon and sent their grotesque shadows racing over the garden and into the looming forest. Raymond, now extremely alarmed at his own intrepidity, made himself as comfortable as circumstances permitted behind the foremost bush and decided he would wait for one hour and not a minute longer.

One fact became clear during the first ten minutes. The forest never slept. Apart from the disturbing hoot of an owl, there were distant cries, the perpetual whisper of wind-teased leaves, the patter-patter of tiny feet, and the occasional crack of breaking twigs.

Then a particularly heavy cloud bank laid a thick blanket of darkness over the entire countryside, and Raymond came to the decision that enough was enough – he was going back to bed. He had got up, stretched, and was about to step out into the open, when the sound of approaching foot-treads made him sink down again. With a pounding heart he listened to the heavy 'crunch crunch', the snap of breaking wood, the crash of a bush being flattened, the swish of pliant branches pushed to one side, and knew – with an awful, unquestionable certainty – that the Mudadora, be it man, beast or monster, was coming in his direction.

Possibly never had a boy so regretted giving in to a mad impulse, as did Raymond, while crouched down behind his meagre bush. The thudding tread drew nearer, small life squealed and scurried through the undergrowth, birds awakened either by sound or pure instinct, twittered with alarm and rose up from nearby trees and became whirling shapes that could just be seen in the dim light.

Raymond, trembling, not knowing if he should stay where he was or run for the house, peered with fearful expectancy into the gloom and waited for horror to come out from the trees. Then a fallen branch snapped, a pine-cone that had been kicked by a massive foot came rolling under the bush – and a black shape loomed up against the cloud-racked sky.

45

Raymond became aware of an overwhelming smell of dank earth, rotting vegetation, plus a cloying sweet odour, and he knew it was no mere wild animal that stood a few metres away, but something that had been born from corruption. But it was still too dark for him to see more than a bare outline; a round blob of a head, the bulk of hunched shoulders, a ragged covering that might have been fur, which in places glimmered with a green, luminous light. Then a flash of lightning momentarily turned night into day, and Raymond was quite unable to smother a cry of terror when he at last saw the tall, thickset figure from which tiny twigs jutted out from glutinous mud, sprouting here and there into clumps of wild plants that somehow had taken root in this walking lump of tainted earth. The head came round, and green, glittering eyes glared in Raymond's direction, while that bubbling cough grew into a terrible roar of anticipation. As though in answer, a crash of thunder made the night tremble, went echoing across the shrouded heavens, then sank down into an angry rumbling before dying away.

The Mudadora took one step towards Raymond's hiding-place – then another – and Raymond jumped to his feet, looked anxiously from left to right, then ran towards the house.

He should have reached it without any great difficulty, for the Mudadora was a clumsy creature, only able to move with slow, ponderous steps. But in the darkness he did not see the patch of brambles that hid an ant-hill, and suddenly he was on the ground, held fast by a tangle of thorn-covered stems. Another flash of lightning made every tree, bush, blade of grass stand out in stark relief, and revealed the Mudadora advancing towards him, black, fibre-covered arms outstretched, its mouth a green, yawning cavern, its eyes gleaming like starlit emeralds.

Raymond cried out: 'Grandfather . . . help me . . . help me . . .'

Another peal of thunder mingled with the monster's roar, shattered the darkness into slabs of terror-haunted nightmare, and completely smothered Raymond's shrill cry. He struggled and came up from the ground with torn clothes and scratched hands. Lightning flashes followed one after the other, and the mudborn

creature was now only a couple of metres away, its body a shimmering, green mass that flattened hope with every step. Fear
paralysed Raymond's legs, and he could not run, or even move,
just stand there and wait for an unthinkable end.

The great arms were raised, curved down towards the boy's
trembling shoulders. Then, suddenly, the rains came.

All at once, a veritable deluge poured down from the black,
seething sky; thudded on ground and forest roof, cascaded from
battered leaves and over-filled gutters – and made the Mudadora
cringe as though in abject terror.

It turned and began to lumber back towards the forest, emit-
ting a low, bubbling cry as rain teemed down over its head, sent
cold watery spears into its shoulders, flailing arms and slowly
moving legs. Raymond knew it was trying to reach the trees, where
a certain amount of shelter could provide protection from this
sudden cloud-burst which was gradually washing away the life-
preserving mud.

With fear-inspired desperation he tore his feet free from the
brambles and performed the most courageous act of his entire
life. He ran forward and crashed into the back of the reeling
monster. It fell to the ground with a soggy thud and lay there,
struggling feebly, while rain seeped into the flickering eyes,
gaping mouth; tore holes in the luminous face and glistening
body.

Then he heard his grandfather's voice calling from his
bedroom window: 'Raymond . . . where are you?' before he too
slumped down on to the drenched earth and lay still.

Sunlight had transformed his bedroom into a golden grotto when
Raymond came back into the world of the living, and, for a while,
he could not remember what had taken place. He lay quite still
and looked up at the ceiling and was thinking it must be long past
his normal hour for getting up, when a single word slid into his
brain.

'Mudadora.'

He sat up in bed and became aware that his grandfather was

seated on a chair beside him. The old man creased his face into a smile and gave a vast sigh of relief.

'Thank goodness! I was wondering if I should not go down to the village and bring back the doctor. How do you feel?'

'What about the . . . Mudadora?'

Mr Carstairs cast an anxious glance at the closed door.

'Not so loud, my boy. Your grandmother – she mustn't know anything about – you know what. She would worry herself ill. Suffice to say that due to your courageous action, the – the creature was almost dead when I carried you back into the house. The heavy rain washed the skeleton clean. I buried it in the forest this morning. Your grandmother thinks you walked in your sleep, and you must never tell her what really happened.'

Raymond promised he would keep the story to himself; but was quite unable to retain his curiosity.

'But why wasn't it washed away by the rain long ago?'

Mr Carstairs shrugged. 'I can only guess, although our friend Jasper can probably give you a more detailed answer. Its entire existence was spent deep in the forest, where the large trees would provide cover and no doubt it had a den of some kind, possibly a cave or a hole in the ground. You lured it out into the open, and the unusually heavy downpour caught it completely unawares.'

Later, Raymond, a little the worse for his adventure, went downstairs, where his grandmother gave him an enormous breakfast and said he must never, never walk in his sleep again. But when he again accompanied his grandfather for a walk through the forest, and they both told Jasper of how the Mudadora came to its watery end, the little man smiled grimly and said: 'So, it walks no more! But the forest still lives, and there be other things that crawl, slither and wriggle through the undergrowth. Aye, that there be.'

Ghoul at Large

Henry Marlow peered from behind the desk at the tall, lean young man who sat bolt upright on a straight-backed chair and stared at his prospective employer with black, sunken eyes. Mr Marlow decided he did not really like the look of him. That long white face was not one that would bring cheer and goodwill to a children's party, and the mouth bulged slightly as though it were confining a set of rebellious teeth, that were fighting to get out. Come to think of it, when the fellow spoke, two ugly eye-teeth slipped over the lower lip and slid into two little indentations on either side of the ridiculously wide mouth. But a man could not help his face, so Henry Marlow sighed and fired his first question.

'Mr . . . eh . . .' he consulted his notepad, 'Mr Lough, why do you wish to enter the undertaking profession?'

Mr Lough smiled. It was not a nice smile and could be likened to the anticipatory smirk of a wolf who had just spotted a succulent little Red Riding Hood.

'I think it might be rewarding.'

The voice was harsh and there was a strange, almost imperceptible lisp after each word. Mr Marlow wished there had been at least one more applicant for the post of mortician's assistant.

'There's nothing rewarding about this job, lad. People are tardy about dying in Brankwell and only do it when there's no alternative. So I can't pay much.'

Mr Lough smiled again and Mr Marlow just could not tear his gaze away from those jutting fangs.

49

'There are fringe benefits, sir.'

'Fringe benefits! Oh, I see what you mean. Yes, the mourners do sometimes cough up with a bit extra for the pall-bearers, but I wouldn't bank on it. What was your last job?'

The smile had grown into a grin and Mr Marlow momentarily closed his eyes.

'You could say, sir, I was in the refuse disposal business.'

Mr Marlow digested this piece of information. When one came right down to it, there was an irreverent, tenuous line between undertaking and waste disposal, but not one that a respectable Mortician Director would recognize. He said, 'You will have to live in of course.'

'That will be *most* satisfactory.'

'Well,' Mr Marlow slapped his hands down on the desk several times. 'We'll give it a go, shall we? See how you get along?'

'You are most kind.'

Sir Daniel Makepiece in life had not been a pretty sight; in death he was appalling. Twenty-four stone of bulging, sagging corpse was laid out on the dining-room table, and seemed ready to burst if it were given the slightest encouragement. When Mr Marlow and his newly-engaged assistant entered the room, the dying rays of the sinking sun were high-lighting the dead man's face, emphasizing the deep creases around mouth and eyes and transforming the sparse white hair into a silver halo. A little, old woman led the way; a shrivelled, brown, apple of an old woman, who wrung her hands, jerked her head and spoke in a high-pitched voice.

' 'Ere 'e be. Large as life and dead as mutton. Fit only for a snack for them things that do slink round graveyard.'

Mr Marlow winked at his assistant, then tapped the old lady on a bony shoulder.

'None of that, Matilda. Your old master is to be cremated and nothing or anyone will be able to get at him.'

Matilda shook her head.

'Them ghoulies won't like that. They'll be 'opping mad. Gnashing, their old fangs . . .'

Mr Marlow interrupted. 'Come, Matilda, surely you don't believe in ghouls. There's no such animal.'

'Not believe in ghouls!' She stared at the undertaker in speechless astonishment. 'But there's always been ghouls in Brankwell graveyard. Any fule knows that.' She cackled and did a little dance. 'A prutty thin time they be 'aving of late though. What with all these cremations and folks living longer than they ought. I wonder's why they don't come sniffing round the 'ouses ...'

'That's quite enough,' Mr Marlow barked. 'Now, listen to me. We're going to take your master to my chapel of rest. So, pay your last respects, then go about your business.'

Matilda grinned. 'I didn't pay 'im no respect when 'e was alive, and I won't pay 'im any now 'es dead. And I bet you can't get 'im down the steps without dropping 'im.'

She went out, slamming the door behind her and Mr Marlow and his assistant were left to their onerous task. The undertaker sighed. 'A lot of him, lad. Take a bit of shifting.' He looked up and gave a snort of disgust. 'For heaven's sake wipe your mouth.'

Mr Lough pulled a piece of coarse rag from the pocket of his rusty-black trousers and wiped the moisture from his gaping mouth.

'Sorry, sir ... Sort of infliction, sir. Can't help meself ...'

'You'll have to help yourself. Can't have you slobbering all over the place when the mourners are present. Bad for business.'

Mr Lough thrust the piece of cloth back into his pocket and made a serious effort to control his obvious emotion.

'I'm all right now, sir. You can trust me. Shall I fetch the meat-wag ... I mean the bier, sir?'

Mr Marlow nodded, then watched the ungainly figure as it lurched towards the door. Odd to say the least. But certainly keen. One could say dead keen, but one shouldn't. He might do, so long as that slobbering affliction could be kept under control, and he could be prevailed upon to take a bath and wear a decent suit of clothes. Those that he wore now looked as if they had been stored in a damp box, then buried for a couple of years.

The door opened and Mr Lough entered, carrying a long,

wooden structure that had handles at either end. This he placed beside the vast corpse, then looked enquiringly at his employer.

'Would you like me to . . . to sling it on, sir?'

Mr Marlow sighed. 'Look, Lough, you don't refer to the dear departed as "it", neither do you sling anything anywhere. We gently lift the mournful remains on to the bier. Is that clear?'

Mr Lough said, 'Yes, sir,' but there was a distinct impression that he was not convinced. The undertaker, having delivered his admonition, turned round and slowly removed his jacket. He then carefully rolled up his shirt-sleeves, spat on his hands, rubbed them together and turned to face an arduous job of work. He took one pace forward, then stopped. His mouth fell open, his eyes widened and he said, 'Bloody 'ell!' – and it would be reasonable to suppose he was completely unaware of this lapse.

The body was on the bier.

A full minute passed before Mr Marlow spoke again.

'You lifted 'im all by yourself?'

Thin eyebrows seemed to crawl up the white face.

'Wasn't I supposed to, sir?'

Mr Marlow then asked a silly question, but he was in no condition to ask a rational one.

'Did you do it reverently, lad?'

The tombstone teeth; the gleaming yellow slabs that were lined up between those awful jutting fangs were bared in another disconcerting grin.

'I bowed me head three times, before I put it – put him down.'

'This,' said Mr Marlow in a suitably low voice, 'is our chapel of rest.'

He did not mention that the ancient structure had once been a barn, and the neat little cubicles, which were fitted with long, wooden tables, were the rightful habitat of evicted cows. On one of these stood a very large coffin and Mr Marlow closed his eyes when his assistant filled it.

'Screw him down, lad,' he murmured.

For some reason this did not please Mr Lough, for his white

brow crumpled into a frown, his fearsome teeth made a distinct grinding noise and he said,

'Must we, sir?'

'We need not, but we will. There's no near relatives who will want to see the old devil. Last of his line, see. So get cracking with the screwdriver. And wipe your chin – you're dribbling again.'

Mr Lough drove screws home. Mr Marlow watched and pretended not to hear a low muttering, that had much in common with a sulky child who has been ordered to lock its toys away. Presently he said,

'No need to do 'em too tight, lad. The cremation chaps will want it off again tomorrow.'

The muttering ceased, the head came round and Mr Marlow was once again the recipient of a toothy smile. 'That will be handy, sir.'

Mr Marlow was asleep and enjoying a very pleasant dream, where he was supervizing twelve funerals, each one with a top-grade, polished oak coffin, equipped with gold handles.

Possibly he would not have slept so soundly, had he known what was taking place in the chapel of rest.

Mr Lough was again wielding a screwdriver. The screws came out in a most satisfactory manner. Sir Daniel also, came out, but with not so much ease, for he appeared to have expanded a little during the night, and Mr Lough had to jerk, pull and finally heave, before the defunct baronet could be induced to leave his shell.

Then Mr Marlow's new assistant slung the inert mass round his shoulders, took a firm grip of dangling hands and stiff legs, and trotted out into the moonlight. He cast no shadow as he moved quickly along the silver-tinted road.

Brankwell Churchyard was a place where moonlight and tombstones conspired together and manufactured shadows. Marble crosses smiled down upon their black counterparts that lay across the tall grass; a green-tinted angel watched its dark twin flutter grotesque wings, as the night wind stirred sleeping columbine and yellowhaired dandelions. An upright headstone, cold and proud, ignored the rectangular slab that sprawled across the weed infested gravel path, and flaunted its own naked whiteness in the bright moonshine.

Mr Lough came over the churchyard wall in one effortless bound and landed on an unmarked grave with a soft thud. He crept forward, his sunken eyes peering from side to side, then he threw back his head and howled.

It could have been the cry of a mating cat, or the high-pitched wail of a stray dog, but somewhere – something, heard and sent back a whimpering answer. Mr Lough slung his burden down on a weather-stained marble slab and waited.

It wriggled up from a mound of raw earth. Naked, white, bloated – like a monstrous slug endowed with arms and legs – hairless – the eyes almost buried in jutting rolls of fat, the thin mouth slightly parted by projecting fangs, that curved down and dimpled the moist chin. This was the common or churchyard ghoul. The outcast, a member of the lower orders, the scavenger – something born from corruption. But still a not-too-distant relative of Mr Lough.

It came prancing over the graves, loping forward on all fours, moisture seeping from the now gaping mouth, making little wailing sounds, that gradually took on the semblance of words.

'Me . . . eat . . . liver and lights . . . ju-icy kid-neys . . . tear and rip . . .'

Mr Lough raised his hand and the lowly one lapsed into reluctant silence.

'Hold it. I'm the brains round here. Who educated himself from the tombstone lettering? Eh! Who thought of going out and getting, when the supplies no longer came here?'

The little eyes glittered like hot coals. 'You di-d. It's yer vam bl-o-o-o-d.'

Mr Lough smiled complacently. 'My gran'dad was a vam, and I'm not ashamed of that. Now, we partakes when I say so.'

The common – one might say purebred – ghoul, looked down

upon the object on the marble slab. A long tongue came out, flickered for a brief while, then slid back in again.

'When you go-ing to s-a-a-a-y so?'

Mr Lough folded his long, thin hands on his flat stomach and murmured, 'Not before grace.'

The little eyes disappeared into their beds of fat, the yellow fangs grew longer as the lips parted. The scavenger-ghoul was grinning. Mr Lough intoned the traditional grace.

> *'Before we crouch and partake of meat,*
> *Let us be grateful for what we eat.*
> *It used to put on lordly airs,*
> *Then bend its head and say its prayers.*
> *Now it's stark, cold and stiff,*
> *And we'll be through it in a jiff.'*

The lowly scavenger and the educated – the brainy – the go-out-and-get ghoul – crouched either side of the marble slab and – partook.

Mr Marlow never did explain how he came to lose a twenty-four-stone corpse. Neither did he understand how it was that his recently acquired assistant vanished at the same time. It never occurred to him to connect one disappearance with the other.

Matilda of course knew, but no one took the slightest notice of her.

In the meanwhile a tall, ungainly figure walked a lonely, moon-lit road. A replete Mr Lough was going towards the nearest town. He had a feeling that more people did dear-departing there.

The Third Eye

IT ALL BEGAN WHEN Uncle George gave Michael a lecture on keen observation.

'Everyone can see,' he stated, 'but few observe.'

'Same thing,' Michael protested. 'If you can see something, you must observe it. Stands to reason.'

Uncle George wagged his finger pontifically. 'That's where you're wrong. Read the Sherlock Holmes stories and you'll know what I mean. For example – you must have seen the steps leading up to your front door. How many are there?'

Michael made a quick guess. 'Ten.'

'Wrong. There are thirteen. You saw the steps, but didn't observe them.' He got up and walked over to the window, which, being on the first floor, commanded a clear view of the street. 'Come here and I'll give you a practical demonstration of EOP.'

'EOP?' queried Michael.

'Extra Ocular Perception. You've heard of ESP, perhaps – Extra Sensory Perception – telepathy, and that kind of thing? Well, EOP concerns your powers of observation. "Ocular", from the Latin *oculis* – "eye".'

To be honest, Michael thought his uncle was an old show-off, who had only the slightest idea of what he was talking about but was good for the odd pound note if treated with respect. So the boy joined the tall, grey-haired man at the window, prepared to express admiring astonishment, no matter how mundane the performance. Uncle George pointed to a plump lady who was trudging along the far pavement.

'What can you tell me about her?'

Michael creased his forehead into a thoughtful frown. 'She's quite old – sixty, at least. Is fat. Wearing a blue dress. And – oh, yes – she's been shopping. Carrying a full shopping bag. I think that's about all.'

His uncle emitted a vast sigh.

'You must be half blind, boy. Even without using EOP it must be obvious that the lady is a grandmother, has recently returned from abroad, was once quite well-off and is prudent by nature. For heaven's sake, use your eyes.'

Michael stared at his uncle with unfeigned astonishment before asking: 'How on earth did you work all that out?'

'Elementary,' Uncle George replied with irritating complacency. 'Let us take each point in turn. You should have noticed that a toy rifle is poking out of the shopping bag. This suggests the lady has a young male relative, who will not be more than ten years of age. As she is too old to have a son of that age, it is reasonable to assume the little wretch is her grandson. Her arms and face are deeply sun-tanned, and as there is nowhere in Great Britain where the sun shines that strongly at this time of year, she must have acquired it abroad. Had she been back in this country for any length of time, the tan would have started to fade. It hasn't. So – she recently returned. Are you with me so far?'

Michael nodded, albeit reluctantly, then scratched his head.

'Yes, I suppose you're right. But what about her once being well-off and being prudent by nature. I can't see how you know that.'

Uncle George narrowed his eyes. 'Wait a minute – she's stopping to have a rest. Respiratory trouble, I wouldn't wonder. Too much weight. Now she's sitting down on that low wall and we'll be able to *observe* her more closely. Don't fiddle with the curtain, you little idiot. We don't want her to know she's being watched. Look at that dress. I'm willing to bet that when new that cost all of two hundred pounds, but now it's worn and faded, suggesting she no longer has the money to replace it. Not even with a cheaper model.

'Now, observe that she has with her an umbrella. Is there a cloud in the sky? No, there is not. Never have I seen a day with less promise of rain. Therefore, the lady is prudence itself – and no doubt a pessimist as well, if she considers it might rain. You see, boy? It's a simple deductive process that comes easily to a man who has developed his sense of EOP.'

The fat lady clambered laboriously to her feet, took up the shopping bag and continued her slow progress along the pavement.

'Well, young fellow,' Uncle George went on, 'I trust that I have lit a tiny spark of enquiry in your brain. Start developing your sense of EOP and there'll soon be a blazing fire of knowledge.'

Michael wandered back across the room and flopped into a chair, where for a while he sat staring blankly at the artificial-log electric fire. Presently he said: 'It all sounds most convincing, but you could be wrong about some of it. I mean, she could have bought that toy rifle for a nephew or a neighbour's child.'

Uncle George helped himself to a drink from the sideboard.

'Maybe. But surely she's far too old to have a ten-year-old nephew and most certainly too poor to buy presents for neighbour's children. The trouble is, I started to develop my powers of EOP too late in life. My eyes aren't what they used to be. Mind you, I could still spot that her hair was tinted. It was almost white at the roots . . . But at your age! My word, if you work hard at it, you'll achieve wonders. Be very useful in later life.'

'I'll certainly try,' Michael promised. 'Gosh, it'll be like having a third eye.'

Uncle George went to America the following week, and although Michael never saw him again, he most certainly had reason not to forget him.

Developing a sense of EOP is not easy – at least, not at first. Michael found that the mere fact that a man has mud-caked trousers does not automatically mean he has been trudging across fields just after a rainstorm. He more than likely has slipped into a water-logged hole that a road worker had left inadequately lit, or been splashed by a passing vehicle. Neither could one assume that a lady with a black eye has an unkind husband. She might have walked into a lamp post.

But after several months spent in watching, taking elaborate notes and learning to spot that little *extra something* that non-observant people never see, Michael began to achieve some remarkable results. For example, he soon realised that the burly man in the grey suit that was much too small for him, who had a blister on the index finger of his right hand, walked with a pronounced limp and kept looking back over one shoulder, could be none other than the convict whose escape from Marston Prison had been reported in the national press a few days earlier.

'Blister on finger – sawing through cell bars. Limp – rope broke when climbing down wall. Stole suit much too small for him. Looking back over one shoulder – afraid of being followed.' Michael explained the results of his EOP in a brisk, professional style to a passing policeman; who merely smiled and said: 'Mustn't let your imagination run away with you, lad,' while the escaped convict disappeared round a corner.

Michael would have voiced his indignation, had not the little two-way radio that policemen carry in their top pocket suddenly erupted into rasping life. 'Escaped prisoner James Bradley seen in Plumstead Road area. Description – five feet ten inches high, heavy build, wearing over-tight grey suit. Walks with a pronounced limp . . .'

'He went round that corner,' Michael said gently. 'If you run you should catch him.'

The policeman gave him one startled glance, said: 'Strewth!' and lumbered off in the indicated direction, blowing his whistle furiously as he went.

That incident was really the turning point in Michael's career as a professional practitioner of EOP. As time passed he all but developed X-ray eyes. A smile, a frown, the flick of an eyelid, when coupled with such irregularities as odd socks, a missing coat button, a frayed shirt collar, told him where a person worked, lived, the size of their income, if they were married or single and what they had been up to during the past twenty-four hours.

Practice makes perfect – too much practice can result in over-perfection. Or, to put it another way – over-perception. Michael suddenly observed something he would rather not have seen.

Mr Manfield was a commercial gentleman.

He had a nice glossy car that was owned by his company and spent five days a week travelling across the country, selling a very superior brand of kitchen hardware: gleaming aluminium saucepans, non-stick frying pans, glazed oven dishes of every size and description, and rather terrifying pressure cookers.

When not travelling, Mr Manfield was a lodger in Michael's house. He slept in the spare room and took his meals with Michael and his widowed mother, Mrs Carrington. Of course Michael's EOP told him a lot about Mr Manfield that was not apparent to those who had not developed this extraordinary gift. He knew a blonde lady; occasionally replaced missing buttons; a left-handed barber cut his hair: a careless person (most likely the blonde lady) scraped mud from his shoes; he had a weakness for brown ale and pickled onions; he threw away his socks when they acquired their first hole.

He also had a ghost that walked behind him.

Michael suspected the ghost had been following Mr Manfield for some time, but due to his previous lack of EOP he had not seen it. When the commercial gentleman had first entered the dining-room, accompanied by what appeared to be a little old lady with white hair and a large curved nose, and attired in a shabby green dress, he all but fainted. His mother asked: 'Aren't you well? Why are you staring like that?'

Michael just could not tear his horrified gaze from the apparition, which seemed solid enough at first glance, but revealed a hint of transparency when subjected to prolonged inspection. But the really frightening aspect was the ferocious expression on the old lady's face and the futile efforts she made to punch Mr

Manfield in the ribs. Michael watched her clench tiny fists, drive them with considerable force in the direction of the tall man's ribs, then do a little dance of rage when he appeared to feel no effects.

'Michael, I'll not tell you again,' Mrs Carrington protested. 'Really, I will think there's something radically wrong with you if you keep staring at Mr Manfield in that fashion.'

'What's the matter, son?' Mr Manfield enquired. 'Have I got egg on my tie?'

Michael gasped: 'No,' and ran from the room, quite unable to watch the antics of that grim spectre any longer.

Having reached the reasonable security of his own bedroom, he sat down by the window, and after giving the matter his full consideration, came to the conclusion that in developing his sense of EOP he had also given life to another inborn gift: the ability to see ghosts. Or, at least, one ghost.

Michael spoke his thoughts aloud. 'Why couldn't Uncle George keep his big mouth shut. I was quite happy not observing anything. Now I've got to watch that old woman following Mr Manfield and trying to punch him in the ribs. Which means I must find out why. A thirst for knowledge is a dreadful thing.'

Then he stopped and jerked his head forward, for Mr Manfield had just come out of the front door and was walking sedately down the garden path. And behind him trotted the old woman, her white head bobbing up and down while she unsuccessfully tried to aim a punch at the bottom of his spine. He opened the front gate and closed it carefully behind him – not, however, before the old woman had slipped through and taken up a position by the near door of his car. When he climbed in behind the steering wheel, she somehow seemed to flow on to the seat beside him, where she swung a really wicked right hook in the direction of his protruding stomach. Michael was unable to see if it made contact.

He decided that here was a problem that might well have baffled Sherlock Holmes, although that rather irritating gentleman would doubtlessly have tried to find a rational explanation for it. Uncle George would have stopped drinking whisky and taken to his heels. But Michael knew he must find out 'Why' and 'How' if he were ever again to know peace of mind.

'What do you know about Mr Manfield?' Michael asked, while watching his mother peel potatoes in the kitchen sink. She frowned and shot her young son a suspicious glance.

'All I need to know. He's quiet and well-behaved and pays his rent regular as clockwork on the first of every month. Why are you so interested in Mr Manfield, all of a sudden?'

Michael shrugged and considered the possibility of telling his mother the truth, but quickly dismissed the idea as impracticable. She was not a lady who would accept the presence of a ghost in the house with anything like equanimity. He would most likely be dosed with something vile and made to stay in bed for several days. So he said quietly: 'I'm just interested in people. Like to know what makes them tick. Do you suppose Mr Manfield was ever married?'

Mrs Carrington prised two eyes from a large potato, cut it in half, then popped both portions into a saucepan.

'He may have been. In fact, now you mention it, I believe he did say he was a widower. That means he was married, but his wife died.'

Michael exclaimed: 'Ah!' and followed it with an equally expressive: 'Oh!' before realising that the shade that followed Mr Manfield around did not look much like a defunct wife. He asked another question. 'Do you suppose Mr Manfield would have married someone much older?'

His mother laughed softly. 'I wouldn't think so. He can't be more than forty-five, and I can't see him tied to an old woman. More likely one younger than himself. Your poor father was ten years older than me.'

Michael sighed deeply and once again wished he had never developed his sense of EOP. The entire business was becoming much too complicated and required more courage and judgement than he could manage. Michael knew nothing at all about ghosts, but clearly Mr Manfield must have done something dreadful for that old woman to be continually trying to punch him in the ribs. Michael shook his head, thereby causing Mrs Carrington to ask: 'What's wrong with you now? I must say you're acting very strange lately.'

'I'll have to watch some more.' Michael answered thoughtlessly.

'Watch what?'

'Oh, what's going on around me.'

'Sometimes,' Mrs Carrington remarked caustically. 'I think you're not quite right in the head.'

Mr Manfield did not arrive back until the end of the week, and then only a little before midnight, so Michael did not see him before breakfast time the next morning. On entering the dining-room Michael experienced a feeling of relief, blended with disappointment, on realising that there was no apparition standing behind Mr Manfield's chair. The commercial gentleman looked up as Michael entered and gave him a wan smile.

'Good morning, Michael. I trust you are well.'

The boy seated himself opposite and endured his mother's kiss when she placed a bowl of Shredded Wheat before him. He gave Mr Manfield a conventional reply: 'I'm quite well, thank you. Did you have a successful trip?'

The man sighed gently and brushed back a lock of grey hair with a not over-steady hand. 'Mustn't grumble. Managed to nail one or two respectable orders.' He looked up at Michael's mother. 'Mrs Carrington, I don't think I can tackle your excellent breakfast this morning. To be honest, I feel a wee bit under the weather.'

Mrs Carrington at once expressed grave concern. 'I am sorry to hear that, Mr Manfield. I do hope you're not sickening for something.'

'Mr Manfield shook his head. 'No. I don't think so. But lately I've had a kind of dull ache in my left side. Around the kidney. Anyway, that's where it seems to be. Probably a touch of wind. But I don't feel much like eating.'

'I've some milk of magnesia in the kitchen,' Mrs Carrington stated. 'A spoonful will work wonders. Let me fetch it.'

Mr Manfield smiled bleakly. 'You are too kind, but I'm beginning to feel a little better. I've probably been overdoing things lately. Tension, you know, upsets the old tummy.'

It was then that Michael realised that the old woman had not been so far away after all. He suddenly saw her standing in the gap which separated the sideboard from the left hand wall, an almost imperceptible figure that lurked in the shadows, for the early morning sunlight did not reach that part of the room. When Mr Manfield had finished speaking, and Mrs Carrington was insisting he have a fresh cup of coffee, the old woman left her hiding place and walked with terrifying slowness towards the table. Michael trembed when Mr Manfield said:

'No need to look so frightened, son. I'm not going to die.'

Her face creased into a grimace of pure hate, the old woman took up a position behind her victim and drove a clenched fist into the small of his back. Mr Manfield emitted a hoarse cry and jerked forward, until his nose was only five centimetres from the butter dish, an action that had Mrs Carrington shouting instructions to a petrified Michael.

'Don't sit there staring. Help me get the poor man up to his room. If he's not better soon, I'm calling in the doctor.'

Together they managed to raise the groaning man from his chair and guide him towards the door, while Michael did his utmost not to look at the apparition, which was now standing to one side, apparently well content with its handiwork. Mr Manfield seemed to have partially recovered by the time they had propelled him up the stairs, and kept muttering: 'No need to worry . . . overwork . . . only a pain in my back.'

They got him on to the large bed, and Mrs Carrington removed his shoes and loosened his tie, then gave Michael some unpalatable instructions.

'Now, you stay here and keep an eye on him. If he has another turn, call me. Then I'll ring the doctor.'

Michael looked anxiously around the room. There was no sign

of the old woman, and he could only suppose she had remained behind in the dining-room. He expressed grave concern.

'You mean – I'm to stay here – all by myself?'

'Of course you won't be by yourself. Mr Manfield's here, isn't he? Don't be so silly.'

And she left the room, leaving the door wide open so as to hear Michael, should he have occasion to call out. The boy sat down on the very edge of the bedside chair and ejected a muffled cry when a cloud passed over the sun, causing a shadow to go racing across the far wall. He managed to produce a pale smile when Mr Manfield stirred on the bed and opened his eyes.

'No need for you to stay, son, I'm feeling much better.'

'Mother said I was to sit by you,' Michael said, 'so I'd better do that. How long have you been – well – feeling these pains?'

'Three or four weeks,' Mr Manfield replied. 'They were only little twinges at first. Scarcely felt them. But lately they've been getting worse.'

Michael jerked his head round and stared wide-eyed at the open doorway, for there had been the suggestion of a figure flitting across the landing. He smothered a cry and asked in a tremulous voice: 'Mr Manfield, do you know an old woman with a big nose, wearing a shabby green dress – someone who doesn't like you?'

For a while. it seemed as if Mr Manfield had not heard the question, for he lay completely motionless and stared up at the boy with unnaturally bright eyes. Michael laid a hand on his arm and shook it gently. 'Mr Manfield. are you all right? Did you hear what I said?'

The man's thin lips parted, and a hoarse voice, so unlike his normal gentle tone, manufactured fear-tinted words.

'What are you talking about, son? How can you know anything about that old hag? Who have you been talking to?'

Michael was not far from tears what with Mr Manfield speaking with such a strange voice and the prospect of that dreadful phantom appearing in the doorway at any moment. His next words did not appear to reassure the man on the bed.

66

'I've developed Extra Ocular Perception – I can see her. She's punching you – that's why you have those pains. And I think she may have something to do with that nice, but not very bright lady, who sews your missing buttons on with the wrong-coloured cotton, leaves blonde hair on your coat collar, and scrapes mud from your shoes with a blunt knife.'

His voice died away as the man gripped his arm and vainly tried to speak. Michael felt a rising wave of pity drive the fear from his mind, for no matter what he had done, no one deserved to look so terrified as Mr Manfield did now. He tried to think of something to say that would at least create an illusion of normality, but before he could speak Mr Manfield collapsed back on to the bed. Michael was about to call his mother, when the old woman entered the room and walked round to the far side of the bed, where she stood looking down upon the motionless man.

Michael whispered: 'Why? Why?' but the apparition did not spare him so much as a single glance, merely turned and moved slowly towards the dressing-table. Michael thought he saw the mirror gleam brightly just before she disappeared.

The doctor said Mr Manfield's illness was due to overwork and nervous exhaustion, and only complete rest and quiet would ensure his recovery. Michael took him at his word and kept well away from the sick-room while he tried to solve the bizarre riddle. Then, on the third day after Mr Manfield's collapse, the unexpected happened.

When the door bell sent its melodious chimes through the house, Mrs Carrington called out from above the stairs: 'Answer that, Michael. I'm making Mr Manfield comfortable.'

The woman who stood on the front doorstep was possibly thirty-five to forty years of age, had well-groomed blonde hair and a round, unlined face, enhanced by large blue eyes. She wore a bright red coat and carried an over-large handbag. She spoke with a voice that was tinged with the suggestion of a Northern accent.

'Hello, love, I do hope I've come to the right house, bet Gerald is a shocking writer, and I couldn't be sure if the number was thirty-two or fifty-two.'

'Gerald?' Michael asked.

'Yes, dear Gerald Manfield. He rings me up regular every Monday and Friday, and as I haven't heard a dickybird from him for the past three weeks, I thought I'd pop down and see if everything was all right.'

Michael stood to one side. 'You'd better come in. Mr Manfield is ill.'

The woman exclaimed: 'Oh, dear! I knew something was wrong,' and all but ran into the hall, where she laid the large bag on a chair, then removed her coat and hung it on the hat-stand. Mrs Carrington's voice demanded information.

'Who is it, Michael?'

'A friend of Mr Manfield.'

Michael could see that his mother was not all that taken by the visitor, for she gave the floral-patterned dress and bright blonde hair a disapproving look, while she said quietly: 'You'd better come into the sitting-room. Can I offer you some refreshment?'

The stranger bared her perfect teeth in a polite smile. 'Thank you, love, but I had a cuppa at the station.' She preceded Mrs Carrington into the sitting-room, where, without waiting to be invited, she flopped down into an armchair. 'That's better. I couldn't wait to get the weight off me feet. Well, now . . . I'm Nora Sugden. And you must be Mrs Carrington. Gerald often speaks about you and how well you look after him.'

Mrs Carrington eased herself down on to the sofa. 'He most certainly has never mentioned you. I was under the impression he was alone in the world. Am I to understand that you are a close friend?'

Nora Sugden giggled. 'You could say so, dear. I'm his intended.'

'Intended!'

'Yes, dear. We intend to get married as soon as he's cleared up some business matters. Lawyers, you understand. Never hurry themselves. I told him not to worry. I said: "I've got enough for both of us, until your first wife's estate is sorted out." But he wouldn't hear of it.'

Mrs Carrington frowned. 'But I understood that his wife died years ago. Surely by now . . .'

'Oh no, love. She only passed away last year. Mind you, I gather they hadn't got on together for some time.' She leaned forward and lowered her voice to a confidential whisper. 'Mother-in-law trouble, I believe. Some old hen who kept making trouble.'

Mrs Carrington said: 'Really!' and Michael felt his pulse quicken with rising excitement. Nora Sugden relaxed back in her chair, then looked enquiringly at the door. 'Do you suppose I could see Gerald now? I'm sure the sight of me will cheer him up no end.'

Before his mother could answer, Michael fired a question that just had to be answered. 'Excuse me, but do you know what his wife died of?'

Mrs Carrington exclaimed: 'Michael, really!' while the blonde woman patted her hair and appeared to give the question some thought. 'I'm not all that certain, love. Something to do with her stomach, I believe. Gastro-something. I remember Gerald saying it was very painful.'

Michael ignored his mother's forbidding frown and asked his second important question. 'And what happened to her mother?'

Nora Sugden began to display signs of some impatience. 'My, he is an inquisitive little lad, isn't he? If you must know, love, she died. Quite recently. Fell down some stairs, I believe. Broke her back, at any rate. Gerald said she was no great loss. Now, if I could . . .'

Mrs Carrington rose and moved towards the door. 'Yes, indeed. But you mustn't excite him. The doctor said he must have rest and quiet and no visitors. But seeing that you're his fiancée, I suppose it'll be all right. I must say I didn't expect to have a sick man on my hands.'

The two women left the room, and Michael waited until they had mounted the stairs before hurrying over to the bookcase and taking out a bulky encyclopaedia. He turned the pages until he found the entry he was looking for.

Gastro-Enteritis: Inflammation of the mucous membrane (lining) of the intestine. Unripe fruit, decomposing meat, irritant poisons (e.g. arsenic, mercury) will cause it. Abdominal pains are symptomatic . . .

Michael closed the book. There was no need to read any more. He knew with a dreadful certainty that Mr Manfield had poisoned his wife, and the doctors had probably assumed she had eaten bad meat or unripe fruit. Possibly she had always suffered from some form of stomach trouble. Then her mother had become suspicious, and Mr Manfield had pushed her down the stairs. He whispered the awful truth aloud.

'Now she's in this house, making him suffer in the same way her daughter did. And I am the only one who can see her.'

His deliberations were interrupted by a loud scream that came from the top of the stairs, followed by Mr Manfield's voice shouting: 'Go away! She don't want you near me! Go . . . o . . . o . . . o away!'

Footsteps came running down the stairs, and Nora Sugden burst into the room, her face transformed by an expression of sheer terror. She slumped into a chair and sat trembling so violently that Michael half expected her string of glass beads to rattle. Mrs Carrington came in a few moments later and, after giving her visitor a quick glance, went over to the sideboard and quarter-filled a tumbler with neat whisky. She thrust it into the woman's shaking hand and said abruptly:

'Here, drink this. It will steady your nerves.'

Nora Sugden emptied the glass in a single gulp and gave the impression she would not object to a refill. But Mrs Carrington sank down into a chair and wiped her moist forehead with a lace handkerchief, while waiting for the woman to recover. Presently she said: 'Well, you can see what kind of a state he's in. I don't think I can stand much more of it, not with a young boy in the house. I'd be obliged if you would arrange for him to be taken somewhere. After all, he's more your responsibility than mine.'

Nora Sugden shook her head violently. 'No, I couldn't. I just want to go home and forget that I ever saw him. There's something wrong. Dreadfully wrong.'

Mrs Carrington raised her voice. 'But you can't expect me to look after him, not now he's in that state. Shaking like a leaf, continually staring at the dressing-table, then screaming like that. If you don't . . .'

The old woman was standing in the hall, looking in through the open doorway, her face wearing an expression that suggested complete satisfaction – even triumph. Then she turned to the left and moved in the direction of the front door. Presently Michael – now oblivious to the women's arguing voices – rose and crept from the room. The hall was empty. Impelled by a burning curiosity that was stronger than fear, he slowly mounted the stairs and pushed open the door of Mr Manfield's room. He was propped up in bed, his face frozen into a mask of abject terror. Michael knew he was dead.

The boy turned his head away and whispered: 'I guess, in the end, Mr Manfield must have developed his own sense of EOP.'

Then he went back downstairs to inform his mother that she need no longer worry about who was to look after Mr Manfield. He had been well and truly taken care of.

The Floaters

THEY FLOAT BEFORE THE eyes and so far as I can understand there is no danger so long as they remain transparent and disappear entirely when dropping below eye level. But – and indeed but – there's another factor that I had not noticed before, due possibly to the clarity of my inner sight (my definition) I refer to the illumination that comes after sunset.

Let me start at the beginning, if there was a beginning, and keep my ramblings to the narrow avenue of truth. Let me . . . another swarm has just dive-bombed my eyes, although as yet none have made physical contact . . . describe them as they first appeared. Transparent bubbles that float before the eyes, the result possibly of eye strain, an excess of eye fluid, I cannot explain more fully, but they are commonplace, at least I have always assumed so. From childhood upwards I have played with them, blinked one eye, then closed the other, pulled the lower lid down, then sideways so I looked like a chinaman or as I imagined a chinaman with eye trouble would look.

Maybe it was from such nonsensible action was horror born.

Maybe . . . possible . . . damnation be . . . I should not have walked through that yellow mist, or lusted after white flesh and full red lips immediately after selfishly praying in an over-heated church.

But know this . . . please know this . . . it was by the war memorial that the big (big for those days) one floated up to my left eye and . . . TURNED BLACK.

Mind you when I made a grab for it there was nothing there but empty air. Solid black! I must type that in capitals or you may miss the importance of that statement.

IT TURNED SOLID BLACK.

But I still grabbed empty air and I haven't tried to grab one recently as too many people have taken to giving me funny looks. But the mere fact that one has taken on opaque substance is terrifyingly horrible. Even more soul disturbing is the certain knowledge the lot disappear at sunrise.

They do. I have dared to watch sunrise and believe you me the very moment the first glimmer shoots above the horizon, bang – not a bubble in sight. Of course they may just become invisible, but on reflection I don't think so because during the dark hours I can drive – will – them below the horizon, but they soon come belting back again. No, I'm willing to bet you anything they have some kind of illumination of their own.

Did you ever come to realise that experience can very soon be transformed into the commonplace? The black bubbles – or blobs – did me no harm and the time eventually came when I could actually forget their existence. After all one is not constantly thinking about the transparent bubbles, but I have become aware that they never go away.

Such is state one.

But I could not stop myself from moving into state two.

Time for capitals again.

THEY GRADUALLY GREW BIGGER.

No they didn't.

THEY SUDDENLY BECAME BIGGER.

Exploded in size. For a brief period became large black butterflies, then something very akin to flying black rats. Then . . . then . . . then a large furry tabby's cat tail.

Now . . . we touch reality here. I had a cat. A lovely tabby cat. And yes it died. Of old age I do believe. Tobias was an ordinary self-respecting cat who was very fond of his grub, scratching furniture and generally making my life a misery. But I could think of no good reason why after death its truly magnificent tail should come floating across the lounge.

I entered state three.

Sound was added.

Tobias's tail began to chase flying rats and flying rats began to squeal, then thud when landing on fitted carpet and was it the result of overheated imagination or did I really spot a flying fur-covered snake gliding across the room? And I know what the next state will be. By the Light Lords I do. All right . . . all right I'll tell now.

FEELING. State three. STATE THREE WILL BE FEELING. Writhing fur caressing my neck. Sharp teeth – or fangs – nibbling my toes, fingers, a quick bite of my nose, clawing away part of my left ear . . .

A fur-covered length is slithering up my left leg. Have you noticed always the left . . .

I believe I scream very prettily.

But I am racing ahead of actual action, but I do feel that all this horror comes from some rot worm nest at the back of my mind.

It seems at times as though I am sleeping in a strange country even though I am aware of what is going on around me.

Thud . . . thud . . . thud the ceiling is raining black flying rats and I find myself praying to long forgotten gods for the blessed gift of daylight for horror that can be seen is horror halved, but all that I am granted is the vision of a silver moon shining down on a blue river where eyeless things float eternally towards tomorrow's dawn.

I am now seated in blanket-thick darkness but can still see the flying things that occasionally whisk by my head, without, thank the Light Lords, actually touching me, but suddenly Tobias's tail is on my lap and there is a deep purring sound that comes from every part of the room.

But just a minute why did I assume it was Tobias's tail? I really must not jump to these unwarranted conclusions, for did not a large black cat go scurrying round the wainscoting, a cat moreover with a fine bushy tail, albeit a black one. I grope for the tabby on my lap and find myself clutching a black tail and what a big tail it has become! I had forgotten growth. Everything is growing. Remember state two?

Maybe if I were to sleep again I'd wake up in a new world where the nightmares have at least a dash of reality. SO . . . SO . . . SO. . . SO . . .

DREAM TWO.

I can't remember going to sleep, but one rarely does. Now, let's check on everything and make a kind of list.

One. Tobias's tail is round my neck. Yes, quite firmly so. Tight one might say. Lots and lots of fur with very little underneath and really one has some difficulty in breathing. A not very pleasant nightmare. I am beginning to wonder if I was not better off in the other one. I mean to say the flying things are still here and I still exist in a kind of grey gloom, and plus something else.

Something very nasty.

I can feel it watching me. And that's not all. My eyesight is growing keener or maybe the gloom is being rolled back.

The flying objects are taking off and I can only concentrate all my power on . . . on that little creature standing by the left hand wall.

The Creature. Italics at least. Let me have a shot at describing it. Right?

A long thin tail that an overgrown rat would not be ashamed of. So far – so good. It stood a full eight inches tall and had a black humanoid body, complete with miniature legs and arms; the perfect little fingers and toes were crowned with scarlet talons; the face was goat shaped – I can think of no better description – the eyes bright red and slanting, the ears pointed, while out from a nest of black curling hair grew two tiny horns. The beginning of a red beard covered the sharp chin and when the creature rolled back its dark red lips in a snarl, I saw a set of even white, tapering teeth.

It moved so quickly, frog-like leap that landed it on to my lap and I felt the weight, a sharp pain when a fang-tooth entered my left kneecap, when I jumped up and down a shadow thing went floating across the room.

76

A minute or so later soft thuds told me that solid horror was on its way back and another sharp pain – in my left big toe this time, a prelude for a patch of blood on my recently installed fitted carpet.

Kick, jerk, gasp – not yet scream – then a daring attempt to escape from that room, only the long thin tail became coiled round my ankles and I was down there among transparent things that streamed towards my nose and mouth and it is quite possible some got into my ears, for I know – and only the Light Lords know how – all *under-life* has this great need to take possession of flesh and blood.

I got back into my chair and the transparent things dripped from me, but it was impossible to brush them all off for they could take refuge in *shadow-being*, then somehow get into my hair.

But the Creature? It took some time for me to understand what it wanted from me. Then the penny dropped. It either wanted my left big toe or – food. Yes, I mean pork pie, stewed steak, bread, cake, any bloody thing food. To make absolutely certain I shouted: 'Grub? Nosh? Cakies for tea?' Yes, I was pushing all the right buttons. It squeaked, nodded, did a little dance, until I got up on to uncertain feet, stumbled across a slightly heaving floor, down three steps that lead to my kitchen and opened the fridge door.

The Creature (what else can I call it?) sank talons and teeth into a wedge of Danish–blue cheese and dragged it out of the fridge and on to the floor.

Oh, by Beldaza it ate quickly. Gulped. Swallowed after one bite. Had no regard for table manners. Smashed six eggs and licked white fluid and yellow yoke, then crunched the broken shell. Twelve back gammon rashers disappeared into gaping jaws while the long thin tail grew another six inches. I poured a pint of Gold-Top milk into a pudding basin and I had never heard such a guggling, guzzling, disgusting sound before.

The tiny black horns were not so tiny anymore.

The refrigerator was soon relieved of all food and I was forced to open tins of baked beans, cream, stewed steak, curried chicken, mixed vegetables, peaches in syrup, evaporated milk . . .

I was saved (for that night only) by a bottle of old claret which I poured into another pudding basin and watched it gurgle down a contorting throat. The Creature belched, made a very rude noise, then lay down and became a splodge of black shadow on the kitchen floor.

I was relieved to see it did not grow while in a shadow state.

I slept the daylight hours away like Count Dracula (to whom I am said to be related) and did not wake until the sun had set.

In fact the Creature and I woke together.

I saw his shadow spring into a solid state, then watched as the sinister little figure scurried away to disappear behind a small sideboard.

Flying horror also woke and greeted the dark hours with squealing, eye-charging rejoicing. As did the floor things, which I now realised alternated between shadow and at least semi-solid, their goal seemingly my left big toe. Let no one be surprised that I decided to leave that cursed house and wander the streets of that land we all know too well.

But I am not accustomed to walking under a night sky, so took to haunting entertainment houses where I looked longingly at white flesh and red lips, sometimes seeing one with a dead white face watching me from the other side of a crowded room. A strange world bares its face after sunset. After a while my very soul cried out for my own nest, so I visited a place where food is sold the entire night and purchased enough of sufficient variety to satisfy even the Creature's voracious appetite.

When I re-entered my house, shadow life fluttered up to the ceiling, while my creature (it is – mine) sat with its back leaning against the refrigerator door. When I spread out the harvest I had gleaned, there was once again a dance of joy, a squealing, high-pitched song of praise and I was relieved to see my guest did not consume every thing, every solid ounce, of the food I had purchased, but left enough to provide a feast when the pangs of renewed hunger so demanded.

When the silver bars of dawn framed the window I again sought my bed and arrived in that land which lies beyond the dreams of yesterday.

I awoke in darkness which I shattered by pressing two electric switches and I was at once made aware of the near silence, that was only broken by an occasional squeal, the flap of wings, then a heavy crunching sound. I sat up and cleared my brain of the lingering mists of sleep. All the food had disappeared, even plastic containers bore signs of hungry gnawing. A flying fur-covered snake circled round my head, then glided away with an angry hiss when the crunching sound came from the doorway. A large furcovered rat made a grab for my left big toe, but ran for the wardrobe when I moved my right foot. A stream of transparent things were disappearing up my left trouser leg. But I ignored them.

The crunching sound was growing louder, soon it must stand in the doorway, reinforcing that sound by a demand for food.

I waited for one minute, two . . . It was there. Huge, monstrous. Bloated. It must have eaten everything in sight, hidden, in holes, on the ceiling, on the fridge . . . My Creature was now a giant it was still hungry and the only eatable item left was. . . ?

I'm barricaded in the loo. The Creature is banging its bloated roundness against the door. I can't write much more as I'm running out of loo paper, but I do wish I could explain how all this began and can it happen to anybody? Most likely it can. Just reading about it or even thinking about it is enough to set the thingy-abobs working.

Bang . . . A hole has been punched in the top left-hand panel and the red eyes, to say nothing about the goat shaped face, is watching me. You know something? I swear it seems pleased to see me. Just maybe it doesn't really mean any harm. It's just . . . well . . . just hungry.

The Hoppity-Jump

LONG AGO, BEFORE THE great island continent called Atlantis sank beneath the waves of what is now known as the Atlantic Ocean, there existed the tiny kingdom of Francu. So far as I can understand from the ancient manuscripts in my possession, this pleasant little domain occupied an area that today would be made up from a slice of southern France, a fraction of northern Italy and the merest speck of western Switzerland.

At the time of which I am writing, King Magnus ruled the land from his capital city of Quink; and I am forced to admit that if this estimable monarch had a fault, it was his weakness for magicians. Prince Manfred, the king's son and heir, could not remember a day when there was not a usually nasty old man dressed in a dirty robe and a conical hat, standing in front of his father's throne, engaged in the task of turning snakes into walking sticks, or making a pot boil on a block of ice. And after a while the king would always ask the same question.

'Is that all you can do?'

The magicians – to a man – never failed to cringe, pour out a flow of: 'May it please your majesty . . . your majesty's humble servant . . . the Emperor of Atlantis loved this one, your majesty,' then beat a hasty retreat when the king roared his rage and threw the nearest heavy object that came to hand.

'Not one of 'em worth a pinch of salt,' he informed the queen – who was a quiet, not-much-to-say-for-herself lady. 'Magicians! Charlatans. Buffoons.'

The queen ventured to express an opinion.

'I did think that last one who turned those white mice into a team of sweet little horses was quite good, dear.'

The king laughed. A deep, hollow, mirthless sound.

'Great garbage, that trick has got whiskers on it! I must have been young Manfred's age when I first saw that one. And done a lot better, I may say. Did you notice – one of the horses had six legs?'

One morning the prime minister approached the throne and, after bowing, announced:

'I have found a new magician, your majesty. He has just arrived from the court of Atlantis.'

The king snorted. 'Indeed! And what does this one do? Turn pumpkins into carriages?'

'He claims to turn base metal into gold, sir.'

Now, Francu was a rather poor country, and gold as scarce as oranges on an apple tree, so the king rubbed his hands and said:

'Does he, by Jove! Show him in.'

The prime minister clapped his hands, and instantly a tall, dark man appeared in the great doorway and came striding towards the throne. Prince Manfred did not like the look of him at all. A long, lean face that might have been carved from granite was not enhanced by a pair of black, deep-set eyes and a thin mouth that gave the impression it might spit venom, should the occasion arise. A bald head was barely covered by a black skull cap, which appeared to be fashioned from the same material as the long, clinging robe that completely encased the grotesquely thin body.

This magician from Atlantis gave the king the most perfunctory of bows, then stood perfectly still, rather like a soldier waiting for orders. The king seemed a little put out by the man's appearance, for he hummed and hawed, twirled his moustache, then adjusted his crown, which was rather an uncomfortable piece of headgear, being made of wrought-iron. Then he said

'Yes . . . well . . . what's your name?'

The magician spoke with a deep voice which had much in

common with the croaking of a bullfrog. 'Kernon, if it please your majesty.'

'Doesn't please me a bit. Funny sort of name. I understand you can turn base metal into gold.'

Kernon – for so we must now call him – inclined his head.

'I can, sire.'

'Right – have a shot at this crown of mine.'

The magician raised a clawlike hand and the entire court gasped when blue fire streaked out from the pointed forefinger and momentarily turned the king's crown into a gleaming, seven-pointed star. Then he dropped his hand and again inclined his head.

'Your majesty is now wearing a twenty-four carat gold crown.'

The king exclaimed: 'Good grief!' and the queen murmured: 'Oh, my!' and touched her own crown, which was a miserable tin affair. After Kernon had obligingly turned this into gleaming gold, he pointed his magical fingers at the king's shoe-buckles, the royal sceptre, two iron goblets and finally the very throne itself, which, it must be confessed, had – up to that moment – been nothing more than a metal chair.

King Magnus patted his golden crown, caressed one arm of his golden throne, then picked up one of his gold goblets.

'It beats me,' he said, 'why the Emperor of Atlantis ever let you go. I mean to say – well – you're worth your weight in gold.'

Kernon sighed deeply. 'I fear, your majesty, the Emperor took exception to my assistant. They just couldn't get on together.'

'He must have been mad!' the king exclaimed. 'So far as I'm concerned, you can have as many assistants as you like.'

The magician smiled and absent-mindedly turned the Home Secretary's spectacles to gold, which was not such a good idea, as the poor man could not see through them.

'I only need one assistant, sire, but he is most essential. Would your majesty like to meet him?'

'Suppose I'd better,' the king said grumpily, for he thought all this talk about assistants was a sad waste of gold-making time. 'Get him in and be quick about it.'

Kemon rubbed his hands, muttered some indistinguishable words, then appeared to grab a large egg from the air. This he laid on the floor, then, after walking round it three times, he recited the following rhyming verse:

> 'Wake up, wake up, the sun is high.
> 'Tis time for mortals to sob and sigh.
> Liver, lights and succulent meat,
> Is walking about upon two feet.
> So up you come – mouth agape;
> Snarl, dribble, claw and jape.'

Barely had he pronounced the last word, when the egg exploded with a terrible roaring sound – and there, crouching on the steps of the throne, was the magician's assistant. All the ladies screamed, most of the men said: 'Oh, my blessed knee-breeches!' or words to that effect, and even the king was so frightened he dropped his sceptre, which is a very unlucky thing for a monarch to do.

It might be as well if we start from the top and work our way downwards. Think of an immense red pumpkin; then give it two round black holes for eyes, two shrivelled leaves for ears, a squashed strawberry for a nose, an awful gaping slit for a mouth, and two rows of jagged stones for teeth. As for the body! No one wanted to look at that – except the Home Secretary, who could not see a thing through his gold spectacles and was loudly demanding to know what was going on. It was narrow and thin, covered with red scales, equipped with very long arms that reached down to the floor when the creature was standing up, bent legs and a most alarming tapering tail, that kept lashing from side to side. To make matters worse, the head inflated and deflated at irregular intervals, rather like a monstrous balloon, when someone is blowing it up then letting the air out again. The king was the first to ask a very important question.

'Great, suffering fish! What is it?'

Kernon patted his assistant's shoulder, which resulted in the

84

awful head swelling up to three times its normal size.

'He's called the Hoppity-Jump, your majesty. But just Hoppy to his friends.'

'Has it got any friends?' the king enquired, tucking his feet under the throne when the Hoppity-Jump stared at him and licked its lips with a long black tongue. 'Keep it away from me.'

'I think,' Kernon said, pulling his assistant back, 'he's taken quite a liking to your majesty, which is by way of being an honour, as he's inclined to be a bit stand-offish as a rule. If you could see your way clear to patting his head . . .'

'Under no circumstances. Now, perhaps you will explain why it's necessary for you to go about with a dreadful thing like that.'

Kernon first pushed his assistant in the direction of the prime minister, who promptly took refuge behind the Home Secretary, then said:

'Your majesty must understand that I was born, many centuries ago, in that vast continent that lies beyond Atlantis. My father – may the earth lay lightly on his bones – who was possibly even a greater magician than myself, found the Hoppity-Jump – or rather its egg – on the top of a tall mountain. Having hatched it out by means of his magical powers, he adopted it. So Hoppy is, in a way, my foster brother.'

'Great garden garbage!' the king exclaimed.

'When my father was at last brought low by a curse sent out by an ill-intentioned witch,' Kernon went on, 'he placed the following spell on me.

So long as you keep Hoppy safe and hale,
All with you shall go well.
But once he be lost or come to harm,
Then will you lose both magic and charm.

'So your majesty can quite well understand, whosoever employs me takes Hoppy as well.'

The king looked hard and long at the Hoppity-Jump. The monster was at that moment taking a very lively interest in the prime minister, who had swarmed up an ornamental pillar. Then he examined his golden crown, throne, sceptre, goblets, shoe-buckles and the Home Secretary's spectacles.

'Yes – well – can you keep that thing under control?' Kernon's smile really was a most horrible sight. 'Within reasonable bounds. There may be one or two unpleasant incidents, but – as I'm sure your majesty will appreciate – monsters will be monsters.'

After a long pause the king nodded. 'Yes, I suppose they will. But kindly keep that thing out of my way, that's all I ask. Now – I've always fancied a gold coach . . .'

It was at that moment that the prime minister gave a strangled cry – and fell.

'But, Father,' Prince Manfred pleaded, 'you said only the other day that prime ministers were hard to come by.'

The king reluctantly left the window where he had been look-ing at his golden coach with a great deal of satisfaction.

'I might have said that prime ministers don't grow on trees, but no more than that. After all – I make prime ministers. I'll promote the Chancellor of the Exchequer. He always struck me as being an ambitious fellow.'

'I'm afraid he isn't any more, dear,' the queen said as she threaded a length of gold cotton into the eye of a golden needle. 'That awful creature swallowed him when he bent down to tie up his shoelace.'

For a while it seemed as if King Magnus was really annoyed, for, as anyone knows, although prime ministers are fairly common-place, a good Chancellor of the Exchequer is as rare as ice-cream in a desert. Then he shrugged and said:

'I must have a word with Kernon. Dash it all, if this goes on I won't have a cabinet worth mentioning.' Manfred decided it was no use talking to his father any more, for the king was by now so greedy for gold, he would let the Hoppity-Jump swallow the entire court and only make a token protest. So he left the royal apart-ments and went down to the kitchens, which is normally a place where a prince is not supposed to go.

86

But his friend Marla worked there: a pert young lady whose father had lost all his money, so that she was obliged to train as a cook – a lowly, but, as most sensible people will agree, a very worthwhile occupation. She treated Manfred with scant ceremony, maintaining that after all the bowing and 'your royal highnessing' he received from the courtiers, a few down-to-earth words were very good for him. On this occasion he found her rolling out pastry, a smudge of flour on her pretty face and an impatient gleam in her blue eyes.

'No time to talk now,' she snapped 'Not all of us are princes who have nothing better to do than strut round in satin suits.'

'But this is a serious matter,' Manfred pleaded, 'and I don't know who else I can talk to.'

'What! With all those fine cabinet ministers and privy counsellors eating their heads off – you have come to me?'

'The trouble is,' Manfred said, lowering his voice, 'they're all too frightened to advise anyone. You see, my father has engaged a new magician, and he has an assistant . . .'

'I've heard all about it,' Marla interrupted, 'and far be it for me to criticise his majesty, but those who hanker after gold must expect to pay the price, one way or another.'

'But if this goes on,' Manfred protested, 'soon there won't be any ministers left.'

'Pardon me while I cry.'

'But you don't understand. When that awful monster has swallowed all the ministers, it might well come down here.'

Marla dropped her rolling pin and assumed an expression of grim determination.

'That's different. I've no intention of ending up in some monster's stomach. Come into the butler's pantry and we'll talk this matter over.'

The butler's pantry was, in fact, a very comfortable room where that gentleman had a quiet snooze after a hearty dinner. Marla sank into a chair and waited until Manfred had seated himself in one opposite.

'Now, what's your plan?'

'I haven't actually got a plan. I was hoping you might have some idea as to how we can get rid of that thing.'

Marla raised her eyes ceilingwards.

'And to think that one day he'll be King of Francu!' She tapped her foot for a while, then asked: 'Where does this beastly thing hang out when its not swallowing cabinet ministers?'

'It becomes a large egg.'

'A what!'

'An egg. Kernon always grabs it from mid-air – the egg, I mean – before putting it on the floor and reciting some dreadful poetry over it. Then there's a flash of light, a roaring sound . . .'

Marla waved her hand impatiently. 'All right, you don't have to go on. All these magicians grab things out of the air. I expect he has the egg up his sleeve. I wonder what he does with it when he goes to sleep?'

Manfred said: 'Ah!' and succeeded in looking very knowing, although he could not understand how it mattered where the magician put his awful egg when he went to sleep.

'You do see what I mean?' Marla enquired.

'Absolutely. Well – almost.'

'Really, you are the limit! *Think.* If we can steal the egg and destroy it before Old Thinny can mutter his poem over it, then all our troubles are over. By the way, where does he sleep?'

Manfred frowned. The prospect of entering a magician's bedroom at night was not one he relished. 'The room at the top of the tower. But suppose the monster isn't an egg? What happens if we find it sitting on the foot of Kernon's bed?'

'Then we'll have to run very fast – won't we?'

Manfred nodded and wished he had never asked Marla's advice.

'Yes, I suppose we will.'

King Magnus was snoring, the queen – as befitted such a quiet, well-spoken lady – was sleeping quietly, and all the courtiers were trembling in their beds, when Prince Manfred and Marla crept up the long flight of steps which led to the tower room. Manfred allowed Marla to go first, for, as he explained, that was the only polite thing to do, but was fully prepared to turn about and run, should there be the slightest suspicion that the Hoppity-Jump was on its way down. Once he tripped, and Marla whispered:

'For goodness' sake pick up your royal feet! And don't lag behind. Anyone would think you were afraid.'

Up they went, one step at a time, pausing every once in a while to listen, their ears strained to detect the slightest sound. Then at long last they came up on to a narrow landing, and there, directly in front, high-lighted by a ceiling lamp, was an immense door. Originally it had been reinforced by thick iron bars, but Kernon must have been practising, for now they were solid, twenty-four carat gold.

'We'd better peep through the keyhole and see if he's asleep,' Marla whispered.

'Yes, perhaps you should,' Manfred agreed 'I'll keep guard at the top of the stairs.'

Marla bent down and applied her eye to the keyhole, then turned her head from side to side as though to obtain a full view of the room beyond. Presently she stood up and said softly:

'Old Nasty is stretched out on the bed with his mouth open. He doesn't appear to be moving, so I think he's in some kind of trance. These magicians do that sort of thing, you know. Go into trances, I mean.'

Manfred took a deep breath. 'Is there . . . is there anything else in sight?'

'Not a sign of a monster. So I think it's all right to go in. Are you ready?'

Manfred had never felt less ready in his entire life, but he nodded and, with deep concern, watched Marla turn the door handle.

King Magnus did not believe in spoiling his magicians, maintaining that it should be an easy matter for them to conjure up their own furniture. All the room contained was a narrow iron bed (which was now solid gold), a chair and a chest of drawers. Kernon was lying fully dressed on the bed, and a very nasty sight he looked, too.

Manfred clutched Marla's arm and whispered: 'Where do you suppose he has put the egg?'

She pointed to the chest of drawers. 'Use your eyes. What do you suppose that thing is – a loving cup?'

Manfred blinked, then muttered: 'My word!' when he saw a gold egg cup, which supported the monstrous egg, standing on the chest of drawers.

'Well, don't stand there looking like a lost dog,' Marla ordered. 'Grab it, and let's be on our way.'

The egg was exceptionally heavy for its size, and very cold. Manfred could not dismiss the thought that it might explode at any moment and he would find himself clutching a wriggling monster. So he tip-toed towards the door, holding this fearsome object at arm's length, then almost dropped it when a voice shouted:

'Wake up! Wake up!'

'It's all right,' Marla whispered in his ear, 'that's only Old Nasty talking in his sleep.'

'Yes, but what's he saying?'

They both stood perfectly still and looked back at the recumbent Kernon, who was twisting and turning in the most alarming fashion. Again he shouted:

'Wake up! Wake up! The sun is high . . .'

'That's the verse for making the egg explode!' Manfred gasped. 'What on earth are we going to do?'

Kernon made a deep snarling sound, then began talking again.

'Wake up! Wake up! The sun is high.

' 'Tis . . . 'tis . . . time for mortals to sob . . . sob . . . sob . . .'

'Don't you dare drop that egg,' Marla snapped. 'Tuck it under one arm and give me a hand. We must stop him talking in his sleep.'

'. . . and sigh,' Kernon continued. 'And sigh . . . sigh . . .'

'How can we stop him talking, apart from waking him up?' Manfred demanded.

'Fiddle-di-dee!' Marla waved her clenched fists. 'Don't they teach princes anything? Cross the right leg over the left and turn the hands downwards. Every *educated* person knows that.'

The sleeping Kernon simply poured out a torrent of words.

'Liver lights and succulent meat is walking about up on two feet . . .'

Manfred needed no further prompting. He reached the bed in two gigantic strides and leaning over the twisting body, turned Kernon's right hand palm downwards. Then he directed his attention to the left. Presently he said:

'Marla, his left hand is . . . is gripping my wrist. And I can't . . . can't get it free.'

'Really, you are helpless,' Marla complained. 'I can't leave you to do anything.'

She managed to prise the fingers from his wrist, then turned the hand over and placed it gently down on the rumpled bedspread. The result was nothing short of miraculous. Kernon became as a sleeping child that is dreaming of setting fire to its grandmother's best Sunday bonnet. His yellow teeth were bared in a ferocious grin, but he now lay still and – most thankfully – no longer talked.

'Now, let's get out of this place,' Marla instructed, 'and please do try not to make any noise.'

They crept from the room, and Marla closed the door quietly behind them, then followed the young prince down the stairs and finally into the warm kitchen.

'What shall I do with this?' Manfred enquired, laying the egg down upon the table and surveying it with distaste.

'Destroy it,' Marla replied. 'I'm going to stoke up the stove so there's plenty of hot water for tomorrow morning's breakfast. That great pot takes about six hours to boil.'

'But what shall I destroy it with? I mean to say – if I just crack the shell. . . !'

'Use the coal hammer,' Marla interrupted with more than a hint of impatience. 'And don't be afraid to hit that dreadful thing really hard.'

The coal hammer was heavy, having a massive head, and appeared to be an excellent implement for disposing of unwanted eggs. Manfred rolled up his sleeves, spat on his hands, gripped the handle – in fact, displayed every sign of a boy who is determined to do a very unpleasant job in the shortest possible time. Then he raised the hammer high in the air and brought it down on to the egg with all the strength he could muster.

The ensuing crash caused a long split to go shuddering along the table, made three plates fall off the dresser; sent a large black cat, which had been sleeping peacefully in front of the stove, running up the stairs – but did not even crack the egg. Manfred cried out and clutched his arm.

'What's the trouble now?' Marla asked. 'Don't tell me you can't even break an egg!'

'It's like hitting a lump of iron,' Manfred said. 'I'll be surprised if I haven't broken my wrist.'

'Give me that hammer. Honestly! If you want a job done, do it yourself. Stand back.'

Manfred had to admit that Marla was very good at wielding coal hammers. She placed both hands round the handle, took a deep breath, then, after spinning round on her right foot, dealt the egg a blow that made Manfred's effort seem like a gentle tap.

The table collapsed, a veritable avalanche of crockery fell from the dresser, two sides of bacon dropped from the ceiling – and the egg, with not even the slightest crack or chip, rolled over the floor.

'It can't be harmed!' Manfred gasped. 'What are we going to do?'

'Certainly not get into a tizz-wizz,' Marla retorted. 'My word, you do carry on. Now, if that egg can't be broken, there's not much point in dropping it from the palace roof, or burying it, or trying to burn it. But – we can boil it.'

'Boil it!'

'Yes – why not? The pot is beginning to simmer, and come daybreak it will be boiling away like anything. I can't think what the effect will be, but I'm willing to bet the monster won't like it.'

'Suppose – it sort of hatches out when the water gets warm?' Manfred asked.

'Don't think it can. There's certain rules to this magic business, you know. Old Nasty upstairs will have to be nearby and do his reciting act first. Any rate, here goes.'

And without further words she picked up the egg and dropped it into the pot, then placed the massive lid into position and weighed it down with a dozen flat irons.

'Well – that's that. No point in hanging about. So off to bed with you. I should imagine, come what may, tomorrow will be a hectic day.'

Manfred knew it was not much use trying to argue with Marla when she was in this kind of mood, so he said goodnight and wandered dejectedly up the stairs.

It would be nice to record that, being a brave prince, with no nerves worth mentioning, he went straight to bed and slept soundly for the remainder of the night. In fact, he was unable to sleep at all and once jumped out of bed and grabbed a ceremonial sword when a passing owl woke all the palace dogs.

The royal family were eating breakfast.

King Magnus was working his way through a heaped plate of fried eggs, grilled bacon, devilled kidneys and braised liver, with remarkable rapidity. The queen was nibbling a slice of buttered toast, while Manfred ate hardly anything at all. The king had just ordered a footman to supply a second and more generous helping, when there was a tap on the door, and the Court Chamberlain entered and took up a position at the end of the table.

'What do you want?' the king demanded. 'Can't you see I'm engaged?'

The Chamberlain bowed low and wiped his forehead with a lace handkerchief.

'I regret disturbing your majesty, but the court magician has requested an immediate audience.'

'Tell him to wait until I've finished me breakfast. Dash it all, the fellow never gives me a minute's peace.'

'I fear he rather insists you see him at once, your majesty. He's in a very bad mood.'

'Insists!' the king roared. 'Insists! Tell him to go take a running jump.'

'I think, dear,' the queen said quietly, 'it might be as well if you saw him at once. After all, we really can't afford to lose any more ministers yet awhile.'

'What! Um! Perhaps you're right. I wanted to have a word with him on that subject. All right, show him in.'

Manfred emptied his coffee cup in one mighty gulp then cast an extremely anxious glance at the retreating Chamberlain.

'Could I be excused, Father?'

'No you can't. I want you to see how I deal with this fellow. And stop fidgetting. I can't think what's wrong with you this morning.'

The door was suddenly flung open, and Kenton, his face creased into a ferocious scowl, all but ran into the room. Without so much as a bow or a 'your majesty', he roared:

'Where is it? Who's taken it? I warn you . . .'

King Magnus choked on a piece of kidney, and it was only after the queen had thumped his back that he was able to speak.

'Who do you think you are? What! Bursting in here, shouting at me. Eh! Making me choke! You're asking for a spell in a dungeon. A quick trip to the block. Never been so insulted in all me life.'

Kernon appeared to be in no way put out by these threats, but continued to glower and grimace and stamp his feet.

'Someone has taken it. Stolen it while I was asleep. And if it's not returned in two minutes flat, I'll turn your tinpot kingdom into a rubbish heap. I'll blight all the crops, dry up all the rivers, make the sky rain blood, call up a plague of rats . . .'

'Here – hold on,' the king ordered. 'Keep your robe on. Now, what's all this about? Am I to understand that you've lost something?'

Kernon went quite black in the face.

'I haven't lost anything. Someone has stolen *the* egg. Purloined my assistant. Taken my dear little Hoppity-Jump while he was in his embryo stage. I want him back – now. This very minute.'

'And do you imagine I've got the horrible little wretch here?'

94

the king demanded. 'Wouldn't give it house room. In fact, I was going to have words with you on the subject. There's to be no more swallowed cabinet ministers. People are beginning to talk, which is only one stage from them not paying their taxes.'

'I see,' Kernon said grimly. 'I must resort to action.'

'Yes.' The king nodded. 'You can turn these forks to gold. Earn your keep.'

'I was thinking of turning your wife's hair to snakes,' Kernon retorted, bending and cracking his fingers in a most disgusting fashion.

'I don't think I'd like that,' the queen protested. 'Neither would my hairdresser.'

'If I'm not told where my little Hoppy is by the time I count ten,' the magician went on, 'get ready for a hissing hairdo. One . . .'

The king turned pale and half rose from his chair.

'Look here – you really don't intend to . . .'

'Two.'

'But dash it all, man, you can't . . .'

'Three.'

'I always said you shouldn't encourage these magicians, dear,' the queen said reproachfully. 'Now I'll never be able to wear a decent hat again.'

'Four.'

'Don't worry,' King Magnus promised, 'from now on I'll make sure not one of the scoundrels sets foot in the kingdom.'

'Five.'

'I suppose you haven't got his beastly egg tucked away some-where?' the queen enquired. 'I know how absent-minded you are.'

'Of course I haven't got it. Now, Kernon, I've had just about enough of this . . .'

'Six.'

Manfred knew he would have to confess. The prospect of his mother with a crop of snakes for hair, plus all the other dreadful events the magician had threatened to bring about, was more than he could even contemplate. He jumped to his feet and shouted:

'I know where the egg is. It's in the kitchen.'

Kernon stopped counting, then nodded and said softly: 'You just wait, my lad, until I've got my little friend back to his old, stomach-filling self. He'll be ravenous after missing his breakfast.'

He turned and ran from the room and knocked the Chamberlain over, before that official had time to remove his ear from the keyhole. The king sighed and placed his hand on Manfred's shoulder.

'Sorry about this, son. All my fault. But I just couldn't resist the prospect of having all that gold.'

'I think,' the queen said quietly, 'we too had better go down to the kitchen. I don't want the cook giving notice.'

The cook, several scullions, umpteen kitchen-maids and Marla were watching a very angry magician and completely ignored the royal family when they entered the kitchen. Kernon was opening cupboards, smashing crockery, overturning tables and shouting: 'Where is it? I know it's here,' then stamping his feet when the Hoppity-Jump egg failed to materialize. Manfred cast a quick glance at the large iron pot which was still on the stove, rattling its lid like a fussy old gentleman demanding attention.

'Excuse me,' he said, 'but – what you're looking for is in that pot.'

Instantly Marla grabbed his arm and hissed:

'You little sneak! Why did you have to tell him?'

'He was going to turn my mother's hair into snakes,' Manfred explained, 'and dry up all the rivers and . . .'

'What do you imagine will happen if that Hoppy-thing gets loose again?'

Kernon grabbed the pot and carrying it over to the sink, tipped a mass of boiled turnips into a bowl, then began to rummage through them, badly scalding his fingers in the process. Presently he roared:

'It's not here! The Hoppy-egg isn't here!'

The cook, a very humble lady who knew her place, came forward and performed a little curtsey.

'Begging your pardon, sir, not wishing to intrude, but if it's an egg you're looking for – why, I found it this morning, when I came to clean the pot.'

Kernon grabbed the cook and shook the poor lady until her hairpins fell out.

'Where did you put it? Tell me, woman.'

'That I will, sir, if only you'll let me speak. As it was a very hard egg and I wasn't able to crack it, why, I thought, there's no reason why it shouldn't be put to good use. So – begging your pardon once again – I used it to prop the larder door open.'

'What!'

'It being a light door, you understand, sir, and it being such a heavy egg. I do hope that I haven't done anything I shouldn't . . .'

Kernon ran to the larder and returned in no time at all, clutching the Hoppity-Jump egg in both hands. Manfred shuddered when he saw the malicious gleam in the magician's eyes and hid behind his father, who kept muttering: 'Never liked the fellow's face.'

'Now,' Kernon said, 'you that have legs, prepare to feel them tremble.'

He laid the egg down upon the floor and quickly recited the rhyming spell, clearly anxious to get his assistant back into full swallow-form in the shortest possible time. There was a faint popping sound, the merest flicker of light, and everyone gasped when the Hoppity-Jump materialized in a cloud of steam.

The magician chuckled. 'A very good morning to you, Hoppy. I expect you fancy a little snack. How about that wretched boy for starters? Then maybe that odious girl? Off you go.'

The Hoppity-Jump did not move. Just crouched at its master's feet and stared with unblinking eyes at the cook, who looked very worried and said: 'Begging your pardon, sir, I'll see about getting them greens on the stove.'

Kernon's voice carried an undertone of impatience.

'Come on, Hoppy. Get a move on. Start swallowing.' The Hoppity-Jump might have been an extremely ugly statue, for there was not the slightest movement, not even a nod, to signify it had heard the magician's instructions. Kernon displayed signs of deep concern.

'What's wrong, boy? Do you feel out of sorts?'

A minute passed, then another, and presently Marla, with courage that Manfred could only admire, stepped forward and laid her hand on the monster's head. Then she patted, poked, shook, kneaded, pummelled and finally kicked.

'Do take care, dear,' the queen advised.

'There's no need,' Marla said calmly. 'The Hoppity-Jump is hard-boiled.'

Kernon clutched his head, tore his hair and generally behaved like a man who has suffered an overwhelming disaster.

'Hard-boiled! Over-cooked! My dear little Hoppy destroyed!'

'Which means you're no longer a magician,' Manfred announced, coming out from behind his father. 'So you can't turn my mother's hair to snakes or dry up rivers.'

'Neither can you transform any more base metals into gold!' the king exclaimed. 'Not much use, are you? Might as well have your head off.'

Kernon flung himself at the king's feet and appeared to be so frightened, Manfred felt quite sorry for him.

'Have mercy, sire. I never intended to turn her majesty's beautiful hair into snakes. Just my little joke. And I'm very sorry about your prime minister and Chancellor of the Exchequer, but Hoppy would insist on swallowing people. I spoke most severely to him many times.'

The cook performed another little curtsey.

'Begging your pardon, your majesty, but if I might be so bold, we be needing a man to do the rough work, peeling potatoes, minding the fires and so forth, so if you'd like me to take him off your hands, I'd be pleased to oblige and that's a fact.'

The king nodded. 'Very well. But stand no nonsense from the fellow.' He jerked his head in the direction of the hard-boiled

98

Hoppity-Jump. 'And send that thing upstairs. It'll be useful to hang me crown on.'

Needless to say, no more magicians were allowed to enter Francu, and everyone remarked what a splendid ruler King Magnus was, now that he could devote his full time to affairs of state. Marla was made lady-in-waiting to the queen, although she occasionally popped down to the kitchen and made certain that Kernon did not neglect his duties.

Eventually she married Prince Manfred, and when, in the fullness of time, he ascended the throne, ruled him and the kingdom most successfully.

And the Hoppity-Jump? What with the king using it as a hatstand, and the queen as a pin-cushion, most people forgot it had ever been a monster.

Bongla

'HAVE YOU,' THE MAN on the park seat enquired while he tied a knot in a piece of sisal string that did duty for a shoe lace, 'ever wondered why many faces you pass in the average busy street are extraordinarily familiar? And I mean extraordinarily familiar. It's not the face you recognize so much as the personality that gleams like a diamond in sunlight behind it.'

I admitted somewhat reluctantly, for I dislike entering into conversation with ragged strangers on park benches, that on occasion I had experienced some such phenomena, but had assumed that it was merely the offspring of an over-active imagination.

The man nodded and his greasy grey hair quivered like wind-whipped sea. 'Most people do. But the facts are simple and not at all fantastic if you reason reasonably – if I might be allowed to phrase – and aren't all that afraid of the unusual. It is the controlling ego that resides in the brain you recognize. The essential self. Know what I mean?'

I shook my head. 'No. Can't say I do.'

The man shifted his lean frame into a more comfortable position and I wondered how old he was and when he had last taken a bath. Had a good soap and water wash. But his voice suggested education, even culture of a kind.

'You must understand that we are all part of an unending whole. You, my dear and patient sir, are repeated many times over this planet. Imagine a line of buckets standing on the seashore. You dip each one into the sea and bring it out filled to the brim.

101

Five Yous. Occasionally you meet up with one of those Yous and all hell breaks loose. When that You is a member of the opposite sex, disaster follows you around as a giant shadow. I mean that. The kind of shadow that you can only see in moonlight. But it's there. You suffer from a disease called love-hate. Often proves to be fatal. One can finish up killing the other. The shadow of course is Death.'

'Really?'

A cold glint came into his eyes and instinct warned me he could turn nasty if I displayed the slightest sign of mockery. These weirdos, who are permitted brief glimpses of what lay behind the curtain, cannot understand the strange darkness that blinds the vast majority of the human race. Alas, I am one of their number.

'I must go,' I exclaimed, rising quickly. 'Sorry.'

His unwashed, bearded face creased itself into a sneer.

'We have met before. Way back when you were a seller of holy water on the pilgrim's way. I used to watch you by the hour. Saw you dip the iron bowl into the filled ditch and bring up the "holy" water. Aye, and once had to push the dead dog aside. The bloated one that had floated down from the farm a mile ahead.'

'You have a rich imagination,' I said.

He again bared ruined teeth. 'Mine is a freak memory, that I could well do without. But at least . . . at least I'm not fleeing before the black shadow.'

'I'm not . . .'

'Look over your left shoulder.'

I ran across the park and did not look back until I reached the main gate.

The bench was unoccupied. There was no one in sight. Not a soul.

The Tele-Mon

It is perhaps to be regretted that the entire Roberts family were television addicts.

Their particular colour set stood in a secluded corner of the sitting-room and was watched most of the day, from one year's end to the next, save for the first two weeks in August, when the family went on holiday and had to make do with a miserable black and white model.

In fact, Mrs Roberts first words after she had opened the front door and watched her bleary-eyed husband dump their cases in the hall, was, 'It's nice to get back to one's own telly.' Then she would all but run into the sitting-room, where she slumped down into the nearest chair and made rude remarks about *Blue Peter*.

It must not be thought that the Roberts were – if I may coin a phrase – finicky viewers. They accepted whatever the clever television people cared to offer, being careful, however, to switch over to another channel whenever a programme threatened to become educational. Nevertheless they did acquire a certain amount of knowledge. Mrs Roberts, for example, knew that one soap powder washed whiter-than-white; Mr Roberts that TV detectives were very clever people indeed, and young Peter could have shot down every badman in the west, if someone had only given him a Colt .45.

Mother, father and son sat and watched the bright screen, day after day, month after month, year after year, sending out bemused thoughts that somehow got mixed up with high-

103

frequency radio-waves; did strange things to a stream of electrons, warped umpteen lines of charged particles and finally started something very nasty in the cathode tube.

'Why isn't there any more?' Peter demanded. 'The screen is still alive. It looks like boiling porridge.'

Mrs Roberts was a very kind mother who believed in answering all intelligent questions to the very best of her ability.

'It's like this, dear,' she explained. 'When the nice man says, "Goodnight, everyone – goodnight", somebody pulls a lot of switches and the power is sort of shut off, and all we can see is that bright mist – which now you come to mention it, does look a bit like boiling porridge. But now you must climb the wooden hill to Bedfordshire.'

Peter was not really convinced, however, for it seemed ridiculous to him that a flourishing television set that could still present a bright screen, was incapable of broadcasting some lively night programme. How could anyone be sure? His father just switched off and said: 'Another telly-day over,' and then they went to bed and slept through what could well be the most interesting telly-time of all.

Peter came to a momentous decision.

One night he climbed out of bed, put on his dressing-gown, armed himself with an electric torch, then crept down the stairs. He switched on the sitting-room wall lights, walked over to the television set and after some hesitation – turned the 'off-on' knob.

Instantly the screen lit up; seething mist crackled and spluttered, looking like a mass of different coloured peas boiling in a square saucepan. Peter sank down into a chair and waited with breathless expectancy for something to happen. After some time he decided that the mist was of a different texture and certainly much more interesting than it had been when his father had switched the set off. It was much thicker and produced an occasional odd-shaped lump that raced round the screen as though seeking a lost companion.

Presently two more lumps appeared – one yellow and the other

104

blue – and they rushed towards the first one, which appeared to blush, for it turned bright pink, before merging with its more colourful counterparts. The result was a large multi-coloured blob which swayed from side to side and seemed to be eating up all the bubbling peas, for they simply teemed in from all sides and fed the pulsating monster until it filled the entire screen.

There was a loud popping sound – the screen momentarily turned black – then the vision returned and presented Peter with a picture, that proved beyond all doubt that a well regulated television set never slept.

The scene was unique and most certainly owed nothing to any of the programmes that entertained the Roberts family during the day.

Peter found himself looking into a large room that appeared to be so real, he felt certain that a very small boy could wriggle in through the screen and crawl along the bright red floor. It had walls that kept changing colour and once in a while dissolved into a quivering green mist; one mauve door and a round window that permitted the viewer to see an expanse of wild moorland.

But it was THAT which walked – if that was the correct expression – down the centre of the room and eventually filled most of the screen, which demanded his full attention. Squat, square-shouldered, it was a television addict's nightmare. A fat, bulging face that had two bright spots for eyes, a broad gleaming slit of a mouth, a small knob for a nose and two larger ones for ears; a pair of indoor aerials rearing up from either side of its bald head, and thin arms that had much in common with interwoven wire flex. The creature was attired in a long robe that had been made from a fine assortment of horror comics: a dress style that would have won Peter's unstinted admiration, had he not been so frightened.

The bright eyes stared at the young viewer with disturbing intensity and a deep hollow voice said:

'Feed . . . feed . . . feed . . . m . . . e . . . e . . . e . . .'

At first Peter thought he must be watching the beginning of a science-fiction film and fully expected a man in a space suit to emerge and start feeding the creature with concentrated food tablets. But the tiny pin-points of light continued to glare at him with a kind of ferocious expectancy and presently the request – or was it a demand? – was repeated:

'Feed . . . m . . . e . . . e . . . e . . .'

Three times Peter opened his mouth to reply and three times he closed it again. Although Mrs Roberts sometimes shouted at the television and had been known to make such remarks as: 'Look behind, you silly sausage! He's got a gun trained on you!' it still required a great deal of will-power to actually start a conversation with a televised monster. Apart from any other reason – there was no telling how it would end.

But when the squat figure moved a little closer and gave the impression it might well come out of the screen, he thought it might be wise to say something.

'I don't know what you like to eat.'

The Tele-Mon raised a long thin arm and turned the knob which did service for a nose and instantly the gleaming eyes grew larger, until they resembled round mirrors which were reflecting a very bright light. The action alarmed Peter greatly and he would have run from the room, had he been able to rise from his chair. The hollow voice spoke again.

'Want . . . soap . . . de-ter-gent . . . tea-bags . . . toothpaste . . . hair-cream . . .'

'Please,' Peter, interrupted, 'I really can't give you any of those things. I mean to say – I'm here – and you – well – you're in there.'

The monster appeared to consider this point for some little while, then it nodded its head thoughtfully as though coming to an important decision; turned around and walked ponderously back along the room. It opened the mauve door, went out into what appeared to be a very dark passage, then disappeared from view.

Peter heard heavy footsteps pounding what sounded like a stone floor; door hinges that screamed an oil-starved protest; then a muffled tread, which suggested that the monster was descending a flight of dust-covered steps – and finally the creak of a large key being turned in a mighty lock.

A few seconds passed before a soft thud-thud came from behind the television set; a sound that was even more disturbing than those which had gone before. Then the Tele-Mon lumbered into view. With every step it grew larger, until a terrifying figure that was at least as tall as Peter came to a halt in front of his chair. The hollow voice again sent out a flow of mangled words:

'Want . . . nour . . . ish . . . ment . . . crunch . . . y . . . bis . . . cuits . . . choc . . . o . . . late . . . ice . . . cream . . . lip . . . stick . . . hair . . . dye . . .'

The Tele-Mon appeared to have an insatiable appetite and continued to demand a seemingly unending list of items that Peter realised had been advertised on commercial television at one time or another. Finally he decided that an interesting night programme was one thing, a starving monster was quite another, so he shouted: 'In the kitchen – help yourself,' before running from the room and not stopping until he was safely behind his bedroom door, which he barricaded with a chair as an added precaution.

Although Peter got up several times during the night and pressed his ear to the keyhole, he did not hear a solitary sound. Eventually he fell asleep and dreamed he was being chased down a long passage by the Tele-Mon, while repeating its perpetual demand for something to eat.

Mrs Roberts was so put out she forgot to sprinkle sugar over Peter's porridge.

'Burglars! What on earth is the world coming to!'

Mr Roberts shook his head sadly and stared at his cup of black coffee.

'And they drank all of our milk!'

'Milk!' Mrs Roberts pointed a shaking forefinger in the direction of the kitchen. 'And what about my *Whiter-than-White* soap-powder? Then there's my *Bridge-that-gap* biscuits and *Polish-*

with-a-wipe floor polish. All gone. To say nothing of my twelve boxes of *Add-an-egg* cake-mix.'

'Even took my *Rub-it-in* back liniment,' Mr Roberts observed dourly. 'I can't think what a burglar would want that for. It never did me any good.'

'Moreover,' Mrs Roberts found difficulty in finding words to express her horror, 'they . . . they actually . . . without so much as by-your-leave . . . turned our telly on . . . and . . . didn't bother to turn it off again. My heart went up into my mouth when I came down this morning and heard a voice coming from the sitting-room. It was some professor rabbiting away on *Open University.*'

Peter had contributed nothing to the discussion, fully aware that it was not burglars who were responsible for the disappearance of household commodities, but – from every point of view – something far worse. He almost choked on his *Warm-glow* porridge when Mrs Roberts announced:

'We must ring the police. Pity we can't get that little man in a dirty, raincoat. He'd track the scoundrels down in no time.'

The plain-clothes policeman who arrived later in the morning, wore a nice new raincoat and therefore failed to merit Mrs Roberts' full confidence.

'Are you going to pull in all the likely suspects?' she asked, eyeing the young man with cold disapproval. 'Round 'em up from all the clip-joints and blow cigarette smoke in their faces?'

The policeman scratched his head.

'The trouble is, ma'am, I can't place any criminals who could find a market for soap-powder, floor-polish, cake-mix and back-liniment. I mean to say – burglars have to make a living like the rest of us and there's no money in stuff like that. Not in such small quantities at any rate.'

After refusing a cup of milkless tea, he departed, having promised to call again should anything turn up. Mrs Roberts slammed the front door, then returned to the kitchen.

'He wouldn't last ten minutes on television,' she said scathingly. 'Made no attempt to look for clues, like loose buttons and things.'

In the meanwhile Peter was worried about what would happen when the television set was turned on again. When Mrs Roberts settled down to her afternoon viewing, would she experience more drama in two minutes, than most TV plays packed into two hours? Certainly she would not take kindly to a lumbering monster with a peculiar appetite, particularly if it came out in the middle of an interesting programme.

But as it happened there was no need for worry. When Peter came home from school and ran into the sitting-room fully expecting to find his mother prostrate on the hearthrug, he was greeted by a beaming smile.

'Hullo, love. You're early! My, you've been running!'

'Yes, I wanted to see if you were – all right.'

'Of course I'm all right. Here – have a *Long-Chew* chocolate.'

Peter accepted the chocolate and looked anxiously at the television. A young man was explaining how to make lampshades out of old hats.

'Anything – anything unusual on this afternoon?'

Mrs Roberts waited until she had swallowed her *Long-Chew* chocolate before answering.

'There was a nice sad film. All about a rich young woman who fell in love with a musician, then committed suicide.'

Peter expelled his breath in a deep sigh of relief, realising that the monster would not put in an appearance before midnight. He cleared his throat and made a dreadful suggestion.

'Do you think we should watch so much television?'

Mrs Roberts's mouth gaped, her eyes bulged; in fact she had not looked so unhappy since that awful time when power cuts had curtailed viewing to a mere hour per evening.

'Oh, dear, you're ill!'

'No, I'm fine,' Peter hastened to reassure her. 'But I do think – well – we ought to do something else – sometimes.'

'What else is there to do?'

Peter racked his brains and finally supplied a reasonable answer.

'We could talk.'

'But if we don't watch television, dear, what would we talk about?'

This was a problem that Peter had never faced before, but he was spared the immediate necessity of solving it, for at that moment the front door opened and Mr Roberts called out:

'I'm home. Anything good on the box?'

Mrs Roberts rose abruptly from her chair and walked very quickly into the hall. Peter heard her say: 'I'm sure he's sickening for something.' Then his father exclaimed: 'He never did!' followed by a lot of agitated whispering.

Presently both parents entered the room looking so worried, Peter felt quite sorry for them. Then his father sank into a chair and spoke in a subdued voice.

'What's all this, then— Eh? Wanting to talk instead of watching the old telly! Wouldn't be civilized.'

For a moment Peter was on the point of telling them the truth, but fortunately commonsense came to his rescue, for such an admission would have resulted in him being packed off to bed, chock full of *Bonfield's Well-Quik*, a panacea for all ills that had been strongly recommended on a recent commercial.

'I only thought,' he said quietly, 'that viewing all the time might not be good for our television set.'

Mr Roberts laughed and Mrs Roberts positively beamed, so great was her relief.

'So that's it! Listen, son. We rent the old telly, don't we? And if it should go on the blink, all I have to do is ring up *Telly-Rent* and a mechanic will be round here in two shakes of a lamb's tail. So there's no need for you to worry.'

Peter had grave doubts if the most talented mechanic alive would be willing to replace *That* which had come out of their television set, but he pretended to be convinced and did not speak again until Mrs Roberts brought the *Watch-and-Eat* snack in on a trolley.

All went well until the final programme.

This was a weekly serial which featured a white-haired doctor, who not only cured a lot of sick people, but settled their family quarrels, patched up failing marriages and sometimes brought the odd criminal to justice as well. Both Mr and Mrs Roberts agreed he was a very remarkable man, who might well have apprehended the nocturnal thief, if only he had been in the locality at the time. Peter – who was feeling the effects of a broken night's sleep – had dozed off, when he was jerked back into full awareness by his father exclaiming:

'Heck – what's that!'

Peter felt his heart-beat quicken when he was once again in a condition to look at the bright screen. The good doctor was pacing up and down in front of a window, apparently explaining to a young couple that they must help each other – and morever – be exceptionally kind to the lady next door, because her son had just been kidnapped by a New York gang. Normally Peter would have wondered why those clever policemen who either wore dirty raincoats or Stetson hats had allowed this band of son-stealers to slip through their fingers, but now he could only gape and do his best not to cry out.

For the Tele-Mon had its face pressed to the windowpanes and was flashing its bright eyes from side to side, as though waiting with ill-concealed impatience for this nonsense to end. Then it vanished – leaving behind an unimpeded view of distant hills and the doctor's car parked under a tree.

'Here,' Mrs Roberts registered a protest, 'that thing wasn't mentioned in the *TV Times*! I mean to say – it don't actually fit into the plot.'

Mr Roberts nodded with ponderous solemnity. 'Don't you be so sure. That was one of them gangsters. Trying to frighten that nice young couple so they won't help the lady next door.'

'Do you really think so?'

'You can bet on it. The monkeys!'

'I think,' Peter said, once he had regained his breath, 'we ought to switch off.'

His father looked at him with an expression of faint surprise. 'Why? Surely you aren't frightened of a gangster dressed up? Not after all those horror films you've watched? In any case it won't

111

come back tonight. There's no time. The programme ends in five minutes.'

'Doctor Thingy will unmask it next week,' Mrs Roberts promised. 'Now, who's ready for a cup of *Tum-Like* cocoa?'

Peter was very relieved when his father finally turned the television off and announced that another telly-day was over. But he could not dismiss the impression that the screen was most reluctant to die, for the bright mist faded very slowly and a bright pin-point of light remained for some time, as though the Tele-Mon was peering through a keyhole. Then Mr Roberts made sure that all the doors were locked and the windows securely fastened, while Mrs Roberts hid the newly purchased supply of soap-powder, floor-polish, biscuits, cake-mix – in fact anything that was even remotely eatable or drinkable – under the bed in the spare room.

'A waste of time of course,' Mr Roberts stated. 'Lightning never strikes in the same place twice.'

When Peter snuggled down under the bedclothes, he did so with one comforting thought. So long as the television set was switched off, there was no chance of the monster getting out. Partially reassured by this piece of logic he closed his eyes and was just slipping into unconsciousness when a sudden sound made him sit upright and stare across the moonlit room. He waited for what seemed like an eternity, straining his ears, watching the door, fully prepared to seek refuge under the bedclothes should it open. Then the sound came again. A dull knocking that was taking place somewhere downstairs.

'Please. don't do that,' he whispered. 'You can't get out.'

But the knocking persisted and although his parents were very heavy sleepers, they were bound to wake up if it continued indefinitely. Peter had a mental picture of his father turning the television on and that thing coming out – getting bigger and bigger – and his mother screaming— all because he, Peter, had stupidly wanted to see if there was a late night – or early morning – programme.

Terrified, but resolute, he slipped out of bed and put on his dressing-gown.

*

The knocking was coming from inside the television set.

Peter walked forward and stopped some three feet from the dull grey screen and said in a tremulous voice:

'Please stop. You'll wake my parents.'

A tiny spot of light appeared and the knocking was renewed, but now much louder. Peter trembled as he listened to the heavy *thump-thump* and saw the little bright eye twinkle, rather like a distant star on a frosty night. There was no doubt in his mind as to what must be done – if he did not want his father creeping downstairs with an inverted umbrella. Switch on and trust that he could appeal to the monster's better nature.

It took more courage than Peter knew he possessed to turn the chromium-plated knob, and great self-control not to cry out when the Tele-Mon flashed into being, standing in the foreground of that long room and glaring out of the screen with gleaming, circular eyes.

Peter took refuge behind the sofa when the creature turned and began to slowly walk back along the room, then opened the mauve door and went out into the darkness. The tramp of heavy feet descending dust-covered steps, the creaking of another door – then IT came out from behind the television set and advanced towards the frightened boy.

Undoubtedly a mixture of soap-flakes, floor-polish, biscuits, cake-mix and milk contains much that is of nutritious value to a Tele-Mon, for the creature became larger and larger, until it was well over six feet tall and at least three feet wide. After adjusting its ear-knobs it boomed:

'Want . . . more. Lots . . . lots . . . and . . . lots . . . more.'

It was almost a full minute before Peter was able to speak, and even then his voice was not much above a hoarse whisper.

'We . . . we haven't got any more. My mother took . . . took everything upstairs.'

'More . . . e . . . e . . . e,' the Tele-Mon insisted and without wasting further words, began to trudge slowly towards the kitchen.

113

Peter waited for a roar of rage, the baffled cry of a food-bereft monster, but instead heard the sound of contented munching. Presently he crept out into the hall and peered in through the open kitchen doorway.

There was no manner of doubt that the Tele-Mon had an enormous appetite and a really first-class digestion. Peter watched it consume Mrs Roberts's *Kit-de Luxe* plastic curtains, a container of *Soft-Hands* washing-up liquid, six *Wipe-Easi* tea-towels, three *Moonbright* bars of soap, one roll of *Dri-Mitt* kitchen paper and a blue *Smartie-Wife* apron. Then the monster turned its head and looked appealingly at Peter.

'M . . . o . . . r . . . e . . . e . . . e . . . e,' it boomed. 'Much . . . much . . . m . . . o . . . r . . . e . . . e . . .'

'But – gosh – you can't have any more! Not after that lot. You just can't. Why not go back into the television set, like a good monster?'

The bright eyes grew larger, the booming voice took on a menacing tone. 'Want more . . . more . . . e . . . e . . . e.'

Peter had a terrible vision of his parents coming downstairs in the morning and finding rooms which had been stripped of everything, except the larger items of furniture – and he was not too sure that the monster could not eat those as well. Then he was struck by an idea. An idea that was so breath-taking, he could only marvel at his own ingenuity.

'I can find lots more food for you. The dustmen have been on strike for five days.'

The Tele-Mon lowered its voice to a contented rumble.

'Lots . . . more . . . is . . . good. I . . . have . . . gap . . . that . . . needs . . . bridging.'

Peter unlocked the back door, ran out into the passage and returned with a bulging black plastic bag. He dumped it down in front of the expectant Tele-Mon, who wasted no time in ripping the plastic to shreds and gorging itself on a collection of tin cans, bottles, cigarette butts, empty cartons and a pair of Mr Roberts's old shoes.

From then on Peter worked very hard indeed. He carried six

full bags into the kitchen, plus two overflowing dustbins and it was an extremely tired boy who finally sank down on to a kitchen chair and looked fearfully up at the still feeding monster.

It swallowed two more *Pied-Eyed-Peas* cans, crammed three *Gob-Freeze* ice-cream cartons into its mouth, then made an awful belching sound.

'Soon . . . sun . . . come . . . up. Must . . . go . . . back . . . to . . . telly. Tomorrow . . . want . . . more . . . e . . . e . . . e . . . e.'

The sheer horror of the situation made Peter gasp. Night after night he must creep downstairs and somehow find food for a monster, whose appetite would never – but never – be appeased. He said: 'Oh, no!' several times, a choice of words that apparently did not please the Tele-Mon at all.

'You . . . turn telly . . . on . . . or . . . I . . . blow . . . set . . . up . . .'

This was a dreadful threat and Peter could imagine his parents horror if an explosion took place in the middle of one of their favourite programmes. He tried to appeal to the Tele-Mon, but the towering figure was already on its way back to the sitting-room, rather like – and Peter could not suppress the thought – a vampire returning to its coffin at sunrise.

Suddenly he jumped up, quite dizzy with excitement. A vampire had to return to its coffin at sunrise – and a Tele-Mon had to return to its telly. And moreover – and this was a reasonable supposition – to a switched-on telly.

Peter did not have time to consider the matter any further, so he dashed into the sitting-room, gave one quick glance at the monster, who was already shrinking – and pulled the wallplug from its socket.

The picture of the long room disappeared. The Tele-Mon which had now shrank to a little below Peter's height, turned its head and glared at him.

'Put . . . plug . . . back . . . in.'

But Peter, who had watched innumerable horror films, was certain that only one more action was needed to rid the house of this creature forever. He walked calmly to the window and drew back the curtains. The rising sun which was just peering over the garden wall, flooded the room with pale golden light and seemed to disperse the nasty night-shadows that always haunt even the best appointed rooms – then did something disastrous to the Tele-Mon.

It did manage to rumble: 'Put . . . pl . . . g . . . g . . . g . . .' when it started to fade. First the head became transparent, then the horror comic robe sort of crumbled and took on the appearance of old newspaper that had been used to wrap fish and chips in. A few seconds later Peter heard a loud bang, just before the Tele-Mon vanished entirely.

If he had not known better, he might have supposed its cathode tube had burnt out.

Mrs Roberts refused to summon the unsatisfactory policeman.

'There's no point,' she said. 'He'll have no more chance of catching the thief than he would that nice Mr Raffles. Besides,' she smiled wistfully, 'whoever it is – he's got a kind heart.'

'Kind heart!' Mr Roberts exclaimed. 'After pinching all your plastic curtains, washing-up liquid, tea-towels and all that other stuff?'

'Yes, I know.' Mrs Roberts sighed. 'But he did take all our rubbish away and if that doesn't mean he's got a kind heart, I'd like to know what would. Don't you agree, Peter?'

Peter smiled slyly. 'He's got – or had – a big one. Very big indeed.'

I am pleased to say that the Roberts family do not watch television so much as they did. Mrs Roberts has joined the local bingo club and Mr Roberts the *Thorn and Thistle* darts team. Both are doing well in their chosen professions.

And Peter? Well, he's reading a lot of books that explain how a television works.

Just in case.

Big-feet

SOMEWHERE IN THE REGION which separates Ashford from Canterbury is the city of Ashbury. Now, it is no use you looking for it on a map. It will not be found on any bus route, neither is there a railway station. In fact – to be honest – it is very difficult to find. But, at the same time, very easy if you are the right sort of person.

Let me explain what I mean. If you are someone who says: 'I don't believe in Father Christmas, ghosts, flying saucers or little green men from Mars,' then you won't find Ashbury in a million years. On the other hand, if you seriously believe in all these things, and you happen to be in the right mood, while walking in the right place at the right time, then you might just walk slap-bang into the walls of Ashbury.

Cary Bedford was such a boy. He was spending the summer holiday with his Uncle and Aunt at Ashford, and had gone for a long walk along the Canterbury Road. He was thinking of nothing in particular, certainly not about lost cities – for it stands to reason that Ashbury must have been lost at some time or another – when a voice said: 'Look where you're going, boy,' and there stood a man in a green doublet and red hose, looking very worried.

Cary glanced around, then gaped with profound astonishment. Gone were the flat green fields of Kent, the long grey ribbon of a road, the grass verge and the neat hedgerows. Instead, he saw a vast plain, with tall, rolling hills in the background. But the most

117

alarming sight was the city. It stood to Cary's right, a mass of roof-tops and turrets that could just be seen over a surrounding wall. He was standing on a wide dirt path which led up to a massive gateway, through which a vast number of people were moving as fast as their feet would carry them.

'Almost bumped into me,' the man complained. 'This is no time to be wool-gathering, boy.'

'Sorry, sir,' Cary apologized, 'but I seem to be lost. Could you tell me the quickest way back to Ashford?' The man frowned. 'Never heard of it. And I've lived round these parts all my life. You sure you don't mean Ashbury? There it is – and you'd best get in there quick. Big-feet is coming.'

As can be imagined, Cary was both frightened and astonished and was not reassured by the man's last remark.

'What . . . who, sir, is . . . Big-feet?'

The man's face turned to a very bright red. He stamped his foot, clenched his fists and generally gave the impression that he was very angry indeed.

'Don't you try to be funny with me, boy. I've got too much on my mind to bandy words with you. Now get inside the city and no more nonsense. The king has given me the job of warning the shepherds that Big-feet is coming.'

With that he strode away, and Cary – because there was nowhere else for him to go – walked up the path towards the great gateway.

Here he found a number of men who must have been soldiers, for they were all dressed in blue uniforms and bright steel helmets. They were shouting at the hurrying procession of people in an effort to make them move even faster.

'Come on, get a move on,' bellowed an officer, who was distinguished by a golden helmet. 'Do you want old Big-feet to eat you all up?'

Cary approached this personage. 'Please, sir, can you direct me to Ashford? I've lost my way.'

The officer glared down at him. 'I've no time to direct anyone anywhere. Get along to the royal palace and make yourself useful.

All the youngsters are preparing fire-arrows. Although I can't think what good they will be against Big-feet.'

Cary followed the crowd across a wide open space that lay just beyond the gateway and entered a narrow street which was lined with tall and strange-looking houses. All the walls leaned outwards and seemed to be in danger of toppling over, and the windows were fitted with coloured glass, a novelty which met with Cary's full approval. He thought it must be very interesting to live in a house with stained glass windows. Presently he came to a large, open square, and there at the far end was a huge building that could only have been a royal palace. It had a row of tall iron railings, which had two big gates set dead in the centre, and two silver-helmeted sentries paced the pavement outside. But they were certainly not stopping anyone from coming out or going in, for Cary saw a lot of people hurrying through the gateway and milling around in the courtyard beyond. Some carried bundles of arrows, others staggered under the weight of large buckets which were full of thick black stuff. One very small boy was waving a flaming arrow, much to the indignation of several people in his immediate neighbourhood, who were in grave danger of being set on fire.

Cary went through the gateway and made for an imposing flight of steps, quite determined that he was not going to prepare fire-arrows or anything else. He would just find some knowledgeable person who could direct him back to Ashford, then quickly depart. At the top of the steps was a long hall, completely filled with grave-looking people in black robes. They were muttering together and often paused to shake their heads in a most gloom-laden manner. At the end of the hall was an open doorway which led to a vast, brilliantly-lit room, with rows of sentries lined up against each wall. At the far end, sitting on a raised platform, was a man who could be no other than the King of Ashbury. He was a thin, worried-looking person, dressed in an ermine cloak and wearing a golden crown. He was seated on a silver throne, and before him stood a group of men that Cary had no difficulty in recognizing as knights. They were all clad in armour of various

119

colours and conditions. Many looked very grand indeed. They wore gleaming suits of armour of bright gold, silver, blue, red and even green. But a few, presumably the poor knights, had to be satisfied with dull steel – and, in one case – rusty armour. When Cary approached the throne, the King was speaking in a high-pitched and extremely worried voice.

'Look here, you chaps, someone has to have a go. There's this awful monster – this Big-feet – on its way and expecting to be fed. Dash it all, last year we gave it our entire stock of meat and when that wasn't sufficient, the Mayor and Corporation into the bargain. Now, you are supposed to be brave, bold knights. Who will volunteer to fight it?'

There was an unresponsive silence and the King began to appeal to individual members of the knightly group. 'What about you, Sir Bevis? Surely the green knight isn't afraid of a mere monster?'

Sir Bevis, who wore magnificent green armour and sported a large red moustache, shook his head sadly.

'I am grieved, Sire, that I cannot oblige you. There's nothing I'd like better than to put paid to the creature, but . . . My ankle, Sire. Bad sprain. I'd never be able to put foot to stirrup.'

The King tried again. 'Sir Mortimer. I'm sure there's nothing you'd like better than a tilt at old Big-feet. What about it?'

This knight, who was really eye-catching in his blue armour sighed.

'Your Majesty is so right. All my life I've wanted to have a go at the brute, but unfortunately my doctor has strictly forbidden me to fight monsters at this time of year. Regretfully, I must allow someone else to have the honour.'

The King tried several more, but everyone had a perfectly ridiculous excuse as to why he could not fight the monster. Cary was becoming quite angry, because he had been brought up to believe that knights were very brave men, who would take on the odd dragon or giant before breakfast and think nothing of it. Then the oldest, the most decrepit knight of them all, stepped forward. He had long white hair and an untidy drooping moustache, and he was clad in a suit of rusty old armour that a rag-and-bone man would not have given twopence for. But he carried his head high and spoke in a loud, if somewhat quavering voice.

'I will ride out against Big-feet, Your Majesty.'

The King looked rather doubtful and all the other knights rather angry. They began to mutter among themselves and Cary heard not a few rude remarks. 'Who does he think he is? The upstart.' 'Thinks he can do better than us, when he hasn't even the price of a decent suit of armour.' 'Silly old idiot. Big-feet will only have to blow and he will fall off his horse.'

The King shook his head. 'Look here, Sir Morris, do you think you're up to it? Monster-fighting is a young man's game, you know.'

'I'm still hale and hearty, thank you, Your Majesty,' Sir Morris said proudly. 'And I've a stouter backbone than some I could mention.'

This last remark was not kindly received, but all protests were quickly smothered when the King made his final appeal.

'Are you chaps *absolutely* sure that none of you would like to have a go? I mean to say—' He looked unhappily at Sir Morris's rusty armour. 'Well, it would be nice if we could put on a decent show.'

But no one seemed to have found any enthusiasm since the last invitation, so the King, after a deep sigh, was forced to turn to Sir Morris.

'So, it seems that the honour is to be yours. But is that the only suit of armour you've got?'

Sir Morris looked down at his armour with a puzzled frown.

'What's wrong with it? A spot of rust is nothing to worry about and it's never been pierced by lance or arrow these past forty years. No, all I want is a few stout lances and a squire on whom I can rely.'

The King gave a meaningful glance at a crowd of brightly-clad youths who were bunched together in one corner. 'Ah! A squire! That's a point. Now, which one of you brave, ambitious lads is going to help Sir Morris kill Big-feet?'

There was no great rush for the privilege of helping the knight of the rusty armour. In fact Cary noticed a marked reluctance on the part of every boy present, and he would have felt very indignant if his own problem had not been so pressing. He decided that the ensuing silence was an excellent opportunity to renew his request that someone should direct him as to the shortest way back to Ashford. Taking a deep breath, he said loudly 'Excuse me, but I'd like to . . .'

'Would you, by George!' the King exclaimed. 'Well now, there's a brave lad. I must say, you're oddly dressed for a squire, but then I suppose you'll go nicely with Sir Morris's rusty armour.'

'But I only want to . . .'

'Yes, I know.' The King waved his hand impatiently. 'You only want to say how pleased you are that your request has been granted. Don't mention it. I like to encourage you lads whenever possible. Well, Sir Morris, is the boy acceptable to you?'

Sir Morris positively beamed his delight. He stroked his moustache with a rather shaky hand and nodded so vigorously that Cary thought his dented old helmet would fall off.

'First rate, Your Majesty. He looks young and nimble and should be able to dodge Big-feet's tail without any trouble at all.'

The King gave a vast sigh of relief.

'That's settled, then. Well, you two had better get ready. Big-feet will be outside the city walls in no time at all.'

'But . . .' Cary tried to explain that he only wanted to be directed to Ashford, but the King cut in after the first word.

'Please, stop trying to express your gratitude. I can't stand boys who keep on saying thank you. Just go along with Sir Morris and try to be a credit to him. Now – not another word.'

And indeed, before Cary could say another word, Sir Morris grabbed his arm and led him into a side room, where the walls were covered with lances and swords and a gigantic boar's head glared down from over the mantelpiece.

'It was jolly decent of you to volunteer,' said Sir Morris, shaking him warmly by the hand. 'I can't think what has come over people these days. No one wants to fight monsters any more. Goodness gracious, in my young days we used to knock 'em off left, right and centre. Will this be your first monster?'

'Yes,' Cary nodded, 'but actually . . .'

'Don't let it worry you. We've all got to start some time. All you've got to do is hand me a fresh lance after each charge. And help me remount if I get thrown. Nothing to it.'

The old man looked so eager and made it all sound so easy, Cary had not the heart to say he was not keen on monster fighting, but only wanted to get back to Ashford. So he manfully held on to six or seven long lances that Sir Morris laid over his right shoulder and followed the rusty knight out into the courtyard.

There Sir Morris slowly mounted a horse that Cary could not help but feel was not suitable for monster charging. It was a fat horse. It also gave the impression that it was a tired, even, possibly, a lazy horse, who would lie down and have a good sleep if given the slightest opportunity. But Sir Morris seemed well content with his steed, for he patted its head and said proudly: 'We'll show 'em, Erasmus.' Then he looked ruefully down at Cary and said: ' 'Fraid there's no horse for you. But never mind, I dare say you can run if the occasion so demands.'

The route back to the main gate was lined with people who for the main part seemed to regard Sir Morris's brave attempt against the monster as foolhardy.

'Go home, you silly old man,' a plump lady called out. 'That awful creature will flatten you before you've had time to blink.'

But a red-faced man seemed to think that Sir Morris's excursion was a good idea.

'At least the knight and the boy should take the edge off Big-feet's appetite,' he informed those around him. 'Then we won't have to give him all of our meat stocks or the Mayor and Corporation.'

It is to Sir Morris's credit that he ignored these remarks and rode slowly forward with head held high and a look of complete unconcern on his face. But Cary was beginning to be more concerned with every step he took. He had not really thought about the monster up to now. But it was surely a very large creature, going by the remarks these people kept on making. Also, if it ate people, there was no reason to suppose it was a well-disposed monster, or one that would go home if asked in a polite and peaceful way.

However, Cary could not consider deserting the old gentleman at this crucial stage, for they had reached the city gate where the guards were lined up with their swords raised in salute. The guard captain was heard to remark: 'The poor old chap hasn't a chance, but you've got to admire his courage.'

But once the pair were outside the city, the gates were quickly shut, and people began to take up positions on top of the walls, so as to have a good view of the coming contest. Sir Morris gave Cary his instructions from horseback.

'When Big-feet comes over the ridge, I will charge straight at him and drive a lance right into his tummy. Then I'll wheel round and gallop back here, where you'll have another lance ready for me to grab. Then I'll charge again. I will keep doing that – charge – lance in tummy – wheel round – back to you for another lance – until the monster is dead. Have you got all that?'

Cary said, 'Yes,' but he couldn't really believe it would be as easy as Sir Morris supposed.

'Now there's just one more thing,' the rusty knight went on. 'I like to look me best on these occasions, so—' He fumbled in his saddle-bag and produced a long red feather. 'I'd be obliged if you'd poke this into my helmet.'

He then lifted the dented, rusty old helmet from his head and handed it down to Cary, who promptly dropped it.

'Look here, be careful,' Sir Morris protested. 'If you've damaged it, I'll be extremely annoyed.'

Cary hastily turned the helmet over and brushed some dry grass away from the battered crest. 'It's all right. Where shall I put the feather?'

'The plume,' Sir Morris corrected. 'You'll find a hole on the left side. That's it. Now, hand the helmet back up again – and do be careful.'

Presently the knight was fully attired again and Cary thought he looked rather like a battle-scarred cockerel. Then there came the sound of a muted roar and the tread of heavy feet, and all eyes were raised to a sloping crest that was situated some two hundred yards away.

Cary did not know what to expect, but he was certainly unprepared for the creature that lumbered into view. Try to imagine something that is forty feet long from gaping snout to lashing tail-tip. Then cover that body with bright golden scales and give it a pair of red, glaring eyes, flanked by immense flapping ears. But, worst of all, support that body on four, thick legs, each one terminating in a huge, six-toed foot. Cary would not have lieved that any creature on earth could have had feet that big. When the monster took a step forward, two of his feet – one fore one rear – crashed down with such force that the ground shook. Stones and small rocks were crushed to powder, large cracks ran across the ground in every direction, and one man fell off the wall.

'Excuse me, Sir,' Cary appealed to Sir Morris, 'but isn't it – too big for you to fight? He must weigh all of forty tons.'

'The heavier they are, the heavier they fall,' Sir Morris said cheerfully. 'Just hand me a lance and I'll have the brute down in no time.'

Cary handed the knight a lance, although what possible use it would be against the towering monster was more than he could imagine. It was standing perfectly still, with its mouth wide open as though waiting for the first course of a hearty meal. It did not appear to be in the least interested in Sir Morris and his preparations for immediate attack.

'Now the first charge,' the rusty knight said, digging his heels into Erasmus's plump flanks. 'CH . . . A . . . R . . . G . . . E!'

Erasmus was clearly a horse who did not believe in charging anywhere. Instead, he began to amble forward and, after Sir Morris had jumped up and down in his saddle and yelled at the top of his voice, presently broke into a reluctant trot.

Big-feet looked down at the approaching horseman with an expression of mild surprise, and when the rusty knight bravely rode in between the thick forelegs and thrust his lance at the

125

heavily scaled belly, Big-feet actually seemed to laugh. The great, snoutlike mouth opened, the sharp teeth gleamed like wet tomb-stones and a strange neighing sound emerged from the long throat. Of course, the lance just bounced off the scales, and Sir Morris dropped it when Erasmus – who did not seem to be happy on finding himself in close proximity to a monster – suddenly turned and came trotting back to Cary.

The rusty knight was a little out of breath, but still confident.

'I think I've got his measure,' he stated 'You can see he's fright-ened of me. Let's have another lance and I'll make the second charge.'

Erasmus, who struck Cary as being a horse of rare common-sense, was most reluctant to move, let alone charge. But after Sir Morris had made a lot of noise and again jumped up and down in his saddle, the animal was induced to move very, very slowly forward. This time Big-feet watched their approach with just a hint of annoyance. He gave the impression that he thought a silly and not very funny joke was being carried too far, and it was time for him to put a stop to it. After all, he had come to Ashbury to be fed – not to have lances thrown at him.

When Sir Morris came within striking distance, he thrust the lance forward with all his strength and did succeed in driving the tip between two scales. I do not suppose this caused Big-feet any real discomfort; it probably pricked him slightly, or gave him a faint itching sensation, but he clearly decided this was an indig-nity that could not be tolerated With an ear-splitting roar, he raised one huge foot and tapped Sir Morris on the left shoulder with his big toe.

The rusty knight seemed to leap from the saddle and went hurling to the ground with a mighty clatter. His helmet came off, the red feather became detached and Sir Morris lay winded and helpless between the great forefeet of the monster. As for Erasmus, he decided to break a lifelong rule – and charge. He charged for the open plain and did not stop until he was a safe distance from the battle area. There he found himself a nice patch of green grass and settled down to a quiet snack.

To be honest, Cary was very frightened, but he was also gravely concerned about Sir Morris's predicament. The old gentleman, due possibly to the weight of his armour, was finding it very difficult to rise, and Big-feet was raising one foot in a most menacing manner. The boy took a deep breath, then raced forward. He entered the shadow cast by the towering monster and grabbed Sir Morris's arm.

'Quick, get up . . . please, let me help you.'

The words died in his throat. Something very large, very white and very nasty was hovering above his head. Looking up, he saw the mighty foot which was slowly descending and which would, without any possible doubt, flatten them both in a matter of seconds. Cary dropped to his knees and, as he did so, his right hand clutched something that was lying nearby. It was the red feather which had dropped from Sir Morris's helmet.

Without any clear intention, apart from an impulse to defend himself, Cary lashed upwards with the feather and succeeded in lightly brushing the descending foot. The immediate effect was electrifying. The monster gave a kind of low, rumbling giggle, and hastily withdrew its foot. Greatly daring, and encouraged by this reaction, Cary pushed the feather between the huge toes. Big-feet repeated his giggling sound and hopped back a few paces, thereby making Sir Morris, who had at last regained his feet, fall down again.

But Cary was bubbling over with excitement. Big-feet was lance-proof. Who knows – perhaps he was bulletproof. But now one thing was certain – he was not featherproof. In fact, he was extremely ticklish.

Cary waved the red feather at the monster, who instantly retreated a few more steps. He darted forward and brushed it down the scales on one thick leg, and Big-feet went into a fit of monsteral hysterics. Then Cary rolled up his sleeves, as though preparing to do a thorough, workmanlike job and blew on the feather so as to ruffle it up into a first class tickling instrument. Big-feet, deciding to make one more attempt to flatten this maddening midget, raised his foot, but after Cary had flicked it twice with his red, fully-fluffed weapon, Big-feet all but collapsed into a fit of growling giggles. Finally, after trying to swipe the boy with his long tail – which Cary easily evaded and proceeded to tickle afterwards – the monster, turned about and lumbered back the way it had come. Both Sir Morris and Cary waited until it had disappeared over the horizon before returning to the city.

As can be imagined, all the inhabitants of Ashbury were highly delighted (with the exception of a few disgruntled knights) and the King wanted to knight Cary there and then, only he was doubtful if they could find a suit of armour to fit him. But he did make a new law which stated that from then onwards, all knights would throw away their swords and carry red feathers instead.

'Well, young man,' he said, 'we owe you a great debt. You certainly put paid to old Big-feet.'

Cary felt rather sorry for Sir Morris, who was looking very depressed because he had not done very much towards the victory, and decided to say a few words in his favour.

'I think you should thank Sir Morris, Your Majesty. If he had not cleverly fallen off his horse and distracted the monster's attention, I could never have tickled its foot.'

'Indeed!' The King looked faintly surprised. 'From where I sat it looked as if he was knocked from his horse and couldn't get up again. But still, you should know. Thank you, Sir Morris, you may now call yourself The Knight of the Red Feather. And we will have to do something about getting you a new suit of armour.'

Sir Morris bowed. 'Your Majesty is very gracious.'

'Yes, I know I am.' The King again turned to Cary. 'Now, is there anything else I can do for you?'

'Yes, Your Majesty,' Cary answered. 'Can you please direct me back to Ashford?'

The King said he'd never heard of it, and so did all the courtiers, and the knights maintained that no such place ever existed. Then, just as Cary was sinking into the depths of despair, a little old man pushed his way forward and humbly removed his hat.

'If it please Your Majesty, I have heard tell of such a place. My old grandfather said that it got lost years ago, along with a lot of other cities.'

'You don't say so!' The King shook his head in surprise. 'That was jolly careless of someone. Losing cities! Whatever next? Well, if this place is lost, how's this young fellow going to find it again?'

'My grandfather said that if you happen to wander down the main road at the right time and just happen to be in the right mood, and, most important, happen to be the right sort of person, then – you might just bump into Ashford.'

'There you are,' said the King, who frankly was getting rather bored with the entire business and wanted his tea, 'that's the best we can do for you. Thanks again for your help in getting shot of Big-feet. If he turns up again we will know what to do.'

After having had his hand shaken several times, Cary was escorted to the city gate and left there to find his own way back to Ashford. He walked past the scene of his recent encounter with Big-feet, then came back to the spot where he had almost bumped into the man in the green doublet and red hose. Suddenly there was a twanging sound, a momentary feeling of giddiness – and he was once again walking down the Canterbury–Ashford Road.

At first he could not wait to get home and recount his adventure to his uncle and aunt, but, after some thought, he decided to say nothing.

No one would believe him.

Well – to be honest – would you?

Package Holiday

ALL TOURISTS ARE WARNED the following rules will be adhered to at all possible times and infringement of any or one of the same will result in legal action being taken against the offender.

1. All contact of any kind whatsoever between a tourist and a native must be kept to the lowest possible minimum. A polite smile, a word of apology will suggest a foreign visitor who is unfamiliar with the language, and should ensure immediate isolation for MTCN detest having to help their immediate neighbours, let alone aliens who cannot fully understand the current language.

2. Under no circumstances will a tourist form any kind of emotional or sexual link with a native. Such a relationship could result in a situation of a catastrophic nature that might well adversely affect all dimensions.

3. Tourists will only enter those buildings which are under complete supervision of this agency. No food will be eaten, liquid drank or goods purchased save those on display or supplied by agency accredited establishments.

4. In case of accident or illness contact the agency at once. Merely push the red button on your personal emergency cassette.

5. Although seeking out celebrities is a sport that cannot be discouraged, tourists are instructed most strongly that no

131

personal contact – not even admiring glances – must be made. Often these great ones suffer acute embarrassment when singled out for marked attention, and this too could lead to investigation of a dangerous nature by the current authorities.

6. All tourists *must* – it is stressed *must* – be at a SAFE POINT 1 at not less minus B.U. 2. Any tourist not at Safe Point 1 after that time will be abandoned.

If these simple rules are strictly adhered to, there is no reason why party 218 should not enjoy a happy, exciting and instructive vacation.

Signed: B. Smollet,
Chief Supervisor.

Diana Parsons drove round the corner at a speed that could not have been less than thirty miles to the hour and therefore could not avoid hitting the exceptionally handsome young man just above his left hip, then carry him for a further thirty yards on the car bonnet until he rolled off on to the pavement.

His head shattered the windscreen, so for a few seconds there was the distinct possibility that Diana would add to whatever injuries he had suffered by running over him.

She braked to an abrupt halt, flung open the far side door, then climbed out on to the roadway and ran round to examine her victim.

He still looked exceedingly handsome, even though an enormous bump was making known its presence just over his right temple and a dark blue bulge was fast closing the right eye.

Diana asked a silly question. 'Are you all right?'

He got up and gripped the car door handle for support. When he spoke, every word was uttered with clear precision and enhanced by an almost imperceptible accent.

'I feel far from well. There is an ache in my head and a lack of strength in my legs.'

Diana decided that he was far too handsome for his own – or anyone's – good, having black gleaming hair, large dazzling near-black eyes and a white skinned, well-shaped face that quite took

132

her breath away. She experienced a deeper wave of guilt for having marred this beauty.

'I must get you to a hospital at once,' she said.

The young man took a deep breath and appeared to find difficulty in speaking, but at last he managed to eject a few words.

'Hospital . . . hospital. . . ? That is not . . .'

He sank back against the car bonnet and displayed every sign that was conversant with a man who is about to fall down.

Diana's self-control crumbled and she fast approached the frontiers of panic. 'Good Lord! Suppose you were to die! Manslaughter! Ten years at least!'

The young man shook his head, tried to take two steps forward, clearly decided he could not make it, and sat down on the running board instead. But his speech effort improved considerably.

'If I can be under cover . . . lay down on soft surface and take restorative, I will soon much improve.'

'My maisonette is nearby,' Diana announced eagerly. 'If you can climb a few stairs you are welcome to stay in my place for as long as you like.'

Had she been less agitated, Diana would have doubted the wisdom of making such a far-reaching invitation to a total stranger, but now her main concern was to see this young man fully recovered, on his feet, black-eyed-and-bumpless.

She opened the car door and helped him on to the front passenger seat. Then, having ensured the safety belt was securely fastened, ran round and slid behind the steering wheel, where she punched a hole in the shattered windscreen.

As the car glided – now driven with exaggerated care – in the direction of the general hospital, Diana cast occasional glances at her passenger, taking comfort from his undamaged profile, but becoming deeply depressed when he revealed the closed eye and monstrous bump.

She again asked a silly question.

'How do you feel?'

She suppressed a hysterical giggle when a silly answer flashed

133

across her brain: 'With my hands', and was only slightly less controlled when he answered, 'With much tenderness', which did appear to confirm her suspicion he was a well-educated foreigner who had yet to appreciate the finer points of the English language.

She drove into the parking area, which was hers by virtue of the flat she leased. There she helped the young man alight, then guided him through a long passageway and into the lift.

There he watched her push a button with a faintly amused expression, before shaking his head.

'It is forbidden,' he muttered several times, then once, quite loudly: 'But what can I do?', only to cling to Diana's shoulder when the doors slid open and she began to urge him towards her bright green door that was enhanced by a large brass seven.

She began to be rather irritated by his obvious reluctance to enter her flat, something she could not remember any young man displaying before.

'Keep your shirt on,' she advised him, 'I'll try not to take advantage of you. If I do lose self-control you can dial nine, nine, nine.'

She had the door open when he murmured for the last time: 'It is forbidden,' and then collapsed.

It took all Diana's not inconsiderable strength to pull him into the tiny hall.

A wet towel wrapped round his head, a quarter of a pound of fillet steak (intended for Diana's supper) and a very considerable amount of malt whisky poured down his throat revived the strange young man, who promptly sat up and looked around at Diana's bedroom with evident alarm.

'Feel better now?' she enquired, only to be answered by a rather insulting statement.

'A good example of late twentieth century decor. Complete lack of good taste which so symbolized that period.'

Only his now completely closed right eye and the really enormous bump over his right temple saved him from a scathing retort. After all, with such injuries, to say nothing of the thud he caused by hitting the road, he could not possibly be held responsible for what he might say.

'Now,' she assumed a bright, practical mein, 'who would you like me to contact?'

He frowned and gave the impression he did not understand. 'Contact?'

'Yes, you must have friends, relations who will have to be told about . . . about your accident.'

He stared at her for some while, although if he actually saw her, or was merely looking into that limbo where important decisions are sought but rarely found, was problematical. Then he shook his head.

'No . . . no . . . I must do that from one of the agency telephones,' he said before clasping hand to mouth as though he had committed a nigh unforgivable indiscretion.

It became Diana's turn to frown, and she did so with some warmth, for either this young man was badly concussed or was more than usually stupid. She decided to be charitable and accept the former.

'Right,' she said. 'Just give me the address of this agency and I'll give them a ring.'

'Ring?'

'Yes. You know – call them on the telephone. Then whoever is in charge can contact your nearest and dearest, if that's the way you do things from where ever you come from.'

He looked more confused, ill and appealing than ever. Diana could not dismiss the thought that she was dealing with an attractive but not very bright child. A sharp pang of pity briefly held her in its thrall; a fine blend of a yet to be developed maternal affection and a desire to arouse him to full manhood.

She wondered how old he was. He had the appearance of a man who has retained his youth past its grave-time; a kind of hothouse blossoming that should have faded long ago under the harsh sun of maturity.

Without speaking, she helped him out of his blue serge-like jacket. He did not protest or speak at all, just did as she wanted.

135

He lifted his feet so that she could remove his shoes – they seemed to be made out of one piece of glossy material with a thickening at the base to form soles.

'Lie down,' she ordered, and he obeyed, apparently content that she had not pursued the subject of contacting the mysterious agency. 'Now, close your eyes and try to sleep for a little while. I expect you will feel better when you wake up.'

She most certainly hoped so. If he would only recover to the extent that he could be conducted to someone – some organization who would take care of him, just maybe the problem of what to do with someone you have carelessly knocked down would solve itself.

Brownie

THE HOUSE WAS BUILT of grey stone, and stood on the edge of a vast moor; an awesome, desolate place, where the wind roared across a sea of heather and screamed like an army of lost souls.

Our father drove into a muddy, weed-infested drive, then braked to a halt. He smiled over his shoulder at Rodney and me, then said cheerfully: 'You'll be very happy here.'

We had grave doubts. On closer inspection the stonework was very dirty, the paintwork was flaking, and generally the house looked as unrelenting as the moor that lay beyond. Father opened the door and got out, his face set in that determinedly cheerful expression parents assume whenever they wish to pretend that all is well, even though appearances suggest otherwise.

'Fine people, Mr and Mrs Fairweather.' He gripped Rodney's arm, then mine, and guided us up a flight of stone steps towards a vast, oak door. 'You'll love 'em. Then, there are all those lovely moors for you to play on. Wish I was staying with you, instead of going back to India. But duty calls.'

He was lying, we both knew it, and perhaps the knowledge made parting all the more sad. He raised a bronzed hand, but before he could grasp the knocker, the door creaked open and there stood Mrs Fairweather.

'Major Sinclair.' She stood to one side for us to enter. 'Come in, Sir, and the young 'uns. The wind's like a knife, and cuts a body to the bone.'

The hall was large, bare, lined with age-darkened oak panels; doors broke both walls on either side of a massive staircase, and there was an old, churchy smell.

'Come into the kitchen with you,' Mrs Fairweather commanded, 'that being the only room that's livable in on the ground floor. The rest is locked up.'

The kitchen lay behind the staircase; a grandfather of all kitchens, having a red tiled floor, a spluttering iron range that positively shone from frequent applications of black lead, and an array of gleaming copper saucepans hanging on brass hooks over the mantelpiece.

A tall, lean old man was seated behind a much-scrubbed deal table. He rose as we entered, revealing that he wore a dark blue boiler suit and a checked cloth cap.

'Fairweather,' his wife snapped, 'where's yer manners? Take yer cap off.'

Mr Fairweather reluctantly, or so it appeared to me, took off his cap, muttered some indistinguishable words, then sat down again. Mrs Fairweather turned to Father.

'You mustn't mind him, Sir. He's not used to company, but he's got a heart. I'll say that for him. Now, Sir, is there anything you'd like to settle with me before you leave?'

'No,' Father was clearly dying to be off, 'the extra sum we agreed upon will be paid by Simpson & Brown on the first of every month. The girl I engaged as governess will arrive tomorrow. Let me see,' he consulted a notebook, 'Miss Rose Fortesque.' He put the notebook away. 'I think that's all.'

'Right you are, Sir,' Mrs Fairweather nodded her grey head, 'I expect you'll want to say a few words to the little fellows before you leave, so me and Fairweather will make ourselves scarce. Fairweather . . .' The old man raised his head. 'Come on, we'll make sure the chicken are bedded down.'

Mr Fairweather followed her out through the kitchen doorway, muttering bad temperedly, and we were left alone with Father, who was betraying every sign of acute discomfort.

'Well, boys,' he was still determined to appear cheerful, 'I guess

138

this is goodbye. You know I'd have loved to have taken you with me, but India is no place for growing boys, and now your mother has passed on there'd be no one to look after you. You'll be comfortable enough here, and Miss Fortesque will teach you all you need to know before you go to school next autumn. OK?'

I felt like choking, but Rodney, who had a far less emotional nature, was more prepared to deal with events of the moment.

'Do we own this house, father?'

'I own this house,' father corrected gently, 'and no doubt you will one day. As I told you, Mr and Mrs Fairweather are only care-takers, and they are allowed to cultivate some of the ground for their own use. Back before the days of Henry the Eighth, the house was a monastery, but since the Reformation it's been a private house. Your great uncle Charles was the last of our family to live here. I've never found the time to bring the old place up to scratch, so it has stood empty, save for the Fairweathers, since he died.'

'Pity,' said Rodney.

'Quite,' Father cleared his throat. 'Well, I expect the old . . . Mrs Fairweather has a good hot meal waiting for you, so I'll push off.' He bent down and kissed us lightly on the foreheads, then walked briskly to the kitchen door. 'Mrs Fairweather, I'm off.'

The speed with which the old couple reappeared suggested the chicken must be bedded down in the hall. Mr Fairweather made straight for his seat behind the table, while his wife creased her stern face into a polite smile.

'So you'll be going, Sir. I hope it won't be too long before we see you again.'

'No indeed.' Father shook her hand, his expression suddenly grave. 'No time at all. 'Bye, boys, do what the good Mrs Fairweather tells you. Goodbye, Fairweather.' He could not resist a bad joke. 'Hope it keeps fine for you.'

The old man half rose, grunted, then sat down again. Mrs Fairweather preceded Father into the hall. We heard the front door open, then the sound of Father's car; the crunch of gravel as he drove away. He was gone. We never saw him again. He was killed on the Indian North West Frontier, fighting Afghanistan tribesmen, and, had he been consulted, I am certain that is the way he would have preferred to die. He was, above all, a soldier.

As Mrs Fairweather never failed to stress, food at Sinclair Abbey was plain, but good. We ate well, worked hard, for Mr Fairweather saw no reason why two extra pairs of hands should not be put to gainful employment, and above all, we played. An old, almost empty house is an ideal playground for two boys. The unused rooms, whenever we could persuade Mrs Fairweather to unlock the doors, were a particular joy. Dust-shrouded furniture crouched like beasts of prey against walls on which the paper had long since died. In the great dining room were traces of the old refectory where medieval monks had dined before Henry's henchmen had cast them out. One stained-glass window, depicting Abraham offering up Isaac as a sacrifice, could still be seen through a veil of cobwebs; an oak, high-backed chair, surmounted by a crucifix, suggested it had once been the property of a proud abbot. For young, enquiring eyes, remains of the old monastery could still be found.

Rose Fortesque came, as Father had promised, the day after our arrival. Had we been ten years older, doubtless we would have considered her to be a slim, extremely pretty, if somewhat retiring girl. As it was, we found her a great disappointment. Her pale, oval face, enhanced by a pair of rather sad blue eyes, gave the impression she was always on the verge of being frightened, the result possibly of being painfully shy.

Where Father had found her I have not the slightest idea. More than likely at some teachers' agency, or wherever prospective governesses parade their scholastic wares, but of a certainty, she was not equipped to deal with two high-spirited boys. It took but a single morning for us to become aware of this fact, and with the cruelty of unthinking youth, we took full advantage of the situation. She was very frightened after finding a frog in her bed, and a grass snake in her handbag, and from then onwards, she watched us with sad, reproachful eyes.

It was fully seven days after our arrival at Sinclair Abbey when we first met Brownie. Our bedroom was way up under the eaves, a long, barren room, furnished only by our two beds, a wardrobe, and two chairs, Mrs Fairweather having decided mere boys required little else. There was no electricity in that part of the house. A single candle lit us to bed, and once that was extinguished, there was only the pale rectangle of a dormer window which, in the small hours, when the sky was clear, allowed the moon to bathe the room in a soft, silver glow.

I woke suddenly, and heard the clock over the old stables strike two. It was a clear, frosty night, and a full moon stared in through the window, so that all the shadows had been chased into hiding behind the wardrobe, under the beds, and on either side of the window. Rodney was snoring, and I was just considering the possibility of throwing a boot at him, when I became aware there was a third presence in the room. I raised my head from the pillow. A man dressed in a monk's robe was sitting on the foot of my bed. The funny thing was, I couldn't feel his weight, and I should have done so, because my feet appeared to be underneath him.

I sat up, but he did not move, only continued to sit motionless, staring at the left hand wall. The cowl of his robe was flung back to reveal a round, dark-skinned face, surmounted by a fringe of black curly hair surrounding a bald patch that I seemed to remember was called a tonsure. I was frightened, but pretended I wasn't. I whispered:

'Who are you? What do you want?'

The monk neither answered nor moved, so I tried again, this time a little louder.

'What are you doing here?'

He continued to sit like a figure in a wax museum, so I decided to wake Rodney – no mean task for he slept like Rip van Winkle. My second shoe did the trick and he woke protesting loudly:

'Wassat? Young Harry, I'll do you.'

141

'There's a man sitting on the foot of my bed, and he won't move.'

'What!' Rodney sat up, rubbed his eyes, then stared at our silent visitor. 'Who is he?'

'I don't know. I've asked him several times, but he doesn't seem to hear.'

'Perhaps he's asleep.'

'His eyes are open.'

'Well,' Rodney took a firm grip of my shoe, 'we'll soon find out.' And he hurled the shoe straight at the brown-clad figure.

Neither of us really believed what our eyes reported: the shoe went right through the tonsured head and landed with a resounding smack on a window pane. But still there was no response from the monk, and now I was so frightened my teeth were chattering.

'I'm going to fetch Mrs. Fairweather,' Rodney said after a while, 'she'll know what to do.'

'Rodney,' I swallowed, 'you're not going to leave me alone with – him, are you?'

Rodney was climbing out of the far side of the bed.

'He won't hurt you, he doesn't move, and if he does you can belt under the bed. I say, chuck the candle over, and the matches, I've got to find my way down to the next floor.'

Left alone, I studied our visitor with a little more attention than formerly, for, as he appeared to be harmless, my fear was gradually subsiding.

I knew very little about monks, but this one seemed to be a rather shabby specimen; his gown was old, and there was even a small hole in one sleeve, as if he indulged in the bad habit of leaning his elbows on the table. Furthermore, on closer inspection – and by now I had summoned up enough courage to crawl forward a short way along the bed – he was in need of a shave. There was a distinct stubble on his chin, and one hand, that rested on his knee, had dirt under the finger nails. Altogether, I decided, this was a very scruffy monk.

Rodney had succeeded in waking the Fairweathers. The old lady could be heard protesting loudly at being disturbed, and an

142

occasional rumble proclaimed that Mr Fairweather was not exactly singing for joy. Slippered feet came padding up the stairs, and now Mrs Fairweather's unbroken tirade took on recognizable words.

'I won't have him lurking around the place. It's more than I'm prepared to stand, though why two lumps of boys couldn't have chased him out, without waking a respectable body from her well-earned sleep, I'll never know.'

'But he doesn't move,' Rodney's voice intervened.

'I'll move him.'

She came in through the doorway like a gust of wind, a bundle of fury wrapped in a flowered dressing gown, and in one hand she carried a striped bath towel.

'Get along with you.' She might have been shooing off a stray cat. 'I won't have you lurking around the house. Go on – out.'

The words had no effect, but the bath towel did. Mrs Fairweather waved it in, or rather through, the apparition's face. The figure stirred, rather like a clockwork doll making a first spasmodic move, then the head turned and a look of deep distress appeared on the up to now emotionless face. The old lady continued to scold, and flapped the towel even more vigorously.

'Go on, if I've told you once, I've told you a hundred times, you're not to bother respectable folk. Go where you belong.'

The monk flowed inio an upright position; there is no other word to describe the action. Then he began to dance in slow motion towards the left hand wall, Mrs Fairweather pursuing him with her flapping towel. It was a most awesome sight; first the left leg came very slowly upwards, and seemed to find some invisible foothold, then the right drifted past it, while both arms gently clawed the air. It took the monk some three minutes to reach the left hand wall; a dreadful, slow, macabre dance, performed two feet above floor level, with an irate Mrs Fairweather urging him on with her flapping towel, reinforced by repeated instructions to go, and not come back, while her husband, ludicrous in a white flannel nightgown, watched sardonically from the doorway.

The monk at last came to the wall. His left leg went through it, then his right arm, followed by his entire body. The last we saw of him was the heel of one sandal, which had a broken strap. Mrs Fairweather folded up her bath towel and, panting from her exertions, turned to us.

'That's got shot of him, and you won't be bothered again tonight. Next time he comes, do what I did. Flap something in his face. He doesn't like that. Nasty, dreamy creature, he is.'

'But . . .' Rodney was almost jumping up and down in bed with excitement, '. . . what . . . who is he?'

'A nasty old ghost, what did you imagine he was?' Mrs Fairweather's face expressed profound astonishment at our ignorance; 'one of them old monks that used to live here, donkey's years ago.'

'Gosh,' Rodney eyed the wall through which the monk had vanished, 'do you mean he'll come back?'

'More than likely.' The old lady had rejoined her husband in the doorway. 'But when he does, no waking me out of a deep sleep. Do as I say, flap something in his face, and above all, don't encourage him. Another thing,' she paused and waved an admonishing finger, 'there's no need to tell that Miss Fortesque about him. She looks as if she's frightened of her own shadow as it is. Now go to sleep, and no more nonsense.'

It was some time before we went to sleep. 'Harry,' Rodney repeated the question several times, 'what is a ghost?'

I made the same answer each time. 'I dunno.'

'It seems a good thing to be. I mean, being able to go through walls and dance in the air. I'd make Miss Fortesque jump out of her skin. I say, she must sleep like a log.'

'Her room is some distance away,' I pointed out.

'Still, all that racket I was making . . .' He yawned. 'Tomorrow, we'll ask her what a ghost is.'

'Mrs Fairweather said we were not to tell her about the ghost.'

'There's no need to tell her we've seen one, stupid. Just ask her what it is.'

*

144

Rodney tacked the question on to Henry the Eighth's wives next morning.

'Name Henry the Eighth's wives,' Miss Fortesque had instructed. Rodney had hastened to oblige.

'Catherine of Aragon, Anne Boleyn, Jane Seymour, Anne of Cleves, Catherine Howard, and Catherine Parr who survived him, but it was a near thing. Please, Miss Fortesque, what is a ghost?'

'Very good,' Miss Fortesque was nodding her approval, then suddenly froze. 'What!'

'What is a ghost?'

The frightened look crept back into her eyes, and I could see she suspected some horrible joke.

'Don't be silly, let's get on with the lesson.'

'But I want to know,' Rodney insisted, 'please, what is a ghost?'

'Well,' Miss Fortesque still was not happy, but clearly she considered it her duty to answer any intelligent question, 'it is said, a ghost is a spirit who is doomed to walk the earth after death.'

'Blimey!' Rodney scratched his head, 'a ghost is dead?'

'Of course – at least, so it is said. But it is all nonsense. Ghosts do not exist.'

'What!' Rodney's smile was wonderful to behold, 'you mean – you don't believe ghosts exist?'

'I know they don't,' Miss Fortesque was determined to leave the subject before it got out of hand. 'Ghosts are the result of ignorant superstition. Now, let us get on. Harry this time. How did Henry dispose of his wives?'

I stifled a yawn.

'Catherine of Aragon divorced, Anne Boleyn beheaded, Jane Seymour died, Anne of Cleves divorced, Catherine Howard beheaded, Catherine Parr. . . .'

'I say, Harry,' Rodney remarked later that day, 'I bet Brownie was the odd man out.'

'Who?'

'Brownie, the monk. There's always one in big establishments.

145

You remember at prep school last year, that chap Jenkins. He was lazy, stupid, never washed. The chances are, Brownie was the odd man out among the other monks. Probably never washed or shaved unless he was chivvied by the abbot, then when he died he hadn't the sense to realise there was some other place for him to go. So, he keeps hanging about here. Yes, I guess that's it. Brownie was the stupid one.'

'I don't think one should flap a towel in his face,' I said, 'it's not polite.'

'You don't have to be polite to a ghost,' Rodney scoffed, 'but I agree it's senseless. Next time he comes we'll find out more about him. I mean, he's not solid, is he? You saw how the towel went right through his head.'

It was several weeks before Brownie came again, and we were a little worried that Mrs Fairweather had frightened him away for good. Then one night I was awakened by Rodney. He was standing by my bed, and as I awoke he lit the candle, his hand fair shaking with excitement.

'Is he back?' I asked, not yet daring to look for myself. 'Yep,' Rodney nodded, 'on the foot of your bed, as before. Come on, get up, we'll have some fun.'

I was not entirely convinced this was going to be fun, but I obediently clambered out of bed, then with some reluctance turned my head.

He was there, in exactly the same position as before, seated sideways on the bed, the cowl slipped back onto his shoulders, and staring at the left hand wall.

'Why does he always sit in the same place?' I asked in a whisper.

'I expect this was the room he slept in, and more than likely his bed was in the same position as yours. I say, he does look weird. Let's have a closer look.'

Holding the candlestick well before him, Rodney went round the bed and peered into the monk's face. Rather fearfully, I followed him.

The face was podgy, deeply tanned, as though its owner had

146

spent a lot of time out of doors, and the large brown eyes were dull and rather sad.

'I told you so,' Rodney said with a certain amount of satisfaction, 'he's stupid, spent most of his time day dreaming while the other monks were chopping wood, getting in the harvest, or whatever things they got up to. I bet they bullied him, in a monkish sort of way.'

'I feel sorry for him,' I said, 'he looks so sad.'

'You would.' Rodney put the candle down. 'Let's see what he's made of. Punch your hand into his ribs.'

I shook my head. 'Don't want to.'

'Go on, he won't hurt you. You're afraid.'

'I'm not.'

'Well, I'm going to have a go. Stand back, and let the dog see the rabbit.'

He rolled up his pyjama sleeve, took a deep breath, then gently brought his clenched fist into contact with the brown robe.

'Can't feel a thing,' he reported. 'Well, here goes.'

Fascinated, I saw his arm disappear into Brownie's stomach; first the fist, then the forearm, finally the elbow.

'Look round the back,' Rodney ordered, 'and see if my hand is sticking out of his spine.'

With a cautious look at Brownie's face, which so far had displayed no signs that he resented these liberties taken with his person, I peered round the brown-covered shoulders. Sure enough, there was Rodney's hand waving at me from the middle of the monk's back.

I nodded. 'I can see it.'

'Feels rather cold and damp,' Rodney said, and brought his arm out sideways. 'As I see it, nothing disturbs him unless something is flapped in his face. I expect the monks used to flap their robes at him, when they wanted to wake him up. Now you try.'

With some misgivings, I rolled up my sleeve and pushed my arm into Brownie's stomach, being careful to close my eyes first. There was an almost indefinable feeling of cold dampness, like

147

putting my arm out of a window early on a spring morning. I heard Rodney laugh, and opened my eyes.

It is a very disturbing experience to say the least, to see your arm buried up to the elbow in a monk's stomach. I pulled it out quickly, determined to have nothing more to do with the entire business, but Rodney had only just begun.

'I'm going in head first,' he announced. Before I had time to consider what he intended to do, he had plunged his head through Brownie's left ribs, and in next to no time I saw his face grinning at me from the other side. It was really quite funny and, forgetting my former squeamishness, I begged to be allowed to have a go.

'All right,' Rodney agreed, 'but you start from the other side.'

We played happily at 'going through Brownie' for the next twenty minutes. Sideways, backwards, feet first, we went in all ways – the grand climax came when Rodney took up the same position as Brownie, and literally sat inside him. But there was one lesson we learnt; Brownie was undisturbed by our efforts, as long as his head was not touched. Once Rodney tried to reach up and sort of look through the phantom's eyes. At once the blank face took on an expression of intense alarm, the eyes moved, the mouth opened, and had not Rodney instantly withdrawn, I'm certain the ghost would have started his slow dance towards the left hand wall.

But there is a limit to the amount of amusement one can derive from crawling through a ghost. After a while we sat down and took stock of the situation.

'I wonder if he would be disturbed if we jumped in him,' Rodney enquired wistfully.

I was against any such drastic contortion. 'Yes, it would be worse than flapping a towel in his face.'

'I suppose so,' Rodney relinquished the project with reluctance, then his face brightened. 'I say, let's show him to Miss Fortesque.'

'Oh no!' My heart went out to that poor, persecuted creature.

'Why not? In a way we would be doing her a service. After all,

148

she doesn't believe in ghosts. It does people good to be proved they're wrong.'

'I dunno.'

'I'm going to her room,' Rodney got up, his eyes alive with mischievous excitement. 'I'll say there is someone in our room – no, that won't do – I'll say you've got tummy ache.'

'But that's a lie,' I objected.

'Well, you might have tummy ache, so it's only half a lie. You stay here, and don't frighten Brownie, in fact don't move.'

Thankfully, he left me the lighted candle, having thoughtfully provided himself with a torch, for there was no moon, and being alone in the dark with Brownie was still an alarming prospect. I sat down at the phantom's feet and peered up into that blank face. Yes, it was a stupid face, but can a person be blamed for being stupid? Apart from that, his eyes were very sad, or so they appeared to me, and I began to regret the silly tricks we had played on him. Minutes passed, then footsteps were ascending the stairs; Rodney's voice could he heard stressing the gravity of my mythical stomach ache, with Miss Fortesque occasionally inter-posing with a softspoken enquiry.

Rodney came in through the doorway, his face shining with excitement. Miss Fortesque followed, her expression one of deep concern. She stopped when she saw Brownie. Her face turned, if possible, a shade paler, and for a moment I thought she would faint.

'Who. . . ?' she began.

'Brownie,' Rodney announced. 'He's a ghost.'

'Don't talk such nonsense. Who is this man?'

'A ghost,' Rodney's voice rose. 'He is one of the monks who lived here ages ago. Look.'

He ran forward, stationed himself before the still figure and plunged his arm into its chest. Miss Fortesque gasped: 'Oh,' just once before she sank down on to the bed and closed her eyes. The grin died on Rodney's face, to be replaced by a look of alarmed concern.

'Please,' he begged, 'don't be frightened, he won't hurt you, honestly. Harry and I think he's lost. Too stupid to find his way to. . . .' he paused, 'to wherever he ought to go.'

Miss Fortesque opened her eyes and took a deep breath. Though I was very young, I admired the way she conquered her fear, more, her abject terror, and rose unsteadily to her feet. She moved very slowly to where Brownie sat, then stared intently at the blank face.

'You have done a dreadful thing,' she said at last, 'to mock this poor creature. I am frightened, very frightened, but I must help him. Somehow, I must help him.'

'How?' inquired Rodney.

'I don't know.' She moved nearer and peered into the unblinking eyes. 'He looks like someone who is sleep-walking. How do you rouse him?'

'Touch his head. Mrs Fairweather flaps a towel in his face.'

Miss Fortesque raised one trembling hand and waved it gently before Brownie's face. He stirred uneasily, his eyes blinked, then, as the hand was waved again, flowed slowly upwards. Miss Fortesque gave a little cry and retreated a few steps.

'No.' She spoke in a voice only just above a whisper. 'Please, please listen.'

Brownie was already two feet above floor level, but he paused and looked back over one shoulder, while a look of almost comical astonishment appeared on his face.

'Please listen,' Miss Fortesque repeated, 'you can hear me, can't you?'

A leg drifted downwards, then he rotated so that he was facing the young woman, only he apparently forgot to descend to floor level. There was the faintest suggestion of a nod.

'You shouldn't be here,' Miss Fortesque continued. 'You, and . . . all your friends, died a long time ago. You ought to be . . . somewhere else.'

The expression was now one of bewilderment and Brownie looked helplessly round the room; his unspoken question was clear.

'Not in this house,' she shook her head, 'perhaps in Heaven, I don't know, but certainly in the place where one goes to after death. Can't you try to find it?'

The shoulders came up into an expressive shrug, and Rodney snorted.

'I told you, he's too stupid.'

'Will you be quiet,' Miss Fortesque snapped, 'how can you be so cruel?' She turned to Brownie again. 'Forgive them, they are only children. Surely the other monks taught you about. . . . Perhaps you did not understand. But you must leave this house. Go—' she gave a little cry of excitement, 'Go upwards! I'm sure that's right. Go up into the blue sky, away from this world; out among the stars, there you'll find the place. Now, I'm absolutely certain. Go out to the stars.'

Brownie was still poised in the air; his poor stupid face wore a perplexed frown as he pondered on Miss Fortesque's theory. Then, like the sun appearing from behind a cloud, a smile was born. A slow, rather jolly smile, accompanied by a nod, as though Brownie had at last remembered something important he had no business to have forgotten.

He straightened his legs, put both arms down flat with his hips, and drifted upwards, all the while smiling that jolly, idiotic grin, and nodding. His head disappeared into the ceiling, followed by his shoulders and then his hips. The last we saw were those two worn sandals. Miss Fortesque gave a loud gasp, then burst into tears. I did my best to comfort her.

'I'm sure you sent him in the right direction,' I said, 'he looked very pleased.'

'I bet he finishes up on the wrong star,' Rodney commented dourly. I turned on him.

'He won't, I just know he won't. He wasn't so dumb. Once Miss Fortesque sort of jolted his memory he was off like a shot.'

'Now, boys,' Miss Fortesque dried her eyes on her dressing gown sleeve, 'to bed. Tomorrow we must pretend this never happened. In fact,' she shuddered, 'I'd like you to promise me you'll never mention the matter again – ever. Is that understood?'

151

We said, 'Yes,' and Rodney added, 'I think you're quite brave, honestly.'

She blushed, kissed us both quickly on our foreheads, then departed. Just before I drifted into sleep, I heard Rodney say:

'I wouldn't mind being a ghost. Imagine being able to drift up through the ceiling, and flying out to the stars. I can't wait to be dead.'

Miss Fortesque's theory must have been right. We never saw Brownie again.

The Harpy

Henry WAS NOT ALL that keen on picnics, but Joyce insisted that it would be a crime to stay indoors on such a fine day. So their mother packed a hamper and their father drove them out to a site near the old castle, and Henry had to admit that, once there, with all the good things laid out on a white tablecloth, perhaps it wasn't such a bad idea.

But of course wasps had to commit *hara-kiri* in the jam; ants insisted on marching six abreast across the tablecloth, and a swarm of flies formed a buzzing halo round his head.

'We are providing food and entertainment for the entire insect kingdom,' he complained.

Joyce poured tea from a vacuum flask into blue plastic cups. 'Nonsense. You shouldn't let a few flies worry you. Ignore them and perhaps they'll go away.'

Henry waved his hands frantically in an effort to disperse the irritating horde. 'What a hope! Also, I'm not happy about wasp and jam sandwich.'

'There aren't any wasps in the jam. I dug the last one out with a teaspoon.'

'Ugh!'

'Don't be so silly.'

It was then that something happened that drove all thoughts of flies, ants and other flying or crawling small life out of Henry's mind. From the direction of the ruined castle came a shriek, rather like that of a whistling kettle under full steam, and what at first appearance looked like some kind of large bird swooped down from the high walls and landed right in the centre of the tablecloth.

Joyce screamed and even Henry emitted a loud cry of horror when he was in a condition to examine the creature that had so abruptly descended upon them. It stood about four feet high, had the body of a very large bird and the head and shoulders of an ugly old woman. But possibly the most frightening aspect was the flapping wings and curved claws. Henry was certain they were made of brass. One claw reached out and grabbed a plate of sandwiches, and instantly the bread turned blue. Then the jam pot was overturned and two wasps flew away as the strawberry preserve assumed a green, mildewy appearance, then began to bubble in the most alarming fashion. Next, the sliced ham that dissolved into a heap of maggots, then the pink iced-cakes crumbled and became small heaps of grey dust, and finally the two cups of tea disappeared into puffs of foul-smelling steam.

Having completely destroyed a perfectly good meal, the creature emitted another ear-splitting shriek, then flapped its brass wings and flew back to the ruined castle.

'What shall we do?' Joyce whispered.

Henry answered without any hesitation at all.

'Run.' he said. 'It might come back.'

Mr Harrington was extremely annoyed when the children arrived home and was in no mood to listen to stories about monsters with brass wings – not to mention the head and shoulders of an ugly old woman.

'Where on earth did you run off too?' he demanded. 'You knew I was going to pick you up at five o'clock. And you left the vacuum flask, cups – plates – everything – for anyone to take. Why?'

'There was . . .' Henry began. but was quickly interrupted.

'Another thing. What was the foul mess all over the tablecloth? I have never seen anything like it.'

'And how did you get home?' Mrs Harrington asked the question which had been causing her great anxiety. 'If you had walked along the main road your father would have seen you.'

'We came across the moors.' Henry explained. 'It was the short-est way. But . . .'

'We were attacked by a horrible thing with brass wings and feet and it was half bird and half woman!' Joyce exclaimed, unable to restrain her excitement any longer. 'And it made all the food go bad.'

Mr Harrington looked at his wife and sighed. 'I told you they should not be allowed to watch so much television. Heaven above knows their imagination is vivid enough at the best of times. It's that *Star Trek* . . .'

'But we did see the dreadful thing,' Joyce insisted. 'And it did turn all the food bad. Tell them, Henry.'

Henry nodded. 'Yes, it was like a bird – a vulture, I guess – with the head and shoulders of an old woman. And I know it will sound mad – but the wings and feet did appear to be made of brass.'

Mr Harrington was quite unable to sustain his angry expres-sion, for he suddenly sat down and began to laugh.

'I see nothing funny in the situation,' Mrs Harrington complained. 'They run off and make me almost ill with worry, then tell us this – this outrageous story. It really is too much.'

Mr Harrington wiped his eyes. 'Yes, I know. But you must admit that they are at least original. When you or I played truant we came up with the old worn out excuses – didn't feel well – lost our way – didn't know the time. But these kids have pulled something out of Greek mythology.'

'I'm sure I don't know what you are talking about,' his wife said. 'All I know is we've been told a silly story that has neither sense or reason. I think they should be both sent to bed without any supper.'

'Hey, just a minute!' Mr Harrington raised his hand. 'They display a certain amount of educated imagination, and although I do not approve of lies, nevertheless someone has been doing his homework. Where did you learn about the harpy, Henry? At school? Or have you been rummaging around in my library?'

Fortunately for Henry his father did not wait for an answer, but got up and, walking over to a bookshelf, returned with a leather-bound book which he placed on the table.

'Now.' He began to turn pages over. 'Let's have a look. Gorgons ... Hamehs ... here we are ... Harpies. Listen to this:

' "A combination of vulture and woman. The four harpies were sent by Zeus to torment the blind king of Thrace, whose meals they snatched before he had a chance to eat. Everything they touched turned to corruption, and they were noted for their brass wings and claws. They were afraid of only one thing – the sound of a brass instrument, which put them to immediate flight." '

Mr Harrington closed the book and grinned cheerfully at his irate wife. 'There you are. These young fibbers have dreamed up a harpy. Only one, mark you. I don't know what happened to her three sisters, but perhaps they're being saved up for the next time ants and wasps become tiresome.'

'But we did . . .' Joyce began, then Henry nudged her and whispered: 'Shut up.'

'But . . .'

'Shut up.'

Mr Harrington next turned his attention to the children and did his best to look very stern.

'Now listen to me, you two. I'm going to overlook the matter this time, but in future you will consider your mother's feelings before running off and causing her – both of us – a great deal of anxiety. Is that clear?'

'Yes, Daddy.' Joyce said meekly.

Henry succeeded in looking contrite. 'Right, Dad.'

'Very well, we will consider the matter closed. Now go upstairs and wash your hands.'

Several times during supper, Joyce appeared to be on the verge of rebellion, but a scowl from Henry was sufficient to smother words before they were spoken. However, once they were alone in the small room that was used as a communal study, she raised her voice in outraged protest.

'Why didn't you insist on them believing us? That thing might be dangerous.'

Henry shrugged. 'They never would have believed us, not in a month of Sundays. You know what adults are like. They can never see anything beyond the tips of their noses. Mind you, I can't say I actually blame Mum and Dad for not believing we were attacked by a harpy. I mean to say – would you?'

Joyce shook her head. 'No, I suppose not. But why hasn't it been seen before? Think what the newspapers would do with a story like that! Harpy in ruined castle! It would be even better than the Loch Ness monster.'

'I should imagine,' Henry said thoughtfully, 'it only puts in an appearance when people are eating. From what father told us, making grub go rotten is its only occupation. And who would dream of picnicking near that old castle – except us?'

'But how did it get there? Surely it ought to be in Greece or somewhere.'

Henry shook his head. 'I don't know. The point is – it is there, and I think we should do something about getting rid of it. I mean to say – someone else just *might* decide to have a quick nosh there and be frightened to death when that horror with brass wings swoops down and snatches the lump of pork pie out of their mouths.'

Joyce shuddered. 'I don't think I could face it again. It was so horrible.'

'Don't be so silly. After all it didn't touch us – only the food – and we now know how to get rid of it. Somehow I must find a brass instrument.'

'Why?'

'You don't listen, do you? Father read out the instructions. The sound of a brass instrument will put a harpy to immediate flight. So – we must look for some kind of brass instrument.'

Joyce thought deeply for a few moments then announced:

'There's no brass instrument in this house.'

'I will find one somewhere,' Henry stated, with more conviction than he actually felt.

During the next few days Henry realised that there is an abundance of brass instruments for those who have the money to pay for them. An antique shop in the High Street, for example, had some excellent brass hunting horns, but as the asking price was thirty-five pounds, the children could only stare at them with wistful longing. Then there was the musical instrument shop, which had any number of trumpets, cornets, trombones, tenor-horns – all of which, the assistant informed them, were made of chromium-plated brass, but, again, not one could be purchased for one pound, three pence, which was the total sum Henry and Joyce shared between them.

'Maybe,' Joyce said after a fruitless morning's hunt, 'if we made a noise like a brass instrument, the harpy would fly away.'

After some consideration Henry shook his head. 'No. It struck me as being a fairly bright harpy and would never fall for a trick like that. We really must think of something.'

The search ended when they found that even a toy trumpet cost five pounds, and that was made of some kind of brass-coloured alloy. It was a very dejected pair who returned to the house, then retreated to their study room for a conference.

'I thought,' Joyce remarked caustically, 'you were going to come up with some bright idea. So far we're not even in smelling distance of getting any kind of brass instrument.'

Henry frowned. 'Maybe the job is proving a little more difficult than I thought, but I'm not beaten yet – not by a long chalk. He thumped the arms of his chair with clenched fists. 'The world is full of brass instruments. People are positively wallowing in them – and we can't lay our hands on even one. It's enough to make you spit.'

'If only we could get a brass band to stage a concert in the old ruins,' Joyce sighed.

Suddenly Henry clapped hands to his head and did a little dance around the room. 'What an idiot I am! A brass band! That's the answer.'

Joyce stared at him with some alarm. 'I don't know why you are so excited. We'll never get any kind of band to go out there. It's so isolated.'

'Of course not, stupid – but, don't you see? We can tape a brass band on my cassette recorder – and take that out there.'

After some deliberation Joyce nodded.

'You have some brains after all.'

Henry ignored the insult and grabbed the *Radio Times*. Presently he read aloud: 'Radio 4. 10 a.m. The Bradford Boiler-Maker's Brass Band. There you are! All we have to do is stand the recorder next to the radio – and Bob's your uncle. There won't be just one brass instrument – but dozens. The old harpy will have a heart attack.'

'Um.' Joyce looked doubtful. 'I suppose you're right. But as soon as that dreadful thing puts in an appearance, I'm going to run. It might get very annoyed when a brass band starts blaring from a plastic box.'

'Rubbish,' Henry said scornfully. 'It will be so scared you won't see its brass for dust.'

'No more picnics unless your father and I are present,' Mrs Harrington said. 'All that food wasted and you coming back with an outlandish story about harpies – or some such nonsense. You will eat your meals indoors like civilized beings.'

'What do we do now?' Joyce enquired.

Henry shrugged. 'It doesn't have to be a picnic – just food. We'll buy a loaf of bread and maybe some margarine and pretend we're going to scoff it.'

Joyce nodded. 'And a little jar of strawberry jam just to make it all look right.'

So it was on Tuesday afternoon that the children, armed with a loaf of sliced bread, a plastic tub of margarine, a jar of strawberry jam, a butter knife and a cassette recorder, set out on their long journey across the moor. They had every reason to feel confident, because the Bradford Boiler-Maker's Brass Band had broadcast a most satisfactory programme of ear-splitting music, calculated to put any number of harpies to instant flight. Henry had rewound the tape, but had not played it back, for, as he said, they did not want the batteries to fail at a crucial moment. When the ruined castle loomed up from behind a fringe of stunted trees, Joyce began to display signs of alarm and despondency.

'Look here, do you know what you're doing. When I remember what that thing looked like and the way it snatched at the food – well – I'm all for turning back and heading for home.'

'You're scared,' Henry stated with well-simulated scorn.

'Too true I am – and so are you.'

'No I'm not.'

'Then why did you almost jump out of your skin when that crow squawked and flew out of a tree?'

Henry blushed and pretended to be angry. 'I was just startled, that's all. Now this is what we must do. First spread some marge and jam over the bread, then start to eat it . . .'

'I don't like margarine,' Joyce protested.

'Then pretend to eat it, stupid. When the harpy puts in an appearance. I'll turn on the cassette and we will retire—'

'Run,' Joyce insisted. 'Run very fast.'

'Retire in good order to that little hollow over there and wait for old harpy to disappear over the horizon. Dead simple.'

Joyce shuddered. 'So long as it's not simply dead. All right, let's get on with it.'

They laid out a plastic mac on the ground, then unwrapped the sliced bread, which Joyce – after casting an anxious glance at the ruined castle – proceeded to cover with a generous coating of margarine. When Henry unscrewed the jampot lid, three wasps zoomed in and displayed a lively and unwelcomed interest.

'Pity they aren't frightened of brass instruments,' Joyce said, waving the butter knife at the offending insects. 'I bet the ants are rallying their forces, too.'

'Never mind the ants,' Henry said, 'just bung on the jam and let's get cracking. I thought I saw a movement from behind that far turret.'

Joyce spread jam with more haste than accuracy, and some red-globules dropped on to the plastic mac, much to the satisfaction of an expectant blowfly. Then, when twelve margarine- and jam-coated slices of bread were laid out in a neat row, Henry made her crouch down beside him and asked:

160

'Ready?'

'Well . . .'

'Right – take up a slice and make out you are going to eat it.'

'Gosh – I'm scared.'

'Do as I say – otherwise we'll be here all day.'

They had scarcely raised bread to mouth when a scream of rage made Joyce drop her slice; and the harpy came gliding down from the castle walls, its brass wings glittering in the afternoon sun. Henry – who had inadvertently taken a generous bite of bread and jam – spoke with a full mouth.

'Quick – run for the hollow while I turn on the cassette.'

Joyce ran like a cat that has suddenly spotted an ill-tempered dog, and Henry, after he had pressed the play button on the recorder, was not slow to follow her example. Once they were lying face down in the hollow with only their heads peering through a low curtain of heather, he said:

'I say, that jam wasn't half bad.'

'Never mind the jam – look at that thing!'

The harpy had landed on the plastic mac and was now busy turning the bread and jam into little heaps of blue and red powder, and did not seem to be in the least disturbed when a voice announced:

'This is Radio Four. For the next half hour there will be a recital of early military music performed by the Bradford Boiler-Maker's Brass Band, conducted by Sydney Brassbottom . . .'

'You idiot,' Joyce whispered. 'Why didn't you rewind to the part where the trumpets and things start blowing? That harpy will have finished making a mess of our bread and jam before the racket begins. Honestly – you are the limit.'

'And you could have reminded me that they always rabbit on at the beginning of a musical programme,' Henry protested. 'I can't think of everything. I say – he's finished. Wait for it.'

A veritable cascade of sound erupted from the recorder; a glorious thunder of blaring horns, raucous trumpets, shrieking bugles, wailing cornets and moaning trombones; all against a background of rumbling drums and clashing cymbals. The harpy

161

temporarily suspended her food-corrupting operation and stared down at the cassette with almost polite interest. The deep sunken eyes – one green, the other red – blinked, the head nodded slowly, then one brass claw began to mark time on the plastic mac. Henry groaned.

'She likes it! As far as she is concerned, it's Music While You Corrupt! What a pity they didn't play a tango, then we would have seen a dancing harpy.'

Joyce watched the monster for a few minutes, then, when it began to beat time with a butter knife, assumed an expression of profound disgust.

'Clever dick! "Dead simple," he says! "All we've got to do is wait for it to disappear over the horizon." All you have done is make it a very happy harpy.'

'But the legend says the sound of a brass instrument will drive a harpy berserk – and I've provided an entire brass band.'

'No you haven't.'

'What do you call that noise? An elephant calling to its young?'

Joyce shook her auburn hair. 'Not a brass band. Just sounds on a length of tape. There's not so much as a brass button in sight.'

After a while Henry nodded. 'I see what you mean. A brass instrument has to be seen as well as heard. It's the brass which is important. Old hag face has to see as well as hear.'

'In one word – yes. I had a feeling that a tape recorder wasn't the answer.'

At that moment the Bradford Boiler-Maker's Brass Band appeared to run out of blowing power, for the stirring march suddenly disintegrated into long-drawn-out moans, and one trumpet, which had been sending out a series of particularly well-performed blasts, acquired a sound that was not unlike that of a cat paying compliments to a lady friend on a tin roof. Then, with a final moan, all sound ceased.

'Oh, no!' Henry exclaimed. 'The batteries have run down.'

The harpy dropped the butter knife and stared at the tape-recorder with an almost comical look of surprise on its wizened face. One brass claw reached out and gripped the cream plastic

162

box, shook it, tapped it, then raised it to a shrivelled ear. For a while it appeared that the harpy could still hear some sound coming from the defunct machine, until, with a cry of rage, she flung it down upon the ground and crushed it under her right claw.

'That's it, then,' Joyce remarked when the harpy had completed her task of turning bread and jam rotten and was once again airborne. 'You will have to explain how your new tape recorder was smashed into smithereens, and we are no nearer driving that thing away than when we started.'

Henry watched the harpy until she disappeared behind the castle walls, then nodded his reluctant agreement. 'Yep. I suppose we could bring Mother and Father out here and let them see it for themselves. Only – that's sort of giving up. Also, adults will put her into a cage and charge the public twenty-five pence to have a look. And I don't think that should happen to anything – not even a horror like that.'

'Absolutely not,' Joyce agreed. 'After all, she only turns food bad and smashes up the odd tape recorder.'

Henry grimaced. 'So says she who never owned one. Come on, we had better head for home. I dare say my really first class brain will think up a master plan sooner or later.'

Joyce made a rude noise.

Joyce was asleep when a hand shook her shoulder and a voice said in a loud whisper: 'Wake up – I've got it I've got it.'

She sat up and blinked owlishly, then stared indignantly at Henry, who was standing by her bed with a brass toasting fork in one hand and a tea tray in the other. She peered at the bedside clock.

'Why – why have you woken me up at three minutes past two? Really . . .'

Henry waved the toasting fork. 'I've got it.'

'I can see you have. Well – now you can push off and let me get back to sleep.'

'You are stupid,' Henry protested. 'Now pay attention. What

163

have I got in my right hand?'

Joyce yawned. 'A toasting fork.'

'And what is it made of?'

'Brass.'

Joyce scratched her head. 'So – you have a brass toasting fork! Big deal.'

Henry sighed very deeply. 'I have in my hand not *just* a brass toasting fork, but – a brass instrument.'

For the first time Joyce began to display an active interest.

'Are you sure? I thought an instrument was a thing you played.'

'There speaks a little mind that has yet to be lit by the lamp of imagination. Study your dictionary, girl. An instrument is any implement or tool by which something is done. Such as toasting bread.'

'But it doesn't make a noise,' Joyce stated with some satisfaction. 'So there.'

'It will when I bash it on this tray.'

'But it will be the tray which will make the noise – not the toasting fork.'

Henry's smile was wonderful to behold. 'And the tray is made of brass. And what is a tray but an instrument by which something is done. To wit – carrying grub into the dining-room. So *there* to you.'

Presently Joyce said: 'It might work at that. I say, you are bright.'

'As polished brass,' Henry agreed. 'I thought we might have a go tomorrow morning. Just after breakfast.'

'Thank goodness this is the summer break. Can I go back to sleep now?'

'If you must. For myself, I will sit up for a while and work out a plan of campaign. Nothing must go wrong this time.'

Joyce slid down between the sheets and smiled sleepily.

'Turn out the light and don't make a noise. If you are still awake tomorrow morning you can bring me a cup of tea.'

Next morning, the baker said there had been an unexpected run on bread, but he had a nice stale seed cake that he was prepared to sell for five pence. So it was that the second harpy disposal expedition set out armed with a seed cake, a brass toasting fork, a tea tray, a plastic mac, and a reasonable supply of optimism.

However, when they reached the old castle Joyce discovered Henry had forgotten to bring a knife, so it became necessary to cut the cake with the toasting fork, and the result was crumbling lumps that attracted the attention of a few hungry birds.

'It doesn't look very appetizing,' Joyce complained. 'No one is going to eat it,' Henry retorted. 'Now, don't mess about. You pick up the biggest lump and I'll stand by with the fork and tray.'

'Why can't I stand by with the fork and tray?'

'Because you'd probably be too frightened to do anything but run when old ugly comes swooping down.'

'You have a point,' Joyce agreed.

Scarcely had she raised a piece of stale seed cake to her mouth when the by now familiar shriek came from the castle and the harpy glided down towards the picnic site. Joyce dropped the seed cake and took refuge behind Henry.

'Suppose – suppose the fork and tray doesn't work?'

'I can think of no reason why it shouldn't work.' Henry replied, taking a firm grip of his brass instrument.

The harpy settled down on the plastic mac and had reduced half of the cake into green mould before the loud clanging sound rang out over the sun-drugged moor. A flock of birds that had been preparing to descend and feed on cake crumbs gave united cries of alarm and dispersed in a sudden explosion of fluttering wings. When fork and tray again made violent contact, the harpy became a grey and brass statue, her head to one side, eyes gleaming, one claw raised – the wrinkled face screwed up into an expression of extreme annoyance. Henry – who had assumed the creature would be frightened and take to instant flight – banged his tray with even greater vigour and shouted: 'Shove off! On your way!' for good measure.

Suddenly the harpy spoke, and this was such an unexpected turn of events that Henry dropped the toasting fork and completely ignored Joyce, who was making whimpering noises in the region of his right ear.

'What-do-yer-wanna to make noises like dat?'

It was a man's voice – rather like that of the foreign gentleman who ran the restaurant in the High Street – and had an undertone of intense displeasure. While Henry tried to think of a suitable answer, the harpy spoke again.

'I comma 'ere to turn fooda into rubbish, which is 'ard enough without you childer making da racket. Why for you banga da fork on da tray?'

Henry discovered he still had a voice, even though it refused to rise above a loud whisper. 'We – that is to say – my sister and I – understood, er, that you were frightened of a brass instrument, and—'

'Dat's a loada nonsense,' the harpy, interrupted. 'Dat aw-ful man Jason he banga us over da head with brass trumpets, so we flies away. Not frightened – just 'eadache.'

'Oh!' Henry found that a little of his normal self-confidence had returned. 'Well – you shouldn't go around turning food rotten. It's . . . it's a rotten thing to do.'

The harpy crouched down on the plastic mac and looked rather like a grotesque broody hen. 'Now 'e tella me I shouldn't do ma job. Ven the world was young, Zeus 'e says to us: "Get down thar, gals, and turna da fooda rotten. Dat king of Thrace," he says, " 'e not been comma over with da tribute. Not a sacrifice 'ave I had from 'im in a month of Tuesdays." Then along come dat Jason and 'is wool thieves and banga da 'eads da trumpets.'

Joyce spoke over Henry's shoulder. 'What happened to your three sisters?'

The harpy rolled her eyes. 'You may well ask. Safe and well dey are. Varming da tail feathers on Olympus, while I da food rotten turn. I come down for a little flutter and a Inglisman over me threw da net and brought me 'ere to da castle. Now it fall down, but I still 'ere. No food rotten turn for 'undreds of years. I fed up.'

And one large tear seeped out from the harpy's red eye and trickled down her wrinkled cheek.

Joyce said: 'Oh, what a shame! We'll bring you lots of food. And you can turn it rotten as much as you like.'

'Hey, wait a minute,' Henry protested. 'We're supposed to drive her away, not encourage her. Look,' he addressed the despondent harpy, 'why don't you go home? Back to Olympus? I should imagine your sisters would be very pleased to see you again.'

The harpy yawned and three wasps flew into her open mouth. She gulped, then bared her teeth. 'Tasty. Sisters never did I get on with. If I see them not again, da tears will not flow. Most times I sleep and wake ven smell of food call me to vork.'

'Well, you can't stay here,' Henry said. 'Not everyone is as brave as Joyce and me, and you might give somebody a heart attack.'

'I 'ave to come when peoples eat,' the harpy insisted. 'If drop dead – too bad. Now I go back and da eyes close.'

And without further words she spread wide her brass wings and soared up towards the castle walls, leaving the children to clear up a lot of rotten seed cake.

Now I would like to be able to record that Henry thought of a wonderful scheme that got rid of the harpy once and for all. I regret to say he did not, and, as the prospect of her being shut away in some zoo could not under any circumstances be entertained – well – she's still there.

Sometimes the children take along some stale sausages that the butcher was going to throw away, or a few pork pies that no one wanted to buy, and the harpy has a wonderful time turning them rotten. They have grown quite fond of her and often clean her wings and feet with a well known brand of brass polish, making them shine so brightly that one man maintained he had seen a flying saucer circling above the moor.

But take my advice: should you decide to have a picnic, for heaven's sake do not lay out your goodies near a ruined castle that is not more than fifty miles from London. And if an obstinate – not to say stupid – adult insists, then get well back and watch the fun, which I do assure you will begin the moment the silly creature raises ham sandwich to mouth.

167

And don't bother to take along any kind of brass instrument. Whatever the old books may say, such things will only make the harpy extremely annoyed.

Walk in Darkness

AFTER TWENTY YEARS OR more spent in discussing psychic phenomenon, interviewing those who maintain they have seen ghosts, heard them, felt their atmosphere, I still have to say 'No' when asked the simple question: 'Have you ever had a psychic experience?'

Never.

For I am an essentially truthful creature.

But I once toyed with an experience that could be classed as 'psychic'.

This is surprising as I live in a house that was – with three others – built by my great-grandfather back in 1864, but so far as I am aware, not one of my family who lived and died in those four houses ever came back as a ghost.

Like most youngsters of my generation, I was spellbound by the superb imagination of Dennis Wheatley. Most young men during the war years read his thrillers, which included his fabulous international spy Gregory Sallust, who was setting Europe aflame long before James Bond was a spark in his father's eye. But I have since come to realise the secret of his success was his ability to blend undoubted fact with very convincing fiction. It was said of Cecil B. De Mille that if it suited his current film he would put Moses in the War of the Roses, then swear he had dug up a slice of real history. But there was one book written by Wheatley that had to be based on naked truth – and if it wasn't, should have been: it was called *Strange Conflict.*

In this book three very gifted friends (clearly based on the Three Musketeers), having acquired the ability of leaving their bodies when asleep, either travel to the dark planes of lower earth or those that normally are beyond mortal vision, until summoned to reoccupy this vessel of flesh and blood, or dare to drift into that land from which (according to the Bard) no traveller has returned.

I read the book many times. The idea was enthralling and I, with a few thousand others before me, decided to have a go at Astral Travelling. I obeyed all the rules (as laid down by Mr Wheatley): go to sleep with a notebook and pen beside me; keep the mind empty until sleep comes and, most important, touch nothing while asleep or in the sleep state.

There are hard won instructions for those willing to risk patience or insanity, maybe both, and Sir Oliver Lodge has left a trail for the intrepid explorer to follow. Wheatley likewise, albeit with a dire warning. Beware of the creatures who crawl between the planes, hungry for flesh and blood life.

Weeks passed, and I found it difficult to fall asleep. And most certainly not a sign did I see of the Hidden World. After giving myself a sick headache, I decided to give up. I reasoned I was not the psychic type. On the other hand, the entire business might well be a load of rubbish.

Then one night I placed a notebook and ball-point pen on the bedside table, then set about emptying my mind. No easy task. Never before had I felt so fresh and wide awake. I called out with a silent voice, begging for some kind of help. None came. I decided none ever would. I was too inexperienced.

I closed my eyes and instantly – the result maybe of suddenly relaxing – I fell into a deep, restful sleep. Vivid brain pictures flashed into being: a green valley flanked by fire-tipped mountains. I knew I was experiencing the beginning of a normal dream pattern. In a while I would slip into a deep sleep.

From whence came this knowledge? I could not even surmise,

but I should imagine it is part and parcel of our astral inheritance. Maybe man is immortal. Maybe . . . maybe . . . maybe something really wonderful waits for us beyond the stars.

However, one cannot keep an open mind and philosophize at the same time. My heart gave a mighty thump – and I was standing on the landing immediately in front of the open window.

This must be clearly understood, or my experience will not be fully appreciated. My first impression was I had sleep-walked and I was standing on a thick carpet on the top-most stair looking down on to the first floor landing. And that was the point – the only sense left was sight, so far as I could tell. No sound to let me know if hearing was still mine. Certainly no aroma to announce the presence of smell.

To my left was the bathroom, to my right my office and work-room. In front, the landing window through which I could see a full moon. Its cold light was almost dazzling (I might be wrong, but it did seem unnaturally bright).

Writing this after ten or fifteen years makes me realise that I should have taken greater notice of my surroundings; tried to decide if I (the essential 'me') was housed in some kind of body. I think I must have been, even though I could not see legs or arms.

But, to be frank, I was scared silly – in constant fear that I was going to lose all contact with my body. The everyday earth body, I mean.

But nevertheless, curiosity was beginning to come to terms with fear. Could I move? If so, how? Once again the answer was simple. I thought 'upwards' and found myself (if that is the right term) up under the ceiling. But at the cost of clarity. I was looking down at the landing, but the entire scene appeared to be covered by a faint mist. That mist became more dense even as I watched.

Gradually fear was replaced by curiosity or, if you wish, a lust for knowledge. One thing was certain: I had the use of one sense only – vision. I could see in whatever direction I wished. I also believed I could move in whatever direction I wanted, but was not all that keen to find out.

171

I began to experiment, albeit in a very small way. Was I alone? Maybe. I saw nothing or anyone that looked even remotely human, but there was evidence of small life. What looked like greyish rats equipped with tiny white breasts and red teats. I'm almost sure these lived on blood. Possibly human when it was available. Anyway, they moved at amazing speed and I could imagine them making nests in a spring mattress.

I remembered the experiments and experiences that are dismissed as nightmares, and I wondered how we can live a full life and remain sane at the end.

Gradually I was adjusting to this strange plane, even though I began to see what had to be ruined buildings superimposed over my bedroom. More small life took on visibility. I recognised my defunct cat, Tobias, who had passed over through old age some six months before. She did not appear to recognise me, but sat perfectly still watching the rat creatures with some disquiet. Then a small dog with a red tail and bright green ears disappeared into my bedroom and Tobias, if it was she, glided down the stairs. I did not see her again.

What could have been flying fur-covered snakes emerged from the bathroom, then all but poured into my office, which I am sure will mean a mass of dream horror to be invented in the near future. But that is in the hands of Beldaza (god of the vampires). How strange it was to exist without a flesh and blood body; to see in every direction while I moved in a silent world which, so far as I can understand, exists in more than one dimension.

Remembering Alice and her small cake, I thought 'upwards' again, and I ascended to a bedroom. I believe I not only moved upwards, but sideways as well. This was certainly a new experiment – for me, at any rate.

I was in a young girl's bedroom and she was sitting on the edge of a divan. Stark naked, pulling on a pair of flesh-coloured nylons. And – read this young girls of England – there were watchers. Afterwards I learned they were called Peepers. Men who watch beauty undress and thus derive certain sexual pleasure through their astral bodies.

The girl was a glorious creature, or rather such as she appeared to be, but one must bear in mind that I was only seeing her astral body. But I saw a mass of golden curls, dark blue eyes and large shapely hands that, when not pulling on stockings, were never still.

Suddenly she looked up and a wave of anger transformed her face into a hideous mask, and what should have been a soft lilting voice rose to a shout.

'Push off . . . go on . . . get out . . . go on get . . .'

As her voice was transformed into a shriek, the creatures detached themselves from the walls and ceiling. Others slid from under the bed clothes, and presently – so far as I could judge – only the girl and I were left. She gave me a quick glance and swore.

'Bloody hell! Here's one that won't be so easily dismissed. No Peeper . . . but a Wanderer. Could become a midnight friend.'

She addressed me direct: 'Tell me, young man, do you wear that face wake and sleep? I do assure you it will be acceptable on either side of the sleep-walk line.'

I nodded and wondered how much longer I could retain my astral body on this plane of existence. I was already feeling a need to wake in a warm bed and dismiss all this as a rather startling dream. But once I had returned to my F&B body and normal sleep, who could tell if I would experience dream sleep again.

I was becoming confused, not certain if I were not kneeling before long-forgotten gods who would desert me when I felt certain reality was their one and only gift. The beautiful girl who still was clad only in stockings, spoke to me again.

'Very soon both of us will wake up on the earth we know so well. The strange animals will now and again make themselves known, but there'll be no fear. Only curiosity. We will become as haunted children and play together in the cold moonlight.

'But you look weary and must return. Tomorrow we'll choose some lovely dresses for me and smart uniforms for you. All young men want to wear smart and eye-dazzling uniforms. White, I think, enhanced by medals and orders.'

173

Together we rose above her bedroom (Peepers hid in every corner) and presently came to the landing that lay outside my bedroom. The moon still lit the landing window. Peace reigned in all dimensions.

'Back to bed,' the naked girl ordered. 'Try to wake tomorrow night in my bedroom.'

'I promise with all my heart and soul,' I replied. 'Tell me, what do you look like on the world we know so well?'

'You want the truth? The absolute truth? Very well, since you insist. Ready?'

I nodded.

'I am old and very ugly.'

I sat for some time, just staring at her lovely face and body. Then I asked in a low voice: 'And that is the absolute truth?'

'It is one form of the truth. But in this world, truth is what you make it.'

Then, with no effort on my part, I was standing by my bed looking down at my body. The bedroom was well lit by the bedside lamp (it must be remembered I was planing to take notes the very moment I awoke). My body was lying on its right side and I could only see the back of my head.

Now – for some reason this is the horrible part – my left arm and hand was dangling over the bed edge, looking very white and still. I thought: 'I'm dead! What I was proposing to do was unnatural and the body rebelled and ceased to function.' After all, what I was doing was by no means natural, and my heart (which was not in tip-top condition) could have well decided to call it a day (or night). Then the hand twitched, thereby affording me certain relief until I remembered that a corpse will move as rigor mortis sets in.

My hand moved again, jerked, and something eerie was happening to the 'me' who stood by the bed.

I fell very slowly forward – floated would be an apt description – and found my earth body fighting some kind of battle with the sheets and blankets . . .

*

And that was it. I came awake. Drenched with perspiration, shaking like a leaf in an autumn gale, heart thudding in no pleasant fashion.

There was no need for the pen and paper, I could remember every second of my sleeping adventure. After all, there wasn't much of it. I lay very still for a long time, rather hoping that I would slip once again into that strange sleep, but this time I would advance with full confidence into the Hidden World.

But let me confess here and now: although quite a few years have passed, and I've tried to find the dark path, the return journey has still to be taken.

And maybe it is for the best: I keep remembering how cold and lonely it is up under the landing ceiling . . .

The Wind-billie

In 1889 THE LITTLE moorland village of Munford was a rather
bleak place. For most of the year a restless wind blustered along
the cobble-stoned streets, rattled windows, lifted the hats from old
men's heads, made the few trees bow respectfully, and blew down
chimneys, thus causing smoke to billow out into parlour or
kitchen. But of course this last discomfort was more prevalent in
some houses than others.

'Drat that wind,' Grannie Wyatt complained, once she had
recovered from a violent fit of coughing. 'It's getting so a body
can't sit by the fire in peace.'

'The wind's blowing from the north,' Richard explained.

'When it blows from the south,' Roland added, 'the houses on
the other side of the street are smoked out.' Richard and Roland
Canfield were identical twins. They both had a mop of blond hair,
slightly tilted noses, broad mouths, excellent teeth and ears that
were inclined to stand out on either side of their narrow heads
like jug handles. People were apt to say: 'Like two peas in a pod,'
'Can't tell one from t'other,' and, 'Bless me, if the two of 'em
together wouldn't make a drunken man turn teetotal.' Needless
to say they were both the same age. That is, twelve years, three
months and two days. Although their father maintained that
Richard was the elder by four minutes. Perhaps this advantage in
seniority was why he sometimes adopted an air of patronage
towards his brother. On this occasion he expressed his scorn by a
loud snort.

177

'What utter rot! If our chimney is smoking, so are those on the other side of the street.'

'Well, they don't,' Roland insisted. 'George Hargreaves says his never smokes. So there.'

'That's because his father fitted a cowl . . .'

'Which the wind blew off.'

'Boys, you mustn't quarrel,' Grannie Wyatt said sternly. 'Especially about things you know nothing about. It's wind-billies that make chimneys smoke. Anyone with any sense at all knows that.'

Grannie Wyatt was a veritable storehouse of strange knowledge, but this item of information left both boys speechless for almost one minute. Then Richard asked 'What's a wind-billie?'

'A smallish monster, but no less nasty for all that. When the sun puts on his red nightgown and slips down into bed early; and the north wind comes roaring out of its icy garden, then the wind-billie starts thinking about reproducing.'

'What's. . . ?' Roland began, but Richard quickly interrupted.

'Having children, stupid. Go on, Grannie Wyatt.'

'First it drifts up from some dark place – like a disused barn, or a forgotten attic – where it's slept all summer, and rides the wind until it spots something that's round, hollow and warm.'

'Like a chimney pot,' Richard suggested.

'You're sharp, I'll say that for yer,' Grannie stated with some reluctance. 'Once in the chimney pot it takes on substance. From being nigh transparent, it turns jet black . . .'

'Due to smoke and soot.' Roland was determined to show he was no less bright than his brother.

'Right. It gets bigger and bigger and the smoke can only seep out around it, and when the wind is real cruel,' Grannie pointed to a cloud of smoke that chose that moment to billow out from the fireplace, 'that happens.'

Richard – who was much addicted to original oaths – cried. 'Great galloping carrots!' while Roland looked really frightened.

'Is there . . . really a wind-billie in our chimney?'

'Sure as God made wriggly worms,' Grannie said with unshakable conviction. 'Use yer eyes, boy.'

'Perhaps,' Richard dared to make the suggestion, 'the chimney wants sweeping.'

The old woman made a strange cackling sound and raised her hands in a gesture of horror.

'Sweep the chimney! If you want all the milk to sour, an invasion of rats, cold feet in a warm bed – then you just shove a brush up that chimney before crocus time.'

Richard gave the matter his full consideration and then expressed an opinion.

'I don't believe a word of it. There's no such thing as a wind-billie.'

A glint appeared in Grannie Wyatt's faded blue eyes and Roland – who was not quite so daring as his brother – stirred uneasily in his chair.

'Are you doubting my word, boy?'

'Well – not exactly . . .'

'Because, my lad, I would take that as an insult. And if I'm insulted I usually turn people's hair to seaweed.'

Richard giggled and Roland shivered and there's no telling what might have happened if Doctor Canfield's pony and trap had not at that very moment rattled into the back yard. Grannie Wyatt climbed laboriously to her feet and walked slowly to the window.

'That's yer father come back from his rounds. Out of this kitchen so I can dish up.'

That evening, after Grannie Wyatt had served coffee and retired to the kitchen, Richard looked shyly at his father and asked: 'Father, is it true that Grannie is a witch?'

Doctor Canfield put down his coffee cup and creased his normally smooth forehead into a frown.

'Richard, I'm surprised to hear you ask such a question. Grannie is a poor old lady whose life was made miserable by the superstition of ignorant villagers, until I invited her to live here. Ever since your mother died she has cooked and cleaned for us and looked after you young ruffians. I don't wish to hear any more nonsense of that kind.'

For a while the silence was only broken by the spluttering logs that were burning in the large, iron fireplace, then Richard said quietly: 'But Grannie told us that there was a wind-billie in our kitchen chimney pot.'

Doctor Canfield poured rich port wine into a tall, green glass and chuckled. 'So that's what brought all this on. You must understand, boys, that Grannie is an old country woman who grew up in the days when isolated people really believed these weird folk tales.' He grimaced. 'Come to think of it – some of 'em still do. But I've never heard of a wind-billie.'

'It comes riding in on the north wind,' Roland said, 'and makes a home in a warm chimney when it is going to have children.'

The doctor nodded thoughtfully. 'All old folk legends must have a basis in fact. Who knows, perhaps our remote ancestors knew much that was forgotten when civilization was established. However, enough of this nonsense. How are you progressing with your holiday task?'

Richard groaned while Roland positively glowed with self-satisfaction.

'I've finished mine,' he said.

Richard believed that bed was the place to mull over the events and problems that had arisen during the day and did not hesitate to transform his thoughts into words. 'I've changed my mind,' he told his brother. 'After listening to father I'm not all that sure there isn't a wind-billie in our kitchen chimney.'

Roland made a grunting sound and buried his head under the bedclothes. This action aroused Richard's wrath.

'Say, are you listening to me? I don't like talking to myself.'

Roland realised that sleep was out of the question while his brother was in this mood, so he reluctantly sat up and did his best to stiffle a yawn. 'If there is such a thing as a wind-billie,' he said, 'and one is in our chimney, then jolly good luck to it. Now, let's go to sleep.'

'But don't you want to know what it looks like?'

'No.'

Richard climbed out of bed and began to pull his trousers on. 'Well, I do. I'm going to have a look.'

Roland scratched his head. 'What – look up the chimney?'

'No, stupid. Look down it. The outhouse roof is just below our window and from there I can climb up on to the main roof and reach the chimney stacks.'

'You're mad!'

'No, I'm not. I've a thirst for knowledge.'

Richard pulled a thick jersey over his head, slipped his feet into a pair of rubber-soled shoes, then picked up a small bedside oil lamp. He looked enquiringly at his brother.

'Coming with me?'

Roland shook his head violently. 'No. Absolutely not.'

'You're scared.'

'Too true. Please – forget all this nonsense and go back to bed.'

Richard did not answer, but walked resolutely to the window, opened one casement and after stuffing the small lamp under his jersey, climbed out on to the outhouse roof. A full moon high-lighted the surrounding countryside and enabled him to see the gabled roof which began its upward slope some four feet above and terminated where the massive red-bricked chimney-stacks towered up against the sky. He took a firm grip of an adjacent drainpipe and clambered up on to the red tiles. After wedging one foot in the gutter, he wriggled up the roof and finally reached the chimney-stacks, which allowed him to stand upright and peer down each one of its six pots.

There was some difficulty in lighting the lamp, but eventually he was able to slip the frosted globe over a tiny flickering flame and turn his full attention to finding a wind-billie – or prove for all time that no such creature existed.

The first four pots were mere black, soot-lined holes, but the fifth – which had a large chip out of the near-side – seemed to be unusually clean, and when Richard lowered his little lamp, he saw, some two feet down, a black, unsubstantial – something.

Richard did not hesitate. Holding the lamp with one hand, he thrust the other into the dark hole – and pushed. His fingers became entangled with a moist, cold – so very cold – substance that seemed to seep up over his hand and gently caress his wrist. Richard, despite his determination not to be frightened, made a sound that was not so far removed from a scream, and jerked his hand free. It came away with a faint popping sound and was so cold that he tucked it under his arm in an effort to restore the circulation.

From the chimney pot a long, very thin and extremely black arm, slowly emerged and waved six tiny fingers. The arm was no thicker than a flower stalk, but there was an elbow, a wrist and those waving fingers. Its substance could have been soot-stained mist, but it was as real as uncompleted homework on Monday morning.

Richard yelled and slid down the red tiles to land on the outhouse roof with a loud thud.

Breathless, bruised and very frightened, he looked up and saw Roland's face peering at him through the open window. His twin brother asked a practical question.

'What have you done with the lamp?'

Richard frowned, then after some thought, shuddered. 'I must have dropped it down the chimney.'

A grim-faced Grannie Wyatt served up breakfast next morning. She banged plates down upon the table, ignored Richard's request for another cup of tea and glared when Doctor Canfield remarked that the wind was particularly boisterous.

'Almost blew me off my feet when I went to feed the pony,' he added.

'Yes,' Grannie Wyatt said grimly, 'and it be most remarkable that the kitchen ain't smoking. Very remarkable.'

'No doubt the wind has veered round to another direction,' the doctor suggested.

Grannie Wyatt shook her head. 'No it ain't. Same north wind that's been blowing this fortnight or more. Only now it's a mighty angry wind.'

Doctor Canfield winked at the two boys. 'Really! I wonder what could have upset it?'

The old woman slammed a plate of bread and butter down upon the table. 'I found an oil lamp in the kitchen grate this morning. A small oil lamp.'

The doctor shot an enquiring glance at his two sons.

'A lamp! What on earth was it doing there?'

'You may well ask!' Grannie replied. 'And it came from somebody's bedroom. A body I could touch with a very short stick.'

For a while no one spoke, then the doctor raised an eyebrow and asked: 'Do you know anything about this, Richard?'

Richard tried to assume an expression of hurt innocence, but only succeeded in looking very guilty.

'I dropped it,' he admitted at last, hoping no one would ask where he had dropped it from.

'In the kitchen grate?'

'Yes. I – I was trying to see if the fire was out.'

Doctor Canfield sighed deeply. 'Now I've heard everything. All right, Grannie – thank you for telling me. The young rascals will have to go to bed in the dark for some time to come.'

Grannie Wyatt laughed. It was a particularly mirthless sound; midway between a cackle and a bark.

'They can go to bed in the dark or in the daylight – it don't matter a fig. I'm thinking they won't stay there longer than it takes to say, "What's that cold thing on my foot?" '

Doctor Canfield muttered, 'Good grief!' and hid his face behind the morning newspaper. Grannie stared at him with marked disapproval.

'You'll be laughing on t'other side of your face before another day has dawned. To start with you'd better get some of that new-fangled condensed milk in.'

The doctor emerged briefly from behind his newspaper. 'No thank you. Can't stand the stuff.'

'It's not a case of what you can't stand. It's what you've got to put up with. Cow's milk will curdle now a wind-billie's on the rampage.'

'Oh, really!' the doctor protested.

'And I daresay you fancy some lamb chops for yer dinner. Well

– you won't have any. The ones I bought yesterday have started to go off.'

And after delivering this disturbing piece of information, the old woman left the room and slammed the door behind her. The doctor lowered his newspaper.

'Now, boys, listen carefully. Grannie is a very old lady and has got some strange notions in her head. But you must make allowances for her. No poking fun or rudeness. Should she mention this . . . eh . . .'

'Wind-billie,' Richard prompted.

'Exactly. Wind-billie – just ignore her.'

Later that morning the twins were inclined to wonder how their father would have viewed Grannie's actions, had he been present. From the kitchen doorway they watched the old woman kneel down in front of the fireplace and say in a loud whisper: 'It's nought to do with me. Let me cook dinner in peace.'

But scarcely had she withdrawn her head when a large lump of soot crashed down on to the smouldering cinders and extinguished whatever remnants of a fire that there might have been. Grannie uttered some words that neither of the boys had ever heard before, then did a funny little dance round the kitchen.

Richard watched the old woman with grave concern.

'I feel rather guilty causing all this trouble. I mean to say, it can't be good for Grannie, jumping about like that at her age.'

Roland nodded. 'I agree. But why is she prancing round the room?'

'I guess she's placating the wind-billie or something. I say, do you suppose that if I explained that I meant no disrespect, but was only trying to quench a thirst for knowledge, it might stop messing up our dinner?'

Roland shrugged, then gave a sigh of relief when Grannie Wyatt stopped dancing and sank down into a chair. 'Maybe. But how do we talk to it? The only answer Grannie got was a lump of soot.'

Richard did not answer, but pointed to a trail of tiny sooty marks that ran across the kitchen, out into the hall and up the

184

stairs. He bent down and examined them closely.

'Do you know what I think?'

'I don't care what you think,' Roland replied. 'Just knowing that something nasty is in our bedroom is enough for me.'

'Several nasty things,' Richard corrected. 'There's more than one. And I bet you my collection of spiders that the smaller marks were made by the wind-billie's children.'

'Rot!' Roland retorted, without any great conviction. 'I mean there couldn't be any children – could there?'

'Oh, yes, there could. If you remember, Grannie Wyatt said that was why wind-billies set up homes in chimney pots. To have children.'

Roland looked up the stairs and shuddered.

'Do you think there's an entire family up there?'

'You can bet on it. And we'd better face them now, rather than get to know them after dark. There's no need to be scared. They can't eat us.'

'Are . . . are you sure?'

'Of course. At least, not both of us.'

There was some argument as to who should go first, but Roland pointed out that as it was Richard who had disturbed the wind-billie, the honour of leading the way was rightfully his. Richard was finally prevailed upon to accept this debatable privilege and crept up the stairs with lowered head, clenched fists and a heart that pounded so loudly, he would not have been surprised if a wind-billie had peered through the banisters to see what all the noise was about.

The landing floor was covered with green linoleum, and the trail of sooty footprints was easily discernible on its polished surface. The wind-billie must have been at a temporary loss as to which direction to take, for the tiny marks formed a rough circle, before branching off and going into the twins' bedroom.

They opened the door and looked around with fearful expectancy, fully prepared to find an army of little monsters lined up in front of the fireplace or playing leapfrog on the bed. But the room was much as usual. Richard peered under the beds, cautiously opened the wardrobe doors, and rummaged through the miscellaneous collection of items that had been tossed inside over the years.

'Nothing in here,' he announced, pulling out a pair of football boots and two ancient jerseys. 'At least nothing I can see.'

'Richard,' Roland's voice came from behind him. 'Oh Lord!'

'What's up?'

Roland pointed a shaking forefinger in the general direction of the wardrobe top. 'That.'

Richard stepped back and looked upwards. The wardrobe had an ornamental plinth which surrounded its roof on three sides, and in the centre, looking over the edge, was a tiny head. It was not much larger than a ping-pong ball, was crowned by a mop of black hair, had a pair of microscopic red eyes, green slanted ears and a gaping mouth that revealed pointed white teeth. The face was streaky black, as though it had been well coated with soot which was beginning to wear off. It is fair to say that the tiny head would never have been seen by anyone who was not looking for it.

'What shall we do?' Roland asked.

'Catch it. Hand me my fishing net.'

This piece of equipment was ideally suited for wind-billie catching, as it consisted of a small net fitted to a length of pliable cane and had in its day landed many a tiddler from the nearby river. But when Richard gently eased the net over the wardrobe plinth, the wind-billie leaped towards the ceiling and after performing a long, graceful curve, alighted on Richard's bed. There it raised long, thin arms, as though appealing for mercy, then wiped away a solitary tear which was trickling down its hooked nose.

'It's frightened!' Roland exclaimed. 'Don't try to catch it with that net.'

'But great rolling onions!' Richard protested, 'it's a monster.'

'But only a baby one.'

'If that's a baby, what does the mother look like?' Now the infant wind-billie could be seen in its entirety, there was little that would please the eye or comfort a nervous disposition. A round,

186

hair-covered body, long thin legs that terminated in another pair of hands; the boys were reminded of a grotesque spider that was distantly related to a long dead leaf. But at that moment it was most certainly frightened and wiped one pair of sooty hands on the bedspread while making an almost imperceptible sound that was not unlike wind screeching through a broken window-pane.

'I wonder if it wants something to eat?' Roland enquired.

'And I wonder where the others have got to?' Richard said, looking anxiously round the room. 'I bet the mother will be hopping mad when she finds that little Charlie is missing.'

Roland approached the mini-monster and to his brother's disgust, began to make coaxing noises. The kind that fond, but misguided parents direct at babies.

'Diddums, then. Is the ickle man frightened? Is the ickle, donkerdiddums frightened?. Yes, he is. He's a ickle, frightened, donkerdiddums . . .'

'Great rotting garbage!' Richard roared. 'Stop doing that. You'll be tickling its stomach next.'

'Why don't you shut up?' Roland protested 'I was calming it down nicely, until you opened your great mouth.' He took two steps towards the baby wind-billie. 'Did the nasty boy shout, then? Yes, he did . . .'

'Suffering rhubarb!' Richard ejaculated.

The infant wind-billie did in fact appear to be reassured by this kind of language, for it lowered its arms, blinked at Roland, then opened its mouth and emitted a kind of gusty sigh, that had much in common with a summer breeze, that is playing hide-and-seek in the branches of a tree.

'Come to daddy-waddie,' Roland invited, laying his out-stretched palm on the bedspread. 'Ickle donkerdiddums come to daddy-waddie.'

At first the mini-monster appeared to entertain grave doubts that this was a safe invitation to accept, but after retreating up the slope of Richard's pillow, where it sat watching its would-be comforter with an unblinking stare, it suddenly performed another effortless leap and landed on the welcoming hand.

'There,' Roland said smugly as he carried the tiny creature towards the window, 'kindness to dumb animals always pays off.'

'Mind it doesn't bite you,' Richard warned. 'Those teeth look pretty sharp.'

Roland began to rub the black head, an action which appeared to meet with the wind-billie's full approval, for it closed the red eyes and made a windy roar, which must have been the equivalent of a cat's purr.

'Of course he won't bite. Look, now I'm rubbing the soot away, he's almost transparent. That's why people rarely see a wind-billie.'

'So, you've managed to pacify a baby wind-billie. Now let's put it into something – like a shoebox – and try to find out where the others have got to.'

They could not find a shoebox, but Roland made up a cosy little bed in an old slipper, where the baby wind-billie, after nibbling a grain of soot, coiled itself into a tiny round ball and went to sleep. Despite his brother's protests, Richard insisted on placing this make-shift cradle into the wardrobe and locking the door.

'At least we'll know where one of them is,' he explained to an indignant Roland. 'Oh, come on! You're like a hen with one chick.'

They searched the room with meticulous care; moved the beds, turned out drawers, even looked behind pictures, but not another wind-billie did they find. Then Roland – who had acquired a lot more confidence since taming the baby wind-billie-pointed to a mouse-hole which had been hidden by the dressing-table.

'That's where they went. And as these walls are hollow, they could now be anywhere in the house.'

Richard was forced to agree. 'Yes, and once we're in bed, the mother can creep back and really give us what-for.'

'Then I'm not going to bed.'

'You'll have to go to bed sometime. Say, what was that?'

That was a mighty crash which seemed to come from the room below; and it was followed by a series of loud thuds, which suggested that a number of books were being thrown against a wall.

The boys ran downstairs and were in time to see Grannie Wyatt performing another little dance in the hall. She stopped when the twins appeared and asked the inevitable question.

'What have you young varmints been up to?'

Richard flinched as the sound of breaking glass came from his father's study. 'Nothing, Grannie. Honest.'

The old woman stamped her feet. 'Don't tell me a wind-billie is carrying on like that for nothing. I've been doing a placation dance 'til me feet fair ache, but it ain't no manner of use. Hark at that!'

A sound that may have been caused by a chair being knocked against a table, did much to confirm that the wind-billie was not in a playful mood. Richard took a deep breath, then uttered the bravest statement of his short life.

'I'm going in there and try to arrive at some kind of under-standing.'

'Understanding!' Grannie screamed the word. 'A wind-billie hasn't any time for understanding. I beg to doubt if you'll be standing after a minute in that room.'

'Will you come with me?' Richard pleaded. 'I mean – you do seem to be on speaking terms with it.'

Grannie shook her head. 'It don't talk. Only dance. If you know the right steps, I'm saying you can't converse.' Roland could not withhold his admiration.

'And you know the right steps! Gosh!'

Grannie Wyatt smiled complacently. 'I'm highly educated,' she admitted.

Doctor Canfield's study was in a sad state of disarray. Chairs were overturned, books lay like grounded moths all over the floor, the shattered remains of a glass vase crunched under Richard's foot and every picture was hanging lopsided on the walls. But no one had eyes for anything but the awful creature that was squat-ted on the desk and was at that moment trying to upset the ink-well.

189

The baby wind-billies were ugly, but – in Roland's opinion at anyrate – appealing. Mother was just plain ugly. A head that was possibly a little larger than an average sized cooking apple, ash-grey hair, red protruding eyes, teeth that looked as if they had been yellowed by years of non-stop smoking, wrinkled slanted ears, a really grotesque bulging body and so very thin legs and arms. Roland said: 'Appearances can be very deceptive,' but he did not sound very convinced.

Mother wind-billie suspended her ink-well upsetting operation and glared at the intruders, while numerous little wind-billies chased each other along the mantelshelf and around the skirting board. Roland would have made endearing noises, but Richard stopped him with a forbidding frown. He spoke to Grannie without turning his head.

'Will you ask it – her – what's wrong?'

Grannie skipped two paces to the right and one to her front. The wind-billie performed a veritable square dance. She jumped, hopped from left to right, ran round in a circle, then sat down and stared at Richard with an expression of hungry anticipation.

Grannie Wyatt spoke with a hushed voice.

'It's bad. Very bad. She says, not only did you disturb her winter rest, but murdered one of her children. She's going to wreck the house and let the north wind through broken windows.'

Richard shuddered and tried not to meet the wind-billie's ferocious gaze.

'Ask her if she'll take her family back to our chimney if I restore her lost child, safe and unharmed?'

Grannie rose up on to the tips of her toes, did a little pirouette across the room, then sank down into a low curtsy. The wind-billie – after a rather terrifying pause – jumped up and down three times, then did a kind of minuet on all fours. Grannie translated.

'She will, so long as her missing little one is returned immediately.'

'Roland,' Richard instructed, 'go upstairs and fetch the little horror.'

Roland ran from the room and returned in no time at all,

190

carrying the old slipper in which the baby wind-billie was still sleeping peacefully. He laid the slipper on the desk, then stepped back and watched the joyful reunion with every sign of intense satisfaction.

'I say,' he said, 'you've got to admit she's a good mother.'

There was ample evidence to prove this was indeed true, for mother wind-billie stretched out a long arm, pulled her offspring out of the slipper, blew a tiny cloud of soot over its face and generally behaved in the ridiculous fashion that parents are apt to display when reunited with a mislaid child. Richard thought the entire proceedings were extremely nauseating.

Presently mother did a hop, skip and jump, which presumably was a signal for the entire family to stop all playful activities and prepare for the homeward journey. The little wind-billies floated down from the mantelshelf, or hopped away from the skirting board, then formed a straight line in front of the desk, all the while puffing and blowing and making strange whining noises that suggested an infant wind was in the process of growing into a force nine gale.

The fond parent – still clutching her prodigal offspring – leapt down on to the floor and led her numerous progeny out of the study, across the hall and into the kitchen, where she made a bee-line for the fireplace. Once the family were congregated on the hearth, the little wind-billies jumped on to their mother's back, merged one into the other, until all that remained was a large black ball. Grannie Wyatt spread wide her skirt and sank into a low curtsy as the black ball bounced three times, before floating up the chimney. Instantly the fire, which up to that moment appeared to be nothing more than a heap of grey ash, flared up into a bright orange flame and a thick cloud of smoke poured into the room.

'She might have said thank you,' Richard remarked, once he had recovered from a fit of coughing.

'You just be grateful she didn't do anything else,' Grannie retorted. 'Now let's get yer father's sudy cleared up. What he don't know won't do him any harm.'

*

Doctor Canfield said he had never enjoyed such a well cooked dinner before and that Grannie had excelled herself.

'Although,' he added, 'how she can work in all that smoke is beyond me. And the silly old woman refuses to have the chimney swept.'

'Not before crocus time,' Richard said. 'It wouldn't be safe.'

The doctor laughed and poured himself a glass of red wine. 'These old superstitions! Still, as I've remarked before – they have some basis in fact.'

'Too true,' Richard nodded.

'They most certainly have,' Roland agreed.

The Slippity-Slop

Reginald liked digging holes.

Give him a spade, a patch of ground, and he was as happy as a mouse in a cheese shop. Understandably his father did not approve of this earth-disturbing occupation, which sometimes resulted in young plants being uprooted, aspiring potatoes left to perish under the noonday sun, and a general air of disarray in the garden.

'Look here,' he protested, while looking ruefully down into a most respectable hole that had ruined his rhubarb crop. 'This can't go on. If you must dig holes, find a place that hasn't been cultivated.'

'Where?' Reginald demanded, for he was a lad who did not waste words. He reserved his energy for digging.

'Oh,' his father looked helplessly round the garden. 'Over there in the corner. Nothing will grow there, not even weeds.'

The patch of ground in question was about two metres square, black as a chimney-sweep's face and always rather damp. Not exactly soggy, but moist, inclined to squelch if one jumped on it – which, of course, Reginald did at irregular intervals – and not really a one hundred per cent digging place. But he was not a boy to look a gift horse in the mouth – whatever that may mean – and lost no time in pushing his spade into the dank soil and depositing a glutinous clod on to the newly laid gravel path.

There was no doubt that the hole – if I may be permitted the expression – was most reluctant to be dug. The sides fell in and covered his legs with thick, horribly clinging soil; great fat, slimy worms slithered round his spade, and there was a distinct feeling that he was not so much digging a hole as burying himself.

But Reginald persevered, shovelled out just a little more than fell in and, after a lot of back-breaking work, was rewarded by seeing a respectable heap above, and something that bore a reasonable resemblance to a hole below. Then his spade struck a hard surface and he was forced to stop and investigate.

It was a round slab of stone.

Five minutes later a very muddy, irritated Reginald approached his father, who had just filled in the rhubarb-patch hole and was in no mood to discuss further spadework activities. He gave his young son one horrified glance, then raised his voice in protest.

'Good grief! Look at you! What on earth your mother is going to say, I can't think.'

'Stone in hole,' Reginald stated. 'Can't move it.'

'Never mind stones in holes. Inside this instant . . .'

'Got writing on it,' Reginald interrupted. 'Can't read it.'

Mr Straddlegrass, for such I must admit was Reginald's father's name, was clearly interested by this latest scrap of information, for he closed his mouth, gave the impression that he might well be thinking, then said: 'Writing you say! On a slab of stone? Let's have a look.'

Naturally the pile of earth on the garden-path aroused adverse comment, particularly as it had spilt over on to a bed of prize dahlias, but this was forgotten – if not forgiven – when Mr Straddlegrass looked down into the gaping hole.

'What a ghastly-looking mess! And all those worms! Ugh.'

'Dirt fallen on stone,' Reginald pointed out.

'So I can see. Well, I suppose I'd better go down there. You stay here.'

He slid down into the hole and began to push the loose earth to one side with the toe of his shoe.

'You're right, there is a stone here. And bless my breeches if there aren't some letters etched on it.'

194

'That's what I said,' Reginald insisted.

'I know you did. There's no need to be so cheeky. Hand me the spade.'

The spade made a grating sound as it scraped over stone, then Mr Straddlegrass spoke again, but this time his voice carried an undertone of excitement.

'Throw me down a piece of stick or something. The letters are filled with earth.'

Reginald passed down a length of bamboo which had been supporting a dahlia, then waited with ill-concealed impatience for further developments. Actually he was not in the least interested as to what was written on the stone, only in having it speedily removed so he could continue enlarging his hole. Presently his father began to spell out words, but with great difficulty.

'Dis-turb not that which lies be-neath,
Or you'll run home with chat-tering teeth.
It mat-ters not if you bolt door;
For Slip-pity-Slop come up through floor.'

Reginald was not very impressed with this piece of doggerel and quickly got back to the essential problem.

'Can you get stone up now?'

His father clambered out of the hole, then scratched his head.

' "Disturb not that which lies beneath!" I wonder if there's anything down there?'

'Get stone up and find out,' Reginald continued to stress his point.

'Don't suppose there's anything worth having,' Mr Straddlegrass said. 'But you never know. Might be treasure or something.'

Reginald considered this to be extremely unlikely, but was prepared to encourage any project, no matter how far-fetched, that would ensure the impediment to his hole-digging was removed.

'Bound to be treasure. Get stone up now.'

195

His father appeared to give the matter his full attention for an entire minute, then nodded vigorously.

'I believe I will. Can't do any harm.'

Reginald, without further waste of words, handed him the spade. There followed a period of scraping, earth-loosening, heaving, much use of strange words, and finally, a mighty rending sound. Mr Straddlegrass lifted the slab of stone and, with great effort, tossed it on to the path.

'Now,' he said, wiping his hands on the legs of his trousers, 'let's see what's down there.'

Reginald would have pointed out that he was quite willing to carry on with the good work, but decided that his father was entitled to a well-earned treat after all that stone-raising. So he sat down on the pile of earth and watched his perspiring parent wield a spade with more energy than skill. Presently Mr Straddlegrass made a sound that was a blend of 'Ugh' and 'Ah' and threw something out of the hole. The object rolled along the garden-path and finished up between two rows of runner beans.

It looked like a large black egg – with roots. Oval-shaped, pitted, still covered with moist soil, it was more than half a metre long and possibly fifty centimetres in circumference. The roots were slightly pink and sprouted from one side. Mr Straddlegrass examined this unexpected piece of treasure with interest.

'Horrible-looking thing,' he observed. 'But unusual. I wonder if it's worth anything?'

So far as Reginald was concerned, he would not have paid three pence for it, but he knew adults often gave large sums for the most unlikely things.

'How much?' he enquired, while looking at the eggshaped object with marked distaste.

His father shrugged. 'Depends what it is. There might be some collector who's got a fancy for such things, willing to pay quite a price. I mean to say, how often do you see an egg with roots?'

Reginald had to admit this was a rare commodity, although he personally could jog along quite happily without one on the

196

mantelpiece. He pushed the thing with his foot and thereby earned a rebuke from his father.

'Hey, watch it! That shell don't look all that thick and if it gets cracked, then no one will pay anything for it.' He cast an apprehensive look at the kitchen window. 'I suppose we had better show it to your mother.'

'I don't like the look of it and that's a fact,' Mrs Straddlegrass protested. 'It looks horrible, it smells horrible and I'm sure it *is* horrible.'

'But it is very rare,' Mr Straddlegrass pointed out. 'And rare things are always valuable.'

'Well, take it somewhere else. I don't want it in my kitchen. I wouldn't be happy washing up, knowing that thing was right next to my feet.'

Reginald had to admit that the egg-shaped object had improved after a good wash under the cold tap. It now had a kind of reddish surface, which, although pitted, was rather pretty, if one did not look at it for too long. The roots, of course – which had not taken kindly to the hasty shampoo – rather created the impression that a number of very thin legs had become entangled, but, given time, would sort themselves out and come running across the floor.

'Where can I put it?' Mr Straddlegrass insisted.

'Dustbin.'

Reginald shook his head reprovingly at this example of adult bickering, and said: 'Loft. No one go up there.' His mother smiled and ruffled his hair. 'That's a very sensible suggestion. Apart from the dustbin, that's the best place for it. But make sure you shut the trapdoor.'

'But it's very hot up there,' Mr Straddlegrass objected. 'It might – well – go bad.'

'It can't be badder than it is. That's my last word on the subject. Loft or dustbin. Take your choice.'

The egg-shaped object was put up into the loft, where it nestled between an old wellington boot and a pile of magazines. Mr

Straddlegrass placed an advertisement in the local newspaper, which stated he had a large black egg with roots for sale, but no one seemed interested. In fact, there was not one single reply.

'I tell you there are rats in the loft,' Mrs Straddlegrass insisted. 'I distinctly heard a slithering sound.'

'Impossible.' Her husband rarely answered back, but on this occasion he felt certain he was on safe ground. 'Rats can't get up into the loft. I can't myself, for that matter. The trapdoor's jammed. Anyway, rats don't slither. They patter.'

Mrs Straddlegrass shook her head. 'No pattering. These slither.'

'Birds?' Mr Straddlegrass suggested.

Reginald thought it was about time he aired his knowledge. 'Birds twitter.'

His mother looked upon him with all the pride natural to a lady who has raised a genius, then shot her husband a withering glance. 'There now, at nine years of age he's got more sense in his little finger than you have in your entire body.'

Mr Straddlegrass sighed deeply. 'Well, anyway, it can't be rats. If you want my opinion, there's nothing up there. Imagination.'

Reginald decided the conversation had become a little boring, for personally he could not care less if something in the loft slithered, twittered or pattered. So he went into the garden, which was disgustingly neat, with not a single hole to enliven its rows of sprouting potatoes, feathery carrots, flourishing cabbages and other plant life, that were a source of pride to Mr Straddlegrass. Even the damp patch which had formerly contained the egg-shaped object was covered by an elaborate rockery.

Reginald added his contribution by throwing a stone on the rockery then turned about and looked idly back at the house. It was bright with new paint and gleaming windows and appeared to be smirking at him, as though it knew something that he did not and had no intention of revealing the secret. He muttered: 'Rotten house. Rotten garden. Rotten everything.'

Then he spotted something move behind a chimneystack, and

life took on a fresh glow of interest again. At first he thought a
large bird had set up home in a chimney-pot, and waited for it to
reappear. But after the first flurry of movement, which he had
only seen from the corner of one eye, the roof continued to
present a normal, innocent appearance; a grey slope of smooth
slates, surmounted by four red chimney-pots.

He was about to walk back along the path, for his mother
usually made a cup of cocoa at this time, when a great, round head
reared up from behind the chimneystack. It looked like a big soup-
plate, equipped with eyes and a pair of tapering ears. So far as
Reginald could see, this terrifying head was supported by a long,
scale-covered neck, which wrinkled whenever the creature swayed
from left to right. Having – so to speak – taken the air, it sank down
and presumably disappeared through a hole in the roof.

Reginald ran down the path, fired by a quite natural urge to
inform his parents about this disturbing tenant who had taken up
residence in their loft.

'Ah, there you are!' Mrs Straddlegrass greeted him. 'Just in
time for a nice cup of cocoa and a condensed-milk sandwich.'

'Big head looking over chimney,' Reginald imparted the news
with his accustomed economy of words.

'Yes, dear. And I'm sure it's a very nice head. Now sit down.'

'Wrinkled neck,' Reginald added. 'Face like soup-plate.'

'I think;' Mr Straddlegrass stated, 'I'll dig up some of them
'taters. Be very nice boiled and served up with a bit of roast lamb.'

'Egg must have hatched out,' Reginald insisted, knowing he
must be very patient, as adult brains do not absorb information
very quickly. 'Slippity-Slop grown up.'

His mother beamed. 'Isn't he a one! My dad had a wonderful
imagination. After three pints of beer he said my mother had
three heads and more arms than she knew what to do with.'

Mr Straddlegrass nodded grimly. 'She had plenty of mouth at
any rate.'

'And,' Reginald continued, 'it slithers in loft.'

If I may be permitted to use a hackneyed phrase – the penny
finally dropped. Both parents looked upon their offspring with

growing interest. It was Mr Straddlegrass who broke the rather disturbing silence. 'What did you say, son?'

'Slippity-Slop hatched out. Grown big. Made hole in roof. Slithering.'

Father looked at mother, both turned pale, then exchanged words of disbelief.

'He's having us on!'

'It's just not possible.'

Reginald sighed and wondered – not for the first time – how such a stupid pair had managed to produce an intelligent being like himself.

'Easy to make sure. Open trap door and look.' There seemed to be a marked reluctance to carry out this excellent advice. Mr Straddlegrass shifted uneasily in his chair, and Mrs Straddlegrass took a deep swig of cocoa from an extremely large mug. At length she said: 'Can't do any harm – can it?'

Her husband agreed it could not, but continued to sit in his chair and stare thoughtfully at the floor. Then Reginald, who was becoming a little impatient with all this dithering, got to his feet.

'I'll get pair of steps.'

'But the trapdoor is jammed, son.'

'And hammer to unjam.'

Such praiseworthy zeal was not greeted with the enthusiasm it deserved, for his mother, said: 'Drink your cocoa and don't be so forward,' and his father made a funny face and looked sadly out of the window. After a while, Reginald decided that he would have to let time reveal that which no one wished to see, so he drank his cocoa, ate two condensed-milk sandwiches, then went out to play with the next-door cat, who liked nothing better than chasing a piece of string with a conker tied on one end.

When he came in for lunch, his father was laying the table, this being one of his many household duties, and wearing an expression of subdued optimism.

'Not a thing up there,' he informed Reginald. 'I've banged on the trapdoor, but it won't budge. But there was no sound, so there can't be anything up there.'

'Sleeping. Need screwdriver to remove frame . . .'

'I've had enough of your suggestions. Now, get the pepper and salt out of the sideboard and don't talk so much.'

In fact, no one spoke very much during lunch, except to say: 'Any more sprouts?' and 'That pudding is filling,' and other mundane remarks. Then something made a loud thudding sound above stairs, and Mrs Straddlegrass said how careless Reginald was to leave things in places where they could fall down, and how Mr Straddlegrass should keep an eye on him, as she had only one pair of legs and couldn't be in every place at once. This was an injustice that Reginald could not tolerate, so, after he had eaten his second helping of treacle pudding, he said quietly: 'Nothing fall down. Slippity-Slop wake up. Soon come down through ceiling.'

Both parents told him to shut up and uttered dire threats about him being sent to bed without any supper, then jumped to their feet when a loud splintering sound, followed by a crash, appeared to confirm his prophecy. Reginald, who had a genuine thirst for knowledge and just could not understand this reluctance to face the unknown, got up and walked into the hall, then slowly mounted the stairs.

Most of the landing ceiling had crashed down on to the carpet, and from the midst of a mass of sagging lathes and splintered beams, a long, scaled neck, which was terminated by a large, soup-plate-shaped head, swayed back and forth like a giant, grotesque snake. The round, green eyes surveyed the intruder with a cold, malevolent stare, while the wide, well-fanged jaws crunched a lump of plaster. Then the remainder of the ceiling collapsed, and Reginald was able to view the monster in its entirety.

To say the least, it was an unnerving sight. Imagine a short, round body that tapered down to the neck on one side and a long, thin tail on the other. Then give the body sixteen pairs of legs, each one equipped with a green, sucker-like foot, that most certainly made an awful slithering sound as they slid among the fallen plaster. The creature seemed to be in no way put out by its fall, but reached out its long neck and took an experimental bite out of the bannisters.

Reginald went back downstairs and into the diningroom where he found his parents huddled under the table. He knelt down and did his best to comfort them.

'No need to worry. Slippity-Slop eating bannisters.' It is regretted that neither parent was reassured by this information or thanked Reginald for imparting it. Mrs Straddlegrass was the first to emerge and she proclaimed her fear and indignation in a loud voice.

'It's all your fault, digging holes and letting your father bring that egg-thing into the house. Well, I'm going to shut myself in the kitchen and not come out until one or both of you have found some way of getting rid of that awful creature.'

Mr Straddlegrass clambered out from under the table.

'Of course, dear. I'll ring the police and fire brigade.'

'No you don't. I'm not having the neighbours know we've a monster on the premises. It's not respectable.' And, having uttered these final words, the good lady departed, leaving a very frightened and perplexed Mr Straddlegrass staring hopefully at his completely unmoved son.

'Eh . . . what do you think we ought to do?'

Reginald nodded his approval. His father was at last showing a glimmer of intelligence, in so far as he was requesting advice from someone who thought before speaking.

'Hole,' he said.

'You can't dig holes now. How are we going to get shot of that thing?'

Reginald sighed deeply. 'Egg come from hole – Slippity-Slop go back down hole.'

Mr Straddlegrass again gave the impression that he was thinking.

'Fine. But how do we get it down a hole?'

Reginald did not answer, but went out into the garden, where he half filled one jacket pocket with moist earth before returning to the house and motioning to an agitated parent.

'Upstairs,' he ordered.

But Mr Straddlegrass needed a lot of persuasion before he

202

could be prevailed upon to mount the stairs and, even then, Reginald had to all but pull him up the last few steps. The Slippity-Slop had not found the bannisters to its liking and was now tackling the right-hand wall. It sucked, crunched, slipped and slopped; it consumed wallpaper and plaster at an alarming rate, then made a loud coughing sound when inadvertently swallowing a lump of loose brick.

'Not right food,' Reginald explained to a trembling Mr Straddlegrass. 'Get indigestion.'

He took a handful of soil from his pocket, spread it out on that part of the bannister rail that was still intact, then stood back to await developments. The Slippity-Slop stopped munching, turned its head, and stared at this offering with unblinking eyes. Presently the long neck came down, a black tongue flicked out and the soil disappeared, together with a thin sliver of wood. The monster then gave vent to a high-pitched cry before sniffing the bannisters with keen expectancy. Reginald addressed his bulging-eyed father.

'Earth natural food. Must spread some on stairs all the way to hall.'

'Must we?' Mr Straddlegrass whispered. 'Suppose it tries to eat us?'

'Wants to eat dirt. Sort of big worm.'

And without wasting any more words, Reginald ran down the stairs and out into the garden, where he grabbed a spade and began to dig a really first-class hole in the middle of the cabbage-patch. It says much for Mr Straddlegrass's state of mind that he did not so much as flinch when fat cabbages were tossed to one side, while his son piled up earth with professional skill, going deeper and deeper, until only his head was above ground. Then he climbed up on to the path and began to fill his mother's washing basket with damp soil.

'I don't mind giving you a hand,' Mr Straddlegrass volunteered. 'So long as I don't have to go more than halfway up the stairs.'

In fact, neither had to ascend more than six steps, for the

moment the Slippity-Slop detected a whiff of its natural food, it came slithering down the stairs, smashing bannisters and tearing up the carpet in the process. Of course, Mr Straddlegrass took to his heels, and Reginald had to drag the basket down into the hall, jerking it back whenever the monster tried to bury its head in the soil, while trying to ignore his mother's voice which kept demanding to know what was going on.

Eventually he reached the garden, pulled the basket over the back doorstep, down the path, and finally to his recently dug hole. He straightened up and pointed to the deep cavity.

'Food,' he said.

The Slippity-Slop advanced very slowly, as though not believing that such a splendid supply of natural nourishment actually existed. It sniffed at a few cabbages, sucked up a few parsnips, sampled some of the earth, then looked down into the hole.

Reginald watched this large, fearsome creature and, for the first time, wondered how the egg-shaped object had come to be buried in their garden. Or had it been planted? Was the Slippity-Slop a cross between a plant and animal; the result of some strange experiment performed in a bygone age? Perhaps there had been others which had died or been destroyed, and the last egg – seed – had been buried under a stone, as though the unknown scientist was unable to completely destroy his own work, but could not again face a fully grown monster.

One thing was certain – the Slippity-Slop fully approved of large holes. The soup-plate-shaped head sucked up the loose soil which lay at the bottom, then wriggled into some more and more – all the while going deeper and deeper, until the long neck was completely hidden. Then the round body slid over the edged and sank down into the agitated earth, disappearing from view. Finally there was only the very tip of the tail, waving away like a small worm that had come up to sample the evening air.

Suddenly the entire hole trembled as though disturbed by a minor earthquake; the sides fell in, and a shuddering crack went streaking across the garden. The Slippity-Slop was burrowing a passage to places unknown. Reginald took a deep breath. 'Now I'll fill in rest of hole.'

Which was the first time he had ever volunteered to do anything like that.

I am certain the Slippity-Slop is still alive and slithering. Also, for all I know, it has laid eggs – or shed seeds – and there may well be hundreds of these ugly creatures wriggling around under your feet. So, take my advice – never dig a hole unless it is absolutely necessary. Should you uncover a stone slab with an inscription engraved on it, shovel the earth back in again as quickly as you can.

And finally – if an egg-shaped object with roots should turn up, don't put it in the loft. Wrap it up in brown paper and post it to someone you don't like. Or send it to the Natural History Museum. It might look well in the prehistoric-monster section.

High World

HIGH WORLD WAS NOT a large palace as palaces went, but what it lacked in size it made up for in reputation.

It was very badly haunted, if I may be permitted the expression. My Great Aunt Elizabeth said it was very badly haunted, and she would have known, as she had long developed the habit of talking to spooks and swore on the family Bible they answered back.

Perhaps I'd better explain the situation. My Great Uncle Edward had been a Major General in the Indian Army. He retired at the age of sixty-six and was rewarded by a grateful country with a Grace and Favour apartment in High World Palace. Retirement did not suit him, for six months later his personal standard was flying at half-mast and Sir Edward Sinclair was dead. Lady Sinclair seemed unmoved by her husband's removal, and there is no reason to suppose he had joined the ghostly number. From my point of view that was not surprising.

You see, I did not believe in ghosts. Even after a six month stay (sick leave) I had no reason to believe such as a ghostly finger was waved in my direction. Then it happened. A pillow was snatched from under my head.

I was a mere fifteen years old and could take most unusual events in my stride, but . . .

I switched the bedside lamp on and had what might be called a good look around. The pillow lay on the bedside rug. In place of the mobile pillow, my head rested on a bolster.

I leaned over the rug and retrieved the pillow. I replaced it under my head. I turned the light out. Five minutes later I was wide awake. The pillow was back on the bedside rug! Clearly the time had come for me to express fear, closely followed by terror. My first bellow had my great aunt erupting into the room.

'Mobile pillow?' she enquired.

I nodded. Speech would follow, I was certain.

In fact I was soon explaining the entire business to my mother. Speech had been mine for the last five minutes. My great aunt explained the how and whyfor.

'Like all very old places, High World has retained the personality vestige of certain people who lived and died here in the past – sometimes the very distant past.'

'Why do they pull my pillow away?' I asked.

'We can only assume that one or more persons wish to attract attention.'

'Why?'

Great Aunt Elizabeth displayed signs of being mentally floored. 'Why would you wish to attract attention? So they could talk to you.'

The situation was becoming more complicated, and my mother did not make it any better. 'There are certain things that we do not discuss. We just pray for them to go away.'

'Why?'

'Because it is not good for us to know.'

'Why. . . ?'

'Strange things that happen in the night are God's business.'

The Almighty seemed to have strange occupations. One would have thought running the universe left little time for pillow-pulling. But it was not for me to question His intentions, so I started back to bed, but not before I looked inquiringly at Great Aunt Elizabeth.

'Sleep without a pillow, just for one night. Just until he gets used to you,' she said.

'Who. . . ?'

'Lord George Banfield. One time the king's bed fellow. Not a happy occupation as the king's leg was a bit strong. Ulcer, you understand.'

'Why. . .?'

'Go to sleep and don't worry if Banfield tries to grab the bolster. Rumour has it that someone tried to smother him with it.'

I went for a long moon-lit walk and wished I didn't have to go back to the palace. Pillow tugging has that effect on one. But there is more to come: the spinning wheel behind the panelling.

The sound became most pronounced just before you reached the bathroom. A deep humming sound. I don't know if a spinning wheel is supposed to make that sound, but this one did. Neither was I at all certain if a ghost wheel could make a sound.

But there was one point that gave me comfort: so far I had not seen a ghost of any kind. A snatched pillow; a humming wheel. So what! I went back to bed and slept the sleep of the brave.

After breakfast I sought out Great Aunt Elizabeth. She was playing one-man chess. That is to say she had the board and white pieces on her side of the table – there wasn't anything at all on the other. She gave me a brave smile, or perhaps bright is the better word. Her praise was beyond my merit.

'My brave, handsome nephew. Not like those cowardly old women. Be a good boy and make up the fire.'

I smirked, walked to the ornate fireplace and placed two large logs on the fire. Then I looked into the mirror to see if I had a smudge on my face.

I did have a smudge on my face. And so had the other fellow. I had seen him often: his picture was hanging by the bathroom door. Lord George Banfield. One-time bedfellow to the King.

You know something? I didn't stop running until I reached the front gate. Funny thing was that I only saw Lord George in the mirror. I never saw him anywhere else.

I pray God I never will.

Homemade Monster

Rodney was lost.

That should not be possible in twentieth-century England, where there are signposts standing at every crossroads, but Rodney managed to do it. He had been cycling through a network of country lanes and the signposts had not been helpful. They had said CATCHEM WALLOP 1 MILE and UNDER BASHEM 1½ MILES, and when he reached these places they proved to be sleepy little villages surrounded by open fields. He could of course have asked someone the way to Benfield, which was his destination, but he was rather shy and found it difficult to approach strangers. So he cycled on, hoping that he would sooner or later reach a main road, and now darkness was falling and it was beginning to rain.

Then his rear tyre made a loud popping sound, which was followed by a prolonged sigh, and the cycle began to wobble across the lane. Rodney dismounted and pushed the machine up a steep incline, wishing he had spent his holiday with his family at Bognor Regis.

The rain simply teemed down, and in no time at all he was drenched. Then there was a vivid flash of lightning and a really ear-splitting clap of thunder, and Rodney, although he tried to be brave, was very frightened indeed. He knew he must not take shelter under a tree, because his father had often said that trees attract lightning, and it was hardly the time to find out if this information was true or not.

He crested the hill, wheeled his bicycle around a sharp bend – and saw the house. It was a very large house, standing well back from the road, and surrounded by an unkempt lawn. No curtains veiled the windows, in fact some were boarded up, and it was reasonable to suppose the place was deserted. So Rodney pushed the rusty iron gate open, parked his machine in the large, crumbling porch, then looked for a way to enter the house.

The front door was locked, but when he made his way round to the back, he found a small window half open. It only took a few seconds for him to clamber over the sill and take refuge in the room beyond.

Dust covered the floors, damp had loosened the wallpaper and formed brown stains on the ceiling. The place was cold and, as the window refused to close, Rodney decided to venture further into the house, hoping that he would find a room with a fireplace so that he could light a fire and dry his clothes.

The door reluctantly, and with many creaking groans, slid open to reveal a gloomy passage. This ended at a large hall where a splendid staircase rose up in a graceful curve to a long gallery. A number of closed doors led away from the hall, and Rodney chose the nearest one, pushed it open and entered the room beyond. He found himself in what once must have been a luxurious drawing-room. The upholstery on the chairs and sofa had rotted, the carpet was hidden under a thick layer of dust, and festoons of cobwebs swayed gently from the high ceiling. But there was a fireplace.

Rodney was wondering what he could use for fuel, when he heard a sudden noise. It was the tramp of heavy feet. A slow, thudding tread that suggested a very large person, who did not believe in hurrying, but moved forward with the ponderous approach of a tank.

The footsteps crossed the hall – then stopped, and Rodney realised that his footprints must be clearly imprinted in the dust, leaving a trail to the door of this very room. The footsteps began again and grew louder as they came nearer, then the door trembled, before it flew back and crashed against the wall.

212

A giant stood in the doorway; a massive figure with a completely bald head and an immense barrel of a chest that was barely covered by a worn leather jerkin. A rumbling sound started way down in the stomach, then rose up and emerged from the creature's throat as booming words.

'What you doing here?'

Rodney gulped and tried to speak without stammering.

'I thought the house was empty. It's raining . . .'

At that moment there was a terrific clap of thunder and the giant waited until it had died away before he spoke again.

'I take you to doctor. Come.'

'But I only . . .'

His arm was seized by a gigantic hand and he was pulled towards the door, while his loudly proclaimed objections were completely ignored. They went back across the hall, along another long passage, down a flight of steps and finally entered a small basement room that appeared to be situated at the back of the house. It was furnished with two armchairs, a long bench under the window and a battered desk. Behind the desk sat a little white-haired man, whose small blue eyes were magnified by a large pair of spectacles. He looked up as Rodney was pulled into the room and expressed his astonishment by removing his spectacles, wiping them carefully with a yellow duster, then putting them on again. He spoke in a rather squeaky voice.

'What's the meaning of this, Daniel? Who is this boy?'

Clearly Daniel did not believe in wasting words.

'Found him upstairs.'

The little man raised his eyebrows.

'Found him upstairs! 'Pon my soul! This won't do at all. You know very well, Daniel, my work is reaching a crucial stage and I mustn't be disturbed.'

'Been walking about,' Daniel stated. 'Footsteps in dust.'

Rodney thought it was about time that he again explained the situation. 'I thought the house was empty, sir, and as I am wet through . . .'

'Good heavens, so he is!' the little man interrupted. 'He's dripping water all over the carpet and must be well on the way to catching cold. Can't have that. The germs might get round and fasten their teeth on Henry.'

Daniel shook his head violently. 'Doctor Frankwell – boy has ears.'

Doctor Frankwell adjusted his spectacles. 'So he has. So what? He'd look very funny without them.'

'Hear too much,' Daniel insisted. 'Got mouth. Talk.'

Doctor Frankwell sighed deeply. 'Oh, dear! I keep forgetting not to mention Henry. Now look here, boy, you will forget that I ever did. There's no such person. You will dismiss the name of Henry completely from your mind. Is that clear?'

Rodney, who was really very wet and extremely cold into the bargain, and would have been quite willing to forget his own name for some dry clothes, said: 'Yes, sir. Now, can you please . . .'

The doctor waved his hand impatiently. 'Yes . . . yes. Take him away, Daniel, and dry him out. Better give him something to eat afterwards, but don't let him near Hen . . . I mean near anyone.'

Daniel did not bother to use any more words, he just pulled Rodney out of the room, pushed him along the passage and deposited him in a bedroom. He opened a chest of drawers and took out a pair of trousers and a thick woollen pullover. 'Put on,' he instructed. 'Bring wet clothes to kitchen. First door on right.' Then he went out and Rodney heard his heavy footsteps recede down the passage.

The trousers and pullover must have been the property of Doctor Frankwell, because they were a very tight fit, but they were at least warm and dry, so it was with a lighter heart – and a fully aroused curiosity – that Rodney emerged from the bedroom and made his way towards the first door on the right.

The kitchen was in a mess. Unwashed plates and saucepans were piled on the wooden draining board, the sink was full of cold, greasy water, and the floor was simply littered with turnip tops, potato peelings and screwed-up paper bags. When Rodney entered, Daniel was examining a half-cooked leg of lamb which he had just removed from the old-fashioned iron range. He pointed to a large wooden chair.

'Hang clothes on back. Put in front of fire. No food yet. Not cooked.'

Rodney draped his trousers over the chair back, and laid his shirt, underpants and socks across the seat. Then he watched Daniel's culinary activities.

The huge man was cutting off the red, juicy parts of the joint, but the deeper he cut, the more it became obvious that the meat was under-cooked.

'Excuse me . . .' Rodney, who had taken a cookery course in the Scouts, had to speak up. 'I think you have taken it out of the oven too soon.'

Daniel said: 'Ugh' – or a sound to that effect – and stared at the leg of lamb with an air of complete helplessness.

'May I help you?'

Daniel started as though he had been stung by a wasp.

'Help?'

'Yes, I can cook. And, since you and the doctor have been so kind – I'll be pleased to – well – clear up for you.' Daniel looked slowly round the kitchen. 'Clear up? Nothing want clearing up.'

'Nonsense!' Rodney could not restrain his indignation. 'This place is in an awful mess. Where is the broom?'

'Broom?'

Eventually Rodney found some cleaning materials in a narrow cupboard and set to work while Daniel watched him with growing approval. Presently the leg of lamb, surrounded by a circle of potatoes, still attired in their brown jackets, was back in the oven, a saucepan of brussels sprouts was simmering on the hotplate and the kitchen floor had been cleared of all refuse.

'Perhaps,' Rodney suggested, 'you will give me a hand with the washing up.'

'Washing up?'

'Yes. All these dirty plates and things. They need washing.

'Only get dirty again.'

Daniel was finally prevailed upon to dry up, but he wasn't very

215

good at it, because at least three plates crashed to the floor and one cup lost its handle.

'What does the doctor do?' Rodney asked, assuming an air of casualness.

'He – make things.'

'Oh, really? I thought doctors treated sick people and wrote out prescriptions.'

This was a bit too much for Daniel and he frowned as though his slow-working brain was struggling with a very complicated problem. At last he spoke.

'Must not talk about what doctor do. It's se-se—'

'Secret?' Rodney suggested. 'I say, is he working for the government?'

Daniel frowned again. 'No gov-er-ment. No talk. Se-cret.'

But Rodney did not give up so easily. 'I expect you are a great help. The doctor is very lucky to have such an intelligent person to rely on.'

Daniel thought about this for some time, then his lips parted to reveal large, fearsome-looking teeth.

'I am big help. The doctor let me shift big pieces on to table and once . . . You not tell him I tell you this?'

'Oh, no.'

'Well,' and an expression of almost childish pride transformed Daniel's face, 'once I pulled big switch and made all the lights jump along wires.'

'Gosh!' Rodney displayed all the signs of suitable admiration. 'You *are* clever. What happened?'

Daniel sighed very deeply. 'No good. All the pieces flew apart. Doctor start again. But this time . . .'

He stopped, looked suspiciously at Rodney, then shook his head. 'I not talk any more. Nobody must know. You help get dinner ready.'

Dinner was served in a small dining-room that was situated on the opposite side of the passage to the kitchen. Rodney laid the table and Daniel brought in the, by now succulent joint, then went to fetch the doctor. The little man came bustling in and positively beamed when he saw the sizzling lamb, the crisp potatoes and the steaming Brussels sprouts.

' 'Pon my soul! Daniel, you have excelled yourself. Absolutely excelled yourself.'

Daniel tried to assume a modest expression, but was quite unable to suppress a self-satisfied grin.

'Boy helped,' he admitted with some reluctance.

'Did he now?' Doctor Frankwell seated himself at the head of the table and began to carve the lamb as though he were performing some intricate operation. 'What a bright lad he is, to be sure. Daniel, after dinner I will require your help. Henry has been lapping up the electricity all day . . .'

Daniel made a sound that was half way between a cough and a growl and jerked his head in the direction of Rodney. The doctor gasped.

'Oh dear, I've done it again. Lad, do you realise there is no such person as Henry? As for lapping up electricity – he never did. Never. I mean to say – he couldn't – could he?'

'No, sir,' Rodney agreed.

'That's all right then. I can't imagine what came over me, talking such rubbish. Nevertheless, Daniel, I think it would be safe to say, tonight you will be able to pull the big switch.'

For a moment it seemed as if Daniel would get up and do a little dance. But he contented himself with banging a spoon on the table instead.

'Pu-ll the big switch! And all the lights will jump along wires?'

Doctor Frankwell nodded violently. 'No doubt of it. Henry will be up and about . . . Boy, you must have some more brussels sprouts. Very good for you . . .'

A dramatic interruption cut short his words. From somewhere a little way off came the sound of a loud thud, followed by the tinkle of broken glass. The doctor jumped to his feet.

'Goodness gracious. Daniel – quickly, man, he's fallen off the table.'

He rushed from the room, closely followed by Daniel, turned left and went running down the passage. At first Rodney decided

217

that whatever was taking place was no business of his, but he was soon creeping down the passage, making his way towards an open door at the far end.

He entered a large room that had probably been a larder at one time, for there were long slate shelves lining the walls and a massive table running down the centre. Rodney noted the electrical equipment that stood on shelves, was screwed into the ceiling and sent coils of copper wire to the table. But his full attention was drawn towards Doctor Frankwell – and the *thing* which lay on the floor. It was approximately seven feet long; a grotesque human shape, swathed in a green plastic sheet, and it had various coloured sockets jutting out from the head, chest and ribs. The doctor was fussing about like an old hen whose chick had gone astray.

'Careful, Daniel. He may have loosened something. Gently, man.'

Daniel lifted the huge figure and laid it reverently on the table, then stood to one side as Doctor Frankwell fitted wires to the sockets and made adjustments to a dial that was strapped across the stomach.

'No damage done, Daniel. We did our work well. He's fully charged, and when you pull the big switch he'll be up and about.'

'Boy here,' Daniel pointed out. 'He see all.'

The doctor spun round and there was a most pathetic expression on his face. 'Oh, dear! Now the same thing will happen to me, that ruined the work of my great-great-grandfather – the famous Baron Frankenstein. He left the door of his laboratory open and a little girl called Mary Wollstonecraft Godwin got in and later wrote a full account of what she saw – the little beast – that was read by the entire world. I hope you are not addicted to pen and paper, young fellow.'

'Oh no,' Rodney hastened to reassure the little man. 'I hate writing. But have you really created a monster?'

'Most certainly not.' Doctor Frankwell looked as indignant as his mild features would allow. 'I have designed, manufactured and will shortly activate a Humanoid-Electronic-Non-lethal-Rapid-developer-Youngster. Henry for short.'

'Good heavens!' Rodney could not tear his fascinated gaze away from the shape on the table. 'Did you make it out of – dead bodies?'

The doctor laughed gently. 'Times have changed and we have progressed since the days of my late lamented great-great-grand-father. I have used a special self-adhesive plastic, some blood substitute fluid that I have called GFI and an awful lot of electricity.'

'Now boy know everything,' Daniel pointed out.

'Yes, but what does it matter?' The doctor took his spectacles off, wiped them on a corner of Henry's sheet, then replaced them. 'As soon as Henry is up and about, the entire world will know. Can't you see the headlines? "*Doctor Frankwell Creates a Man*". I expect I'll be invited to appear on television.'

'Shall I pull big switch now?' Daniel asked.

'Well . . .' the doctor looked undecided until Rodney reminded him of a very important fact.

'We haven't finished our dinner yet.'

The doctor's spectacles slipped down his nose and his eyes widened with shocked horror. 'Great Scott, you're right! And the roast lamb will be getting cold.'

They all but ran back to the dining-room and continued their interrupted meal, although the doctor kept jumping up and trotting to his laboratory to make sure that Henry had not fallen off the table again. At length, knives and forks were laid aside, plates were stacked and carried into the kitchen, and Doctor Frankwell beamed at his assistant.

'Daniel – I can think of no reason for further delay. Henry is fully charged, his working parts are in excellent condition – the great moment has arrived.'

Henry certainly appeared to be very lively, if the strange twitching movement that was taking place in every part of the shrouded figure was any criterion. Doctor Frankwell first of all made sure that all the wires were fully connected to the sockets, then turned his head and nodded to Daniel, who was standing by a very large wall switch.

219

'Now,' he said.

Daniel pulled the lever. Instantly, pulsating streamers of coloured light ran along the wires; electric bulbs lit up and flashed on and off like neon signs, and from the far corner of the room a large metal box began to make a loud buzzing sound.

Henry displayed every sign of being well and truly activated. The huge shape was writhing like a cut worm; the sheet-covered head rolled from side to side and there seemed a distinct possibility that the entire bundle would roll down on to the floor again.

'Daniel!' Doctor Frankwell shouted, his voice shrill with excitement. 'Watch him. I am going to increase the current. It's do or burst!'

Rodney sincerely hoped Henry would not burst. On the other hand, he was not at all sure that he wanted to see a homemade monster walk, either. He seemed to remember that the one created by Baron Frankenstein had not behaved in a civilised manner. He watched the doctor turning knobs, pressing different coloured buttons, all of which resulted in the wires becoming brighter, the bulbs flashing more quickly and the buzzing sound rising to an earsplitting shriek.

Suddenly there was a loud bang and all the lights went out. The wires became dull black, the electric bulbs went pop-pop, one after the other, and the metal box which had been making the awful noise became as silent as a Quaker's meeting. And Henry? After the doctor had lit three candles, it was easy to see there was no sign of life.

'All the wires are burnt out,' the little doctor sighed deeply. 'Three years' work gone up in puffs of smoke.'

'Perhaps the fuses want mending,' Rodney suggested, surprised to realise that he was disappointed that Henry was not going to walk. But Doctor Frankwell shook his head.

'No, all my equipment is ruined. I overloaded it, you see.'

'I put kettle on,' Daniel stated. 'Make tea.'

The doctor smiled bravely. 'Well, I suppose we might feel better after a cup of tea. There's not much we can do here.'

They adjourned to the kitchen where Daniel placed a large

iron kettle on the hotplate, then brewed some really excellent tea in a brown pot. There was no doubt that the doctor enjoyed his cup, for he sipped it with every sign of appreciation and had quite recovered from his disappointment after a second one.

'It's back to the drawing board, Daniel. We must use stouter wiring, double the feed-backs and install an even bigger switch.'

Daniel said: 'Ugh,' but did not seem all that keen.

'In the meanwhile,' the doctor went on, 'we might as well get some rest. I dare say we can find our young friend a bed?'

Daniel nodded and poured some of his tea into a saucer.

Rodney was about to express his gratitude when his ears detected a slight sound. A very slow slithering, followed by the creak of protesting floorboards. Daniel also heard it, for his head came up, then turned in the direction of the open doorway.

No one spoke. They just sat, waiting for the impossible to put in an appearance. Now the slithering was alternating with loud thuds. Slither-thud-slither-thud, and the suspense was so intense that Rodney dropped his cup. Then something very large filled the doorway. Still swathed in a plastic sheet, with bits of wire, dangling from the coloured sockets, with the dial still strapped to its stomach, the Humanoid-Electronic-Non-lethal-Rapid-developer-Youngster lurched into the room and stood swaying like a tall tree in a hundred-mile-per-hour gale. Doctor Frankwell was the first to speak.

'It *did* work, Daniel! We gave up too soon. Henry is up and about.'

The plastic sheet bulged as two great hands came out and pushed against the confining material. Rodney heard a tearing sound as a long, ragged hole appeared, and one immense and one smaller fist sprang into view and began to punch the air in a most aggressive fashion.

'I don't think he likes us very much,' he gasped.

'Nonsense.' Doctor. Frankwell adjusted his spectacles. 'He's just pleased to be alive. Daniel, get him unwrapped. Be careful you don't hurt him.'

Daniel displayed praiseworthy caution. He approached the

monster from the rear and unzipped a long fastener that ran from the top of the swaying head down to the gigantic feet. The sheet fell away and it took all of Rodney's self-control not to turn tail and race from the room.

Henry was not at all pretty. A head which resembled a mis-shapen turnip was surmounted by a mop of red hair. One eye was blue and round, the other brown and slanted. The mouth was extremely wide and filled with large, yellow teeth. The nose could have been mistaken for a parrot's beak, the ears for the wings of an ancient bat. A mighty chest was flanked by arms of unequal length. Rodney could not see the legs, for the creature was dressed in a long, flannel nightgown, but the feet had much in common with two overturned vegetable dishes.

Doctor Frankwell beamed his delight and was clearly waiting for everyone's unstinted admiration. 'Well – what do you think of him?'

It took a few seconds for Rodney to regain his power of speech.

'He's – he's not very handsome – is he?'

'Not handsome!' The doctor frowned, then examined his creation with some anxiety. 'How can you say that? Why – he's positively beautiful. Possibly I could have taken a little more care in the matter of his arms and eyes, but I think that a little irregularity of features can be quite attractive. Daniel, let's get him into a chair and invite him to take some nourishment.'

Getting Henry to sit down was not all that easy. He took a wide swing at Daniel, then resisted most forcibly when that person exerted all his strength and pushed him into the doctor's chair. The little man looked at the remains of the leg of lamb and cold baked potatoes.

'Do you think we should cook him something special, Daniel? Perhaps we could tempt him with a nice steak and kidney pie.'

Henry literally took matters into his own hands. The round eye stared at the cold lamb, the slanted one examined the potatoes. Apparently the round eye won the decision. The larger fist grabbed, the smaller one tore and the great teeth began to munch. Perhaps crunch would be a better word, because Henry was not a dainty eater. Meat, bones – all went into the gaping mouth, were crushed and swallowed in a little under five seconds. The doctor was delighted by this display of rapid consumption.

'He's got a healthy appetite. Gracious, Daniel, if this keeps up he'll eat *us*.'

Rodney thought this more than likely and decided he would not like to be around when the supply of roast lamb ran out. Having eaten, Henry slept. First the slanted eye closed, then the round one – having swivelled in its socket as though to make sure all was well – also lowered its lid and for a while there was peace. Then the wide mouth opened and a sound that was rather like a saw being driven through a hard piece of wood filled the kitchen. Henry not only slept – he snored.

The doctor yawned and Daniel rubbed his eyes.

'Well, Henry has set us a good example. Time we were all in bed. Daniel, do you suppose he will be comfortable there?'

'Not like to wake up,' replied Daniel, with obvious deep sincerity. 'If he not comfortable, can go back to lab-ora-tory.'

The doctor rose. 'Yes, you are right. Leave the door open for him.'

As Rodney was taken upstairs and installed in a little dust-haunted room on the ground floor, he could not help wondering if it was wise to leave Henry all by himself. After some reflection he barricaded his door by wedging a chairback under the handle, then lay down on top of the bed fully clothed.

The old house was very quiet. The storm had long ago exhausted its rage and gone to sleep in the western sky. A full moon peered in through the undraped window and tinted the old furniture with silver light, forcing black slabs of shadow to lurk in corners and take on weird shapes. Rodney tried to keep awake, but what with one thing and another (he had had a tiring day) and unconsciousness crept up on him like a soft-footed burglar.

He was awakened by a crash. He lay perfectly still for some time, his heart thudding wildly, trying to dismiss the chilling thought that Henry was up and around. After a few minutes he heard the sound of disturbed broken glass, followed by a low wail that could have been made by an abandoned dog – or by a home-made monster that is not exactly dancing for joy.

Curiosity and fear fought a hard battle. Curiosity – after much serious thought – won. Rodney crept to the door, removed the chair, then went out into the passage. The clatter of broken glass drew him towards a room that was situated a few yards away. Rodney saw the by now familiar neglect, the dust – and the smashed mirror which was scattered over the floor, each separate particle reflecting the bright moonlight, making them gleam like fallen stars. Henry was slumped against the wall, his grotesque face masked by shadow, his ridiculous hands held out as though in supplication. Rodney felt his fear ebb away as he advanced into the room, dimly realising that Henry might be a monster, some-thing designed and manufactured by Doctor Frankwell, but apparently he had emotions. Was unhappy.

'What's the matter?' he asked, not that there was much hope that Henry would understand him, although the R in his name did stand for Rapid-developer.

The ungainly figure came out into the moonlight, the right hand pointing to the broken shards of mirror-glass, and a stran-gled sound escaped from the wide mouth. Rodney picked up the largest piece of glass and stared at it thoughtfully. He held it out and Henry shrank back with a muted cry.

'It won't hurt you. It was only an old mirror and I don't suppose the doctor will be angry that you broke it. He doesn't appear to use this part of the house.'

Henry's large hand came out, pointed to the piece of mirror, then turned and indicated his own face. Understanding flooded Rodney's mind with an all-revealing light.

'You saw a reflection! It frightened you! Gosh, I expect it would. Look – that was you. See?'

He held the piece of mirror above his head and tilted it until his own young face was reflected in the gleaming surface; then turned until it could be seen by the monster. Henry snatched the fragment of glass from him and stared at it intently. Suddenly he pointed to himself and made a growling sound.

Rodney nodded violently. 'You. It's you – nothing to be frightened of.'

Henry did not appear to be comforted by this information. He flung the piece of glass across the room and Rodney was surprised to see a solitary tear trickle down from the large eye, while a little moaning cry seeped out from between the sagging lips. He crashed both hands together and uttered his first word.

'Ye-e-w . . .'

Rodney nodded again. 'It should be me, but you seem to have got the point. I say, you are bright.'

Henry lurched forward. Taking long floorshaking steps, he crossed the room and moved slowly into the passage, with Rodney following a few yards behind. Boy and monster descended the stairs to the basement, and here Henry continued to advance until he reached the laboratory door. A single push from his right fist sent it hurtling back and a terrible suspicion flared up in Rodney's brain.

He called out: 'Doctor . . . Daniel . . . come quickly!'

The doctor emerged from a room on the left, dressed in a long white nightgown and wearing a tassled nightcap. He hurriedly put on his spectacles and peered at Rodney with some irritation.

'Gracious me, what is all this noise about? I must have my eight hours sleep. Absolutely essential.'

'It's Henry.' Rodney explained. 'He saw his own reflection, and now I think he's going to do something awful.'

As though to confirm his words, there came from the laboratory a mighty crashing and thumping; a splintering of wood, a shattering of glass, all intermingled with loud roars of insensate rage.

'What on earth has come over him?' the doctor asked, by now looking extremely agitated. 'Heavens above, he's ruining all my equipment. I will never be able to replace it. Daniel!'

Daniel appeared from another room, looking rather ridiculous in a woollen vest and a long pair of underpants. He ruffled his hair, rubbed his eyes, then asked:

'What's wrong? Somebody making noise.'

The doctor waved his hands frantically in the direction of the laboratory. 'Henry's gone berserk. Get in there and restrain him.'

Daniel did not seem all that keen to obey this last instruction, but he dutifully went towards the laboratory, with the doctor and Rodney walking cautiously in his footsteps. When he reached the doorway, he stopped and motioned his employer forward.

'All finished,' he said simply.

Rodney looked fearfully over Doctor Frankwell's shoulder and came to an immediate decision that Henry had done a thorough job. All the intricate equipment had been smashed, broken wires hung like dead snakes from walls and ceiling, and even the table had been shattered into jagged fragments. Only one item still remained intact, and that was the large metal box that had formerly given out a loud. buzzing noise. Henry was working on that now. He had it raised high above his head and was about to crash it down on to the floor.

'Stop him.' the doctor shouted. 'That is my charger. Thousands of volts of electricity are stored in there. The slightest jar and Henry will be blown to smithereens.'

Everyone began shouting at once, trying to explain to Henry his predicament. He stood perfectly still, the charger clutched in his ill-assorted hands, and it seemed to Rodney that a light of dawning understanding gleamed in the round, large eye.

'That,' the doctor said, pointing to the box, 'bang when you drop. You—' He spread wide his hands. '—Finished. Over. Dead. No more.'

Seconds passed, then Henry's mouth opened and he uttered two more words.

'Ye-e-w fin-ish-ed?'

The doctor nodded. Daniel nodded. Rodney closed his eyes and dramatically pretended he was about to fall down. Henry seemed to get the message, for he nodded, too. When Daniel made a slight movement forward, though, he growled warningly. The doctor sighed.

'Perhaps we had better leave him alone. Come to think of it, we would be in great danger should he drop that charger.'

Rodney felt very sad as they trailed back along the passage, then took refuge on the stairs and waited for what they all knew must happen. The explosion was not very loud, just a muted booming noise, followed by a flash of bright light. The doctor and Daniel went back into the devastated laboratory, but Rodney remained on the stairs. Presently the two men came back. The doctor was dabbing at his eyes with a large pocket handkerchief.

'Nothing left,' he said. 'All my work gone up in a flash. I will never have the heart to start again.'

'Make hair restorer,' Daniel suggested. 'Lots of. men bald. Me bald.'

Doctor Frankwell suddenly, looked much happier.

'I say, that's not a bad idea. Make some money, too. Then I'll be able to get this place done up. Thank you, Daniel.'

Daniel grinned delightedly and produced another gem of wisdom.

'Make hair – not men.'

Later, when Rodney was cycling down a country lane, far away from that house of dust-coated furniture, he felt glad that Henry was no more. After all, there are enough monsters in the world, without homemade ones.

The Great Indestructible

I PULLED THE IRON bell-handle and listened to the mournful clanging sound that took place somewhere deep down in the old house. I waited – not without considerable trepidation – and presently was rewarded by the slip-slop of approaching footsteps. The door groaned its doleful protest as it slid open, and the face of the count's butler peered round the edge. He bared teeth that were too long and sharp for my peace of mind and hissed,

'Y-iss-s?'

I produced my press card. 'Clutcher –*Ghoul Gazette*. I have an appointment with Count Dracula.'

He opened the door to its fullest extent, and I was able to see that his head was tilted over to one side and rested on his right shoulder. A large bump stood out like a monstrous carbuncle on the exposed side of his neck.

'Won't you en-ter, sir? His Excellency is ex-pecting you.'

I entered the hall and noted the picturesque cobwebs that dangled from the ceiling; the friendly rat that sniffed with optimistic expectancy at my ankles; and the bleached skeleton that did service as a hat-stand.

The butler began to pat my pockets and run his green-tinted hands down my person. 'If you would permit, sir. I must ass-ure that you have no cros-ses, sharp stakes or gar-lic. One cannot be too careful.'

Having made certain that I was completely devoid of lethal weapons, he led me towards a fungus-covered door, and after tapping on one spongy panel, turned a handle and announced in a loud voice,

'Mr Hans Clutcher, of *Ghoul Gazette*, your Excell-ency.'

I entered, and there behind a wormriddled desk stood the Great Indestructible. The Unquenchable Thirst. The Mighty Partaker. Tall, surprisingly thin, long, white face, red-flecked eyes, sleek black hair – he was all that I had expected, and more. He motioned me to an upturned coffin, then bared his fangs in an engaging smile.

'Please be seated, Mr Clutcher. Delighted you could come.'

I sat down and the count nodded to his butler.

'Thank you, that will be all, Carlos, unless . . .' He looked at me with meaningful intent. 'Unless you would care for some light refreshment.'

I hastened to decline this kindly offer. The count seated himself, and when the door was closed, said, 'I would be lost without Carlos. Excellent provider.'

'Where did you find him?' I asked.

'On the gibbet. I expect you have noticed he has a broken neck. Fortunately I was able to get a nip-on-time.'

A short silence followed while I digested this piece of information, then I remembered my mission and produced my notepad.

'Count Dracula, you have been called the Great Indestructible. Would you care to comment?'

He shrugged and tore his fascinated gaze away from a small razor nick on my chin. 'Everyone's had a go – haven't they? I've had a stake through my heart six times. Been left out in the sunlight twice. Been decapitated, smothered in garlic, burnt to a cinder, plunged into running water, and disintegrated by innumerable chanted incantations. But I always come bouncing back.'

I said 'Good Heavens!' and instantly apologised for my lack of tact. 'How do you account for this . . . this continuous resurrection?'

'Fortunately, the world is full of long-nosed idiots who can't mind their own business. There's always someone who will pull a stake out of a grinning skeleton; pour virgin blood over my ashes;

hold midnight orgies and gabble unpronounceable words, then scream their fool heads off when I put in an appearance. On one occasion I was revived by a priest's blood. Can you beat that?'

I started to say 'Good G. . . !' but managed to change it to 'Bloody hell!' just in time.

'Yes,' the count put his feet up on the desk and I was able to observe a small hole in the right shoe. 'I was encased in ice at the time. You know, the usual thing – some rotten swine had lured me over a frozen river – thin ice – running water beneath – in I go – become as stiff as a fish finger – and that was that. Then along comes this knee-basher waving a wooden unmentionable – slips on the ice – cuts his text-croaking throat – and I get a mouthful of the red stuff. I was up and about in no time at all.'

It was then that we were interrupted by an ear-splitting scream which seemed to come from somewhere beneath our feet. The count nodded his approval.

'Ah, that must be Carlos drawing off my lunch. Keep a couple of virgins in the cellar, you know. Well, I can't get around so well as I used to. They aren't bad. AB group, 1954 vintage. I suppose you wouldn't care. . . ?'

I shook my head vigorously and the count smiled.

'I won't press you – at least, not yet awhile. Do you know what I've always wanted? The present which would make my eyeballs swivel in their sockets?'

My thoughts toyed with walnut coffins with gold fittings – a central-heated tomb – a new dinner jacket – the one he was wearing was frayed and turning green. Finally I shook my head.

'A magnum of O group,' he stated, while two little rivulets of moisture ran down his trembling chin. 'The last time I wetted my whistle with a drop of O group must have been 1863. Or was it 1849? Anyway, I remember the container was a baker's wife, and I was just getting stuck in when her husband turns up and starts waving two crossed loaves at me. Then the delivery boy shoved a dirty great poker through me gizzard, and the last thing I saw was that precious liquid making a mess of six French rolls and a tray of jam tarts.'

This painful memory seemed to cause him such distress, I could do no less than murmur 'What a bloody shame!'

The Great Indestructible sighed deeply. 'Yes, I've never been what you might call lucky. Scarcely am I up and around, than some interfering busybody has me nailed down again. It's very discouraging.'

I consulted my notes. 'You have had several journeys into the realms of matrimony, I believe?'

'You might call it an invasion. At one time I had three wives – all at once. Though we shared a common taste, we were not really compatible. Women are all right in the kitchen – if you get my meaning – but they're all take and no give.' He was lost in a maze of melancholy thoughts for some little while. Then he said softly, 'Greedy cows. There was that young solicitor – what was his name?'

'Jonathan Harker?' I suggested.

'You may well be right. I remember he had an unfortunate habit of writing long, detailed letters and keeping a diary. Anyway, I intended to put him on ice. A little something for a dry night – and I naturally assumed that he wouldn't be touched. Not a bit of it. I came home early – there they were – fangs dripping, bibs at the ready, squawking away like a flock of starved hens, fighting over a bowl of stewed giblets.' He chuckled. 'I did 'em dirt though. I drained him drier than last year's orange peel. Did they nag!'

This was an aspect of vampiral matrimonial conduct I had never considered. 'You mean to say your wives nagged you?'

'What! Did they nag!' He rolled his eyes until they resembled two milkyglass marbles. 'Evening, midnight and sunrise.' He raised his voice and began to imitate an indignant woman. ' "You never bring us anything *nice* home. Not like Baron Carver over the hill. He gives his wives a couple of fat bankers and a property speculator every Sunday. All you can do is lie-a-coffin all night and expect us to wait on you." He resumed his normal tone of voice. 'Enough to make you want to spit.'

I was about to ask him if he had any interesting hobbies, when he erupted again.

'Then there were the mother-in-laws. Great fat, billowing, parched-throat, bulging-eyed, flap-eared, grasping harridans. Huddled together like a herd of cows at milking time. "You can't get round us," they said. "No, but the exercise will do me good," I retorted.' He smiled complacently. 'I always had a pretty turn of wit.'

I frowned. 'Somehow, I can never think of lady vampires having mothers.'

He bared his fangs in a snarl. 'Did you suppose an owl dropped 'em under a tombstone? They had fathers too. Lazy old has-beens. "Now we've gained a son, we can all take things easy." Nine of 'em all told I had to cater for. You can't wonder the entire countryside was soon suffering from anaemia. That's why I emigrated.'

I closed my notepad, placed it carefully in my pocket, then stood up. 'Well, this has been most interesting. I am certain the readers of the *Ghoul Gazette* will be thrilled out of their skins.'

The count walked round the desk. I backed away a few paces and bumped into Carlos who had somehow entered the room without making a sound.

I think the attentive butler was brushing some mould from the seat of my trousers and possibly he was a little careless, for I felt a sharp pain on the back of my hand. When I looked round, Carlos was straightening up and doing a fair imitation of an excited wine-taster.

An expression of unholy joy transformed his face into a grimacing mask and he had difficulty in imparting the good news.

'Excell-ency, O-o-o-o . . .'

'Are you in pain, my good Carlos? the count enquired solicitously.

'No, Excell-ency. O . . . o . . . o group. A comp-lete body of O group.'

The Great Indestructible moved in with single-minded intent. I tried to appeal to his better nature.

'You wouldn't?'

His smile was gentle. 'I would. I will. My dear fellow, you can't expect me to pass up a chance of a hundred lifetimes.'

'It won't be good for you. Too rich – and diluted with whisky . . .'

He nipped my neck. A genteel little nip – a prelude to a good old-fashioned, get-stuck-in bite, but fortunately I had the presence of mind to thrust two crossed pens in his face. He looked rather hurt.

'That's a dirty trick' he said. 'I expected something better from a gentleman of the press.'

I backed away towards the door, then turned and ran across the hall. The friendly rat looked at me reproachfully.

I know I've been bitten by a vampire. So what? That's no reason for anyone to get worked up about it. As I sit typing this report, my editor is standing in the doorway. He says he's sharpening a pencil. Well – I've never seen a pencil that size before.

If I'm found skewered in the centre of some crossroads, with a sprig of garlic in my mouth, I want the world to know who is responsible . . .

The Werewolf

THE HOUSE WAS OLD and tucked away behind a curtain of trees; a lonely place that had been built by a man who loved solitude.

Mr Ferrier liked the company of his fellow beings as much as the next man, but he did not have much money, and The Hermitage – due, possibly, to its isolated position – had been very cheap. So he bought the property, moved in with his furniture and family and began to extol the virtues of a rustic life.

'Room to move around,' he informed a sceptical Mrs Ferrier. 'A chance to breathe air that isn't contaminated by petrol fumes.'

'But it's such a long way for Alan to go to school,' his wife protested. 'And the nearest shop is five miles away. I tried to warn you, but I might as well have saved my breath.'

'Ten minutes' car ride,' Mr Ferrier retorted impatiently. 'Besides, there's a travelling salesman who has everything you'll ever need in his van.'

'And what about social life?' Mrs Ferrier demanded. 'How will we get to know people, stuck in this out-of-the-way place?'

'Other people have cars, haven't they? At least give the place a chance. If at the end of three months we find the solitude a bit too much, well – I suppose I'll have to look for another house nearer town.'

Alan was more than content with his new home. After years spent in a large industrial town, he found the rolling moors had much to commend them. He also discovered ruined farmhouses with frameless windows and gaping roofs, the exposed inner walls still retaining patches of flower-patterned wallpaper; and he wondered how long ago the last family had moved away, leaving their home to fall into decay.

But one of these relics from a bygone age was not completely deserted. According to an old map which Alan borrowed from the public library, this particular ruin had been called High Burrow: a very suitable name, as the house stood on the summit of a fairly steep hill and commanded a splendid view of the surrounding countryside. Alan climbed the slope, clambered over a low wall, then walked across an expanse of weed-infested ground that had probably once been a front garden.

He mounted three crumbling steps and passed through an open doorway, then entered the narrow hall, where the stone floor was coated with dust, and a large rat jumped down from a window-ledge and went scurrying into a side room. The ceiling had either fallen down or been removed, and Alan could see the room above, which had an iron fireplace clinging precariously to one wall. Higher still were massive beams, each one festooned with writhing cobwebs; the naked bones of a dead house.

Alan was about to leave, for there was an indefinable, eerie atmosphere about the place, when he heard the sound of ascending footsteps, which seemed to come from beyond a gaping doorway situated to the left of a dismantled staircase. The footsteps became louder and were intermingled at irregular intervals by an exceedingly unpleasant barking cough.

Presently a figure emerged from the doorway and walked slowly into the hall. Alan saw a tall young man with a heavily bearded face and long matted hair that hung down to his slightly bowed shoulders, deep sunken eyes that were indescribably sad and a set of perfect teeth which were revealed when he again coughed and gasped in a most alarming way.

Alan waited until the man had regained his breath, then said:

'I didn't realise there was anyone here. I was just exploring.'

The man wiped his brow on the sleeve of his ragged shirt, then spoke with a surprisingly cultivated voice. 'That's all right. But I heard you come in and wondered who it could be. Haven't had a visitor for years. This place is rather off the beaten track.'

'Do you live here?' Alan enquired.

The man jerked his head in the direction of the doorway.

'Yes, down there. The cellars are still intact, if rather damp.' He sighed deeply. 'There's no other place I can go.'

Alan thought there were many places he would rather live than in a damp cellar of a ruined house, particularly if he had such a bad cold. In fact, the man probably had bronchitis, or even pneumonia, for, despite the perspiration that poured down his face, he was shivering and could scarcely stand upright. Alan felt a twinge of pity for this strange, lonely person who appeared to have no one to look after him.

'Look, I know it's none of my business – but shouldn't you be in bed?'

The man nodded and leaned against the wall.

'Yes, I suppose I should. But my stores are running low and I must somehow get to the village before . . .'

Another fit of coughing interrupted his next words, and Alan made the only suggestion that was possible under the circumstances.

'Would you like me to do your shopping?'

The man groaned and shivered so violently that Alan became quite alarmed.

'It's a long way for you to go and come back,' said the man.

'I've nothing else to do,' the boy replied, although the prospect of tramping back across rugged moorland carrying a heavy shopping bag was not all that attractive.

'Well, if you're sure you don't mind. Come downstairs and I'll give you some money and some idea of what I require.'

Alan followed the tall figure through the doorway, down a winding flight of steps and finally into a large underground room, dimly lit by an ancient hurricane lamp. So far as he could see, this dismal place contained little more than an iron bedstead and a rickety chair.

'The nearest village is Manville,' the man said, pulling a tin box from under the bed. 'About five miles as the crow flies. Get some tinned stuff. Soups and stewed steak. I suppose you couldn't carry a gallon can of paraffin?'

'I could try,' Alan said ruefully, determined never to explore empty houses again.

'I'd be greatly obliged if you could. Otherwise I'll soon have to lie down here in the dark. Here's five pounds – that should cover the cost of all you can carry.'

'Right.' Alan cast a glance at the untidy bed. 'You cover yourself up and keep warm. I'll be back as soon as I can.'

'Thank you very much,' the man said. 'You are exceedingly kind.'

Actually, Alan thought he was, too, but just murmured: 'Nonsense, no trouble at all,' before walking towards the steps, carrying a leather shopping bag in one hand and an old rusty paraffin can in the other.

The greater part of four hours passed before Alan arrived back at the ruined house.

He ran down the steps and found the sick man sitting up in bed, his face lit by a smile of intense relief. 'And I thought you were not coming back! I should have known better.'

Alan frowned and put the heavy bag and paraffin can down on the floor. 'Of course I've come back! But it took me a long time to find that village and I lost my way coming back.'

The man shook his head in self-reproach.

'Sorry, I shouldn't have said that. And it must have been very hard work lugging that bag and can over the moors. What have you got?'

Alan began to remove tins of food from the leather bag.

'I spent most of your five pounds. There's tins of stewed steak, mixed vegetables, soups and some nourishing rice pudding. Now, where's your cooking stove?'

The man nodded in the direction of a dark corner. 'Over there. You'll find a saucepan and a few odds and ends of crockery.'

Alan found the oil stove – and a very smelly, decrepit piece of apparatus it was, too – and, after lighting it, heated some oxtail soup, which the sick man consumed with every sign of satisfaction.

'That's marvellous!' he said. 'I'm beginning to feel much better already.'

'Would you like some stewed steak now?' Alan asked.

The man shook his head. 'No, this will keep me going for a bit. Maybe I'll heat something up myself a little later on. But I must thank you for all your trouble. Not many lads of your age would have been so kind.'

'That's all right.' Alan began to back towards the steps. 'I'd better get back now or my parents will start worrying. Would you like me to pop in tomorrow?' For a while the man did not answer, then he said quietly: 'I don't think you should. No – definitely not. Go away and forget you ever saw me. That would be best.'

Alan wondered if the man had done something wrong and was hiding from the police. It might well be the reason why he was living in this awful place. But he did not look like a criminal, nor act like one. After all, he apparently went into Manville to do his shopping. So, just before he ran up the steps, Alan said:

'Don't worry – I won't tell anyone you're here. And I will come to see you again.'

Mr Ferrier brought Charlie Brinkley back from the Grape and Barleycorn, for he was determined to make friends with his nearest neighbours, even if they did live miles away. Charlie was a youngish man with a full red face, a mop of flaxen hair and a hearty, familiar manner which did not go down all that well with Mrs Ferrier.

He sank into a chair, accepted a glass of brown ale, winked at Alan, then directed a slightly bovine stare at the good lady.

'Must be rather lonely for you out here, mam. Not a sight or sign of another body for miles. Wouldn't suit my missus. Likes a bit of company, she does.'

'It takes all sorts to make a world,' Mrs Ferrier remarked coldly. 'It wouldn't do if we were all alike.'

Charlie emptied his glass, then held it out for replenishment. 'Ah, you're not wrong there, mam. Right nice drop of beer, this is.'

Mr Ferrier smiled amicably, rubbed his hands together and all but pleaded with his wife to like their guest.

'Charlie's in the way of being a sheep farmer,' he said heartily.

Mrs Ferrier was clearly not impressed. 'Really! How interesting.'

Charlie shook his head with mock modesty.

'I wouldn't go so far as to say that, mam. Maybe I've got a few hundred head out there on the moors. Got grazing rights, see. Not much money in sheep these days. Just enough to let me have a scrape of margarine on me dry crust and maybe a spoonful of jam on Sundays.'

'How distressing for you,' Mrs Ferrier commented.

Conversation lagged for a little while after that, until Mr Ferrier said desperately:

'Tell Ethel about that dog, Charlie. The one that's been killing your sheep.'

'Oh, ah! Must be a monster, mam. Skulking great brute. Do you know I've found six of my best rams with their throats torn out, over as many months?'

Mrs Ferrier grimaced and gave the impression that such information was not to her liking. But Charlie was not to be deterred from a subject that was clearly of great interest to him.

'Three were ripped to bits, mam. Never seen anything like it. Blood and wool everywhere, there was.'

Mrs Ferrier did not comment, but dabbed her lips with a lace handkerchief, and Alan knew she would speak most sternly to his father, once their guest had departed.

'But you did catch a glimpse of the beast, didn't you, Charlie?' Mr Ferrier prompted.

'Ah, that I did! One bright moonlit night last week, it were, and a body could see for miles. I was on top of Manstead Tor and I see'd this thing go prancing across the moors. Must have been two mile or more away, so there was no chance of me having a pot-shot at it with me old rabbit gun.'

He took a deep swig from his glass, then continued.

'But this is the bit which makes the chaps down at the Grape and Barleycorn curl up. Mind you, it's as true as I sit here. It stopped and stood up on two feet. May I be struck down if it didn't. Reared up on its hindlegs, and . . .'

'Howled, I dare say,' Mrs Ferrier interrupted. 'Howled at the moon.'

'No, mam. Begging your pardon for contradicting such a forthright lady as yourself – but it coughed. Sound travels on those moors when the wind is in the right direction, and I distinctly heard a barking cough. Like a chap who's got a nasty cold on his chest. Then it ran – still on two feet, mam – over Hangman's Ridge, and I didn't see it any more.'

Mrs Ferrier glanced at the clock and assumed an expression of great surprise.

'Good gracious! Is that the time? I never realised it was so late.'

Charlie, in no way put out by this broad hint, emptied his glass and stood up. 'Ah, I must be pushing on. The missus will think I'm up to something I shouldn't. But I'll get the varmint, never you fret, mam. Then everyone will laugh t'other side of their faces.'

'I'm sure we wish you all good fortune, Mr Brinkley,' Mrs Ferrier remarked, before crossing the room and opening the door. 'I do hope you get home safely.'

'That I will, mam. Unless me old boneshaker blows a gasket.'

Charlie Brinkley departed and Alan – without being told – went upstairs to bed. He had a lot to think about.

Three days later, Alan Ferrier once again paid a visit to the ruined High Burrow. He had intended never to go near the place again, but the memory of that poor sick man, lying all alone in a damp cellar, had haunted his dreams and spoilt his enjoyment of the perfect summer days. The man might have died – or be on the verge of death – all because a boy had been too frightened by a silly story to keep his promise.

So he now climbed over the low wall, walked very slowly across the neglected garden and entered the house. He called out:

'Excuse me . . . is it all right for me to come down?' Presently he heard the sound of a match being struck, then a voice that said:

'Yes, come on down, lad.'

Alan crept down the steps, not knowing what he was going to see, determined to turn and run should there be the slightest sign of anything alarming. But to his gratified surprise he found the man standing up and adjusting the flame of the oil-lamp.

He greeted the boy with a sad smile.

'I've been for a little walk and only just got back. I thought I told you to keep away.'

'I was worried about you,' Alan replied, relieved that his one-time patient looked so well – and normal. 'Are you. better?'

'It's very nice of you to be so concerned. Yes, I'm much better. There's no fear of my dying – not from a cold.'

Alan looked around the room. So far as he could see some effort had been made to tidy it up, for the floor had been swept, the bed stripped and the blankets folded into neat squares.

'What about your stores?' he asked. 'Do you want me to fetch you some more?'

'No, thank you. I'm well able to look after myself now. I cook my meals upstairs in one of the empty rooms.'

Alan took a deep breath – and braced himself to ask the question that had been partly responsible for the fear which had haunted him for three days.

'Why do you live in this awful place? You have plenty of money. I saw lots of banknotes when you opened that tin box.'

The man sighed and pushed him gently towards the flight of steps.

'Let's go up into the light of day and I'll try to explain.'

They went up into the devastated hall and out into the over-grown garden. The man led his young friend over to the low wall.

'Sit down, son, and listen very carefully. Once, I lived in this house with my parents. That was a long time ago and, believe it or

242

not, this was a very pleasant place then. My father farmed the entire expanse of this high ground, and although we were by no means rich, we were quite comfortably off. Then one day a stranger came to High Burrow.'

The man stopped and stared sadly out across the wild moors. Alan knew he must not speak, but had to wait for the story to be completed.

Presently the man continued.

'Ah, a stranger! A tall, dark man with haunted eyes. He was lost – or so he said – and my father invited him to spend a night here. One full-moonlit night. Never has anyone been so ill-paid for an act of kindness.'

He lapsed into silence again, and Alan prompted gently.

'What happened?'

'What happened indeed! The stranger had a rare disease. And during that one night I was . . . oh, most merciful God! . . . I was infected. I became as he was. He went away next morning, but I remained. Remained to see my parents die of grief and horror, my old home crumble slowly to the ruin you see now – and watch a hundred summers fade into autumn.'

'A hundred!' Alan gasped.

'Yes. Maybe more. For the rare disease has a strange side effect. I cannot grow old. Or – so far as I know – die a natural death. But I can't expect you to believe that.'

'Then . . .' Alan hesitated, then blurted out what he now knew to be the awful truth. 'Then . . . you must be a werewolf.'

The man jerked his head round and looked down at the boy with shocked surprise. 'You believe that! You can actually accept that I'm cursed with the mark of the pentagram! Indeed, must your generation be gifted with great knowledge!'

'I've seen lots of horror films,' Alan explained, 'and I always thought they were just fantasies. But a man called Charlie Brinkley saw what he thought was a large dog standing up on two feet – and it coughed as you did. So I put two and two together and . . . It must be awful to be a werewolf.'

The man nodded and recited the following words:

A man may be pure of heart,
And say his prayers at night,
But into a wolf he will turn,
When the moon is full and bright.

'You've never killed *people*, though – have you?' Alan asked.

The man frowned. 'No, of course not. Wolves don't unless they're starving and there's no wild life for them to hunt. But I appear to be rather partial to sheep. Disgusting, isn't it.'

Certainly, Alan thought that tearing sheep to pieces was not very nice, and he could only hope they had been killed first. However, he said gently:

'You can't help doing – what you do. But that man called Charlie Brinkley says he's going to shoot you. Doesn't he have to use a silver bullet?'

The man shook his head 'Shouldn't think so. An ordinary bullet can kill a werewolf – or at least injure him. Now, you have heard my story and know why you must not come here again.'

'But you only – well – turn into a wolf when there's a full moon,' Alan protested. 'There's no reason why I shouldn't visit you during the day.'

'I'm sure your parents wouldn't approve of you associating with a werewolf,' the man said sternly. 'I know I wouldn't if you were my son. So – thank you once again for your help and kindness. Now you *must* go.'

And without so much as another word, he got up and walked quickly back to the house. Presently, Alan climbed the low wall and wandered dejectedly down the hill and out across the moors.

The summer days slipped by, and the moon, from resembling a sliver of Edam cheese, began to assume the proportions of a ripe melon. Every evening Alan would peer up at the gradually increasing disc of bright light and try to imagine how his friend in the ruined house was feeling, knowing he must soon be transformed into a dreadful monster.

Then came the night when a full moon rode a cloudless sky

and Charlie Brinkley paid another visit to The Hermitage.

'That awful man has just parked his dreadful car in our drive,' Mrs Ferrier informed her husband. 'I saw him from the bedroom window. And I'm sure he's drunk. Ah, that must be him ringing the doorbell now. Tell him I've got a headache.'

Charlie was not drunk but very excited.

'Saw the brute again,' he gasped. 'Running across Black Heath. Had to come back for me gun – in fact two guns. Thought you'd like to come with me, old chap. You can take up a position on Manstead Tor, and with me patrolling Hangman's Ridge, one of us should be able to pot him.'

Mr Ferrier's eyes sparkled with excitement:

'Count me in. Hang on a second and I'll have a word with the wife, then I'll join you. Do we need my car?'

'No. Have to walk most of the way.'

Alan, who had stationed himself in the hall, did not hesitate. He slipped out of the back door and ran up the narrow path which led to the moors.

The wind, which in this wild place was like a wailing, never-resting ghost, tore at Alan's hair and seemed to be trying to hold him back with invisible arms. But he continued to trot forward, even though his labouring heart and rasping lungs warned him that the limit of endurance would soon be reached. He had no idea what would happen when – or should – he come face to face with a raging werewolf. There was only the overwhelming urge to warn his friend that two hunters would soon be on his track, each one armed with a loaded rifle.

Manstead Tor stood out against the moonlit sky, a gently sloping hill that flowed up from a sea of heather to a grass-covered crown. Opposite, and about a quarter of a mile away, was Hangman's Ridge, a long, high mound that, according to local tradition, had at one time been a place of execution.

Alan stopped running when he saw the sheep. They were bunched together on the lower slopes of the ridge, looking like a large, grey shadow. They stirred uneasily when the boy

245

approached them. Suddenly he knew what must be done.

The sheep were the only reason why the werewolf would come to this part of the moor. If he could drive them from the valley before his father and Charlie Brinkley arrived, then his friend might live to see another sunrise. He shouted, uprooted a clump of heather and waved it from side to side.

The sheep became a protesting, heaving mass that began to slowly move down into the valley as Alan raised his voice to a higher pitch. His was not an easy task, for the disturbed animals insisted on milling round in circles, and one or two would not budge at all, but stood still and stared at him with pathetic reproach.

He finally managed to get them all on the move and might well have succeeded in driving them from the valley, had not a sudden terrifying howl shrieked out from Hangman's Ridge. There was no controlling the sheep after that. They ran in every direction, they burrowed deep into the heather, bumped into each other and raced up and down the slopes. When Alan raised his eyes he all but turned and ran away himself.

Long afterwards, he decided that not one film producer had ever laid eyes on a werewolf, for the creature that was advancing towards him bore not the slightest resemblance to any of the monsters he had seen in the cinema.

The head was round, the ears large, hairy and tapering to sharp points. The face – which was narrow and sloped down to the slavering mouth – was covered with black, matted fur. But it was the eyes that made Alan wish he had stayed at home. They were sunken and bright red. Little pools of liquid fire that appeared to gleam with ferocious hate. The body was that of a deformed man. Bent shoulders, long arms that terminated in curved claws, the ghastly white skin sparsely covered by long strands of reddish hair. The creature still wore a torn shirt and a pair of stained grey trousers.

The werewolf ran forward, its claws brushing the ground, then stopped when it reached a point that was just a few feet from the terrified boy. The grotesque head went back, the jaws slowly parted to reveal sharp, pointed teeth, then a low growl rose to a

246

full-throated roar.

Alan screamed.

'No . . . no . . . I'm your friend! Don't you know me?'

The roar died away, and the monster became still, a dark, menacing figure that gave the impression it might explode into lethal activity at any moment. Then it shuffled forward, lowered its head – and sniffed. Alan shuddered when the long snout travelled up his left arm, across his chest and finally muzzled his right ear. Then the werewolf whined.

A dog that wishes to be patted, fed or taken for a walk, might have made some such sound. It could also have come from any unhappy creature, who, through no fault of its own, has been cursed with the stigma of a monster. Alan's fear drained away and was replaced by a warm flood of pity. His friend – the gentle, kindly man with the sad eyes – was imprisoned in that hideous form, pleading for understanding – forgiveness – a morsel of affection.

Alan was about to lay his hand on that unlovely head – when there came the sound of a rifle shot. A single, muffled report that came from the ridge. The werewolf jerked upright, gave one terrible cry of despair, then went bounding across the valley and disappeared behind Manstead Tor.

Alan was crying when Charlie Brinkley and Mr Ferrier reached him. His father put an arm round his shoulders and said:

'Thank God you're all right, son. When I saw that awful creature so close to you . . .'

'I got him!' Charlie Brinkley interrupted, his voice trembling with excitement. 'Right between the shoulders. He won't last long. Biggest dog I ever saw . . . and did you see? It stood up on its hindlegs! You'll tell those nincompoops down in the Grape and Barleycorn, won't you? It stood upright!'

'I think,' Mr Ferrier said, leading his young son away, 'the least we say about this night's work the better. I would rather not believe what I saw.'

But Alan could only repeat over and over again: 'He couldn't help being a werewolf. He wouldn't have harmed me.'

247

*

It was two days before Alan was allowed to go out on his own, for the doctor said he was suffering from shock and needed time to recover.

When he reached High Burrow he found it sleeping under a benign sky, with moths fluttering among the harebells in the overgrown garden and the wind breathing through the grass, and knew that tranquillity had returned to this once happy homestead.

He walked slowly down the stone steps and directed the beam of his torch round the desolate cellar. The man who had been a werewolf lay on the bed. He was dead – but on his face was the most beautiful smile that Alan had ever seen.

Presently he covered the body with a blanket, then remounted the steps.

He never went back.

The Gale-Wuggle

JUBILEE TOWER, AS ONE might expect, was a very tall building indeed.

Way down at ground level was a supermarket, a television hire showroom, several shops and a cinema. The next three floors housed offices of various kinds, then level upon level of flats right up to the fortieth floor. But perched on top of this human ant-hill of steel and concrete was a penthouse. Built on the roof, it was so high up, Gerald's father said he wouldn't be surprised if, come winter, they had snow on their beards.

Gerald thought this to be extremely unlikely, as neither he nor his father – and most certainly not his mother – had a beard, but he was quite prepared to see an abominable snowman wending its way between the cement tubs of flowering plants. Of course, his sister, who was all of nine years old and considered to be very advanced for her age, said this was complete nonsense, as an abominable snowman would never be allowed on the lift, and, in any case, such a creature – if it existed at all – lived far away on top of mountains that were much higher than Jubilee Tower.

Gerald could do no more than bow before such superior knowledge, but he thought that having moved up into such an elevated position, there ought to be some unusual manifestations. True that on a fine day, when his father carried him out on to that part of the roof which did duty as a garden, and he was able to peer down over the parapet, people did rather resemble ants that were looking for somewhere to hide, but he lacked the strength to stand upright for any length of time to have a really good look.

As the doctor must be a man of great learning, he decided to ask his opinion once the weekly examination was completed.

'Doctor, this is a very high building, isn't it?' Doctor Canfield nodded his grey head.

'It certainly is, Gerald. Way up above the noise. You are very lucky.'

'But shouldn't I – well – see things up here -- that can't be seen down below?'

The doctor pulled the bedclothes back into position, then ruffled his hair. 'Depends on what you want to see. And if you have the right kind of eyes.'

'Right kind of eyes?'

'Yes. Long ago, before even I was born, my father lived in the country. He was about your age at the time. And the old folk said a colony of elves lived in a nearby wood, but the no-nonsense people just laughed and talked about superstition and fairy tales – you know the kind of thing?'

Gerald nodded. 'But didn't anyone go into the woods and look for the elves?'

The doctor laughed softly. Wouldn't have done any good if they had. They could have searched those woods from sunrise to sunset and not a solitary elf would they have seen. Hadn't got the right kind of eyes, you see.'

'But your father had!' Gerald exclaimed.

'Indeed he had. Spotted their village at first glance. Told me there were three rows of little cottages, no bigger than flowerpots, nestling down between the roots of an oak tree.'

Gerald pondered on this most remarkable story for some time, then he asked shyly: 'Do you suppose I have the right kind of eyes?'

'I wouldn't be at all surprised. Let's have a look.'

Doctor Canfield put on a large pair of spectacles, then peered gravely into Gerald's very wide-open eyes.

'Um. Blue – that's a hopeful sign – and round. Long lashes too.

Ah! What have we here? A tiny fleck in each corner! That's it. You've definitely got seeing eyes.'

Gerald said: 'Gosh!' and felt very superior to his wretched sister, even if she did know where abominable snowmen lived. The doctor removed his spectacles and put them away in a leather case.

'All those eyes need is practice. Keep 'em wide open and heaven's above knows what they'll see.'

Then Gerald's mother came into the bedroom, and the doctor rose rather quickly from his chair and picked up his black bag.

'Gerald and I have been chatting away and quite forgot the time, Mrs Grantworthy.'

Gerald's mother creased her face into a bright smile, but he could see the anxious look in her eyes that was rarely absent these days. She said: 'How nice. And he's much, much, better, isn't he, doctor?'

'Good heavens, I'll say he is! Be running up and down those confounded stairs in no time.'

Then both he and Mrs Grantworthy left the room, and Gerald heard them speaking softly in the hall and once was able to understand three words: 'There's always hope.'

He wondered why Doctor Canfield considered it necessary to reassure his mother as to the continued existence of hope, and if it had anything to do with the anxious look in her eyes and the fact that she sometimes cried. But he had long ago given up trying to understand adults and now gave his full consideration to the subject of 'seeing eyes'.

The large French windows overlooked the roof, and it was obviously there that any strange manifestation would take place. From his bed he could see the cement tubs in which flowering plants politely bowed their colourful heads to the prevailing breeze; and one of Marcia's dolls, that was looking rather the worse for wear after spending a rainy night on the parapet. But there was not the slightest sign of an elf.

After some thought, Gerald decided that it was unlikely that these minute people would take up residence on a cement roof.

251

They belonged to dense woods and tall grass and would be very unhappy in these artificial surroundings. No, he must train his special eyes to see something that would be – like this abominable snowman – at home on a mountain top – or in the sky.

Gerald began to watch the sky.

'Your eyes are no different to anyone else's,' Marcia protested. 'And certainly not as good as mine.'

'But I tell you, Doctor Canfield says I have special eyes,' Gerald insisted. 'Like his father, who could see elves.'

Marcia smiled with gentle scorn. 'That proves he was just making it up. Everybody knows that there are no such things as elves.'

Gerald nodded with grave satisfaction. 'That's what all no-nonsense people say. You couldn't see an elf even if you tried ever so hard.'

'Oh, yes, I could.'

Mrs Grantworthy, hearing the raised voices, came into the room and frowned at her young daughter. 'You're not to argue with your brother. You know he's not very strong and mustn't be excited.'

'But he says he has special eyes – and he hasn't.'

'Go and put your hat and coat on. Your father is waiting to drive you to school.'

Marcia ran cheerfully from the room, for like all no-nonsense people, she soon forgot a disagreement and was now looking forward to the coming day. Mrs Grantworthy smoothed Gerald's hair from his forehead and said: 'You mustn't take any notice of what your sister says. She likes to tease you.'

Gerald smiled complacently. 'I don't. May I go out on to the roof?'

She looked enquiringly out of the window.

'It's a bit windy, dear. You mustn't catch cold.'

'I won't. Not if I wear my thick dressing-gown. May I – please?'

Eventually Mrs Grantworthy gave way to his pleading – she always did – and helped him out on to the roof and into a long garden chair. There he lay back and stared up at the cloud-dappled sky. There was no manner of doubt whatsoever – he was learning to see.

Already he had come to understand that small flying objects were not always birds. If a person, gifted with the right kind of eyes, watched them through a fringe of long lashes, and concentrated really hard, then – more often that not – there was a flight of little old women gliding through the air. So far as Gerald could see, they wore tiny top hats and black cloaks that not only covered their entire bodies, but trailed out behind and on each side, so as to create the impression that these aerial creatures were equipped with triangular wings.

Sometimes they made a strange wailing sound, and Gerald would only smile when his father said: 'Those crows are making an awful din,' for he knew it was no use trying to explain to those who could not see. Even the doctor, on being told of the successful development of Gerald's special sight, only frowned and took his temperature.

On this particular morning, the sky resembled a bad-tempered face that might shed rain-tears at any moment, and the clouds kept surging over and under each other, so that Gerald had grave doubts if the airborne old ladies would venture out in such precarious weather. Although the wind was rising and tried to turn his hair into a gold-tinted nest, it was quite warm and did not make him cough once.

His mother called from the open window. 'Don't you think you should come in, dear? I have to go out for a while and I don't want you to be caught in a rain-storm.'

'No, I'll be all right,' he assured her. 'If it rains I can go indoors. I'm much stronger today.'

'Well – if you say so. I won't be long.'

Gerald lay back and watched the clouds through narrowed eyes. The wind, with the perversity of its kind, was tormenting them. They writhed, seethed, built up into great fat billows, then went tumbling across the heavens, as though trying to outrun this terrible, wailing monster.

Then Gerald saw it – *that* which can only be seen by special eyes, which is no reason to suppose it does not exist. It came sailing out of a veritable sea of boiling clouds; roughly shaped like a bull with no legs, a fleecy, white body that was dappled in places with stormy black, and with a gleaming grey streak running down the back. The face – and Gerald could clearly see every feature – was made up of jutting brows, a round snout that alternated between bright pink to vivid red, most innocent-looking blue eyes, and an extremely broad mouth. Taken by and large, he decided it really was a most beautiful creature and much more interesting than airborne little old ladies.

It glided along just under the roof of clouds, turning its head slowly from one side to another, then came to a stop above a tall building which had a flag fluttering from a green mast. There it floated, looking down with bright blue eyes upon the sprawling city. Then, suddenly, it seemed to take an exceedingly deep breath, for its mouth opened and some of the nearest clouds were sucked in. The head grew larger by the second, then the body expanded until it resembled a gigantic balloon, and Gerald put shaking hands over his ears, as he fully expected to hear a mighty explosion.

Then – the air-monster blew.

A seemingly unending plume of cloud poured out of the gaping mouth, and the most terrible wind that Gerald had ever felt or heard went roaring over the rooftops, tore the flag from its mast, rushed in through one open window and played havoc with a lot of papers, then descended to street level, where it doubtlessly lifted hats and skirts without so much as a by your leave.

But Gerald – who expected to have his chair overturned at any moment could only watch the creature who was responsible for all this commotion. As it blew, the snout grew longer, the body shrank, and the eyes took on the appearance of large blue saucers. Then, having regained its original size, it glided over the street and – to Gerald's great alarm – moved to a position immediately above Jubilee Tower.

Now he could look up at the underside of the monster, which resembled an odd-shaped cloud, and gave a loud cry of alarm when he realised that it was about to sink down and completely engulf him. The wind snatched his cry and carried it up into the tumultous heavens – and presumably into the ears of the sky-monster as well, for it bent its head and stared down at him with more than ordinary interest.

Suddenly the wind sank and became nothing more than an innocent summer breeze, which, in some strange way, slowly emerged into a sighing whisper.

'You . . . can . . . see . . . me?'

For some time Gerald was quite unable to answer this simple question, and, in fact, was not at all sure if the whispered words were not the result of his excited imagination. But when the creature continued to stare at him and appeared to be waiting for an answer, he did manage to produce a hesitant: 'Y-yes.'

The breeze sighed again. 'You . . . are . . . ill?'

At that moment, Mrs Grantworthy came running from the open French windows, still dressed in her outdoor clothes and clearly in a state of intense agitation. She put an arm round Gerald's shoulders and all but lifted him from the chair.

'Oh, that dreadful wind! I got back as soon as I could. Are you all right?'

'Yes, but . . .'

'Good heavens, you look so pale! Back to bed at once and I'll ring Doctor Canfield.'

He was half carried, part led into his bedroom, but just managed to glance back over one shoulder and catch a glimpse of the sky-monster, which was gliding away to the west. Once in bed, Mrs Grantworthy turned on the electric blanket, then walked quickly to the telephone and dialled a number. Gerald listened to her begging Doctor Canfield to come round at once, although his thoughts were far away, following the trail of an awesome creature that rode on the back of the north wind.

His mother sank down on to a chair and watched him with anxious eyes.

'I should never have left you out there. Heavens above, you might have been blown off the roof?'

255

'But the sky-monster stopped the wind when it knew I was ill.'

This statement, far from reassuring Mrs Grantworthy, made her clap hand to mouth and stare at him with wide-eyed horror.

'You've got a fever! Oh, why doesn't Doctor Canfield come?'

Although Gerald had never been so clear of mind, he did feel very weak. But it was a rather pleasant sensation, as though his body had become sun-warmed mist and he might float away on a gentle breeze at any moment. Then the doorbell rang, and his mother said: 'Oh, thank goodness, there he is!' before running into the hall and returning with Doctor Canfield.

The doctor put his black bag down on the table and assumed an expression of mock horror.

'What's all this then? Caught out in the freak gale, were we? My word, it was a whistler. Now, let's have a look at you.'

He listened to Gerald's heartbeat through a stethoscope – which was extremely cold – then laid a cool hand on his forehead.

'No more trips out on the roof for a while, my lad.'

Gerald tugged at the doctor's sleeve and waited until the tired face was bent over him. 'I saw a big thing – like a bull with no legs – in the sky, and it blew so hard there was a gale.'

Doctor Canfield straightened up and frowned thoughtfully.

'Did you now! That's strange.'

Mrs Grantworthy shook her head in mock reproof. 'Your imagination, Gerald! You mustn't take any notice, Doctor.'

The doctor waved his hand impatiently. 'No, wait a minute. My father told me an old folk tale which was about a strange sky-monster that looked like a bull with no legs. I gather he got it from the old woman who looked after him and his twin brother. It was called – it's on the tip of my tongue – the . . . the Gale-Wuggle. That's it – the Gale-Wuggle. Ever heard that name before, Gerald?'

Gerald shook his head. 'No. Never. But I really did see it. And it spoke to me. A kind of whisper. Sort of sigh-talking.'

'Has he got a fever?' Mrs Grantworthy asked.

'Maybe a slight one – which might account for monsters in the sky. But – a Gale-Wuggle! Well – keep him warm, Mrs Grantworthy. I'll pop in again tomorrow.'

When his mother conducted Doctor Canfield to the door, Gerald closed his eyes and tried to imagine where the Gale-Wuggle was now. It must be tired after all that blowing and would probably have to curl up on a fleecy cloud and sleep for several days.

Presently, Gerald too fell asleep and dreamed he was riding on the Gale-Wuggle's back, through a blue meadow, which shimmered under a rainbow-coloured sky.

Three days later the weather became hot and sunny, and the doctor said Gerald could get out of bed, so long as he did not walk about too much. So he sat in his garden chair and looked up with almost breathless expectancy, but, of course, there was no wind worth mentioning, or even the smallest cloud, and the prospect of the Gale-Wuggle turning up in a clear sky was very remote. But the airborne old ladies were out in force; entire droves flew in arrow-head formations and appeared to be in a hurry to get somewhere. Others were diving, flying round in circles, and Gerald could not dismiss the thought that they were – well – sort of young old ladies. Some chased each other and made shrill wailing sounds that were not dissimilar to a whistling kettle demanding attention.

Then one dived down to roof-level and came gliding in Gerald's direction, making him gasp when it settled on the parapet and stared at him with tiny, red eyes. He had never seen such an ugly creature before. At close view it became apparent that the top hat and cloak were part of the minute monster – an extension of its body – and could never be removed. The face was dead white, surrounded by a mane of matted grey hair, and the nose resembled a hooked, yellow beak that almost touched the jutting chin. Then a tiny claw came out and pointed a shaking forefinger at Gerald, while the creature emitted a sound that was not far removed from a cackling laugh.

Despite the blazing sun and the stifling heat, Gerald shivered and would have got up and run into the penthouse, had he found the strength to do so. But he could only sit in his chair and hope the nasty little thing would fly away. But it suddenly raised its voice to a shrill shriek, and several more of the airborne little old ladies swooped down and settled on the parapet. They all sat in a long line and watched him with red, unblinking eyes, the black cloaks clinging to their bent little bodies like folded wings.

Such a spectacle was too much for Gerald, particularly as there was no indication as to what these creatures intended to do next, so he called out: 'Help me! Help me!' – not that he really expected anyone to come to his assistance, as Mrs Grantworthy was out shopping. Then suddenly – literally out of a clear sky – came a mighty clap of thunder, followed by a bellowing roar that might have been caused by a passing gale. Instantly there was a united chorus of squawks, agitated flapping of wings, and the entire hideous pack rose up from the parapet and soon became black specks that disappeared behind the distant power station.

After due consideration and careful examination of the now empty sky, Gerald called out: 'Thank you, Gale-Wuggle,' and felt very happy when a gentle breeze caressed his hair.

Doctor Canfield nodded thoughtfully. 'Little airborne old ladies, you say! 'Pon my soul! And dressed in cloaks and top hats! Goodness gracious! They could be banshees.'

'But the Gale-Wuggle drove them away,' Gerald pointed out. 'Does that mean it likes me?'

The doctor slipped his stethoscope into a side pocket and shrugged. 'It would appear so. Mind you, I've always understood that a Gale-Wuggle made people disappear. Sort of came down on top of 'em. But I suppose it has likes and dislikes and could well have taken a fancy to you.'

Mrs Grantworthy was clearly not at all happy with this conversation and hastened to register an objection. 'Don't you think that Gerald should be discouraged in these fanciful notions, Doctor? I'm sure they can't be good for him.'

'Imagination is a good friend, so long as it provides a happy ending,' the doctor retorted. 'And Gerald's Gale-Wuggle certainly did that. But it is extraordinary how he manages to describe these creatures, when, so far as I can understand, he has never read or heard about them. I mean to say, there isn't one person in a hundred thousand who even knows about a Gale-Wuggle.'

'I still think he should read a nice book,' Mrs Grantworthy insisted. 'It really is most disturbing to hear him talking about horrible things that float in the sky, and awful little old ladies who wear top hats.'

But Gerald could not wait for the next windy day, even though his special eyes had by now become so keen he was able to see much that had been hidden from him up to now. There were, for example, the tiny people who came out from the wainscotting and played hide-and-seek in the hearthrug. And the long, almost transparent, snakelike thing, that undulated through the air and sometimes draped itself round the ceiling lamp. But he was fast getting used to this kind of thing and nothing – not even the disembodied head that rose up from the floor and disappeared through the ceiling – could rival the great Gale-Wuggle that rode in on the north wind.

So the long, hot, summer days slid out, one after the other, from the great storehouse of time, and Gerald grew a little stronger and was able to stand up and look down over the para-pet. Toy cars continued to race along a narrow grey ribbon of road, and ant-like people scurried here and there, not one of whom knew or cared about the existence of a Gale-Wuggle. And the dazzling blue sky was like a vast steel dome that permitted only the stray passing bird, or a roaring jet plane to disturb its serenity.

Then one day Mr Grantworthy – after a long talk with Doctor Canfield – came into Gerald's bedroom and said: 'Seaside for you, my lad. Sea air will set you up in no time.'

Normally Gerald would have been very excited at this prospect, but now he felt a strange reluctance to leave his rooftop home and forego the weekly visits of Doctor Canfield, who was the only person he could confide in. Also, would the Gale-Wuggle know where he had gone? But there was no argument that would prevail against his parents – and Marcia's – enthusiasm. Mrs Grantworthy spoke of cool sea breezes, Mr Grantworthy of

259

wonderful castles that could be built of sand, and Marcia went into a state of disgusting rapture when she pondered on the delights of wearing a straw hat and bathing her feet in salt water.

Cases were packed, milk and newspapers cancelled for two weeks, electricity switched off at the main, then Gerald was helped into the lift by his father and finally made comfortable on the back seat of the family car. Marcia sat in the far corner and loudly proclaimed her impatience when they were held up in a traffic jam, their father shouted at several motorists who refused to allow him to overtake, and Mrs Grantworthy expressed grave concern that so many drivers had not bothered to learn the highway code. All in all, it was a fairly normal journey.

When they arrived at Mrs Brown's Guest House, that good lady welcomed them on the doorway and said how nice it was to see them again and how well Gerald was looking – under the circumstances. He was installed in a front bedroom, which commanded a fine view of the sea, and at once developed a keen interest in the scene laid out before him. The beach was packed with holiday-makers. Elderly gentlemen sat in deck chairs with white handkerchiefs draped over their peeling faces; young ladies in bikinis lay roasting on the golden sand; and children screamed with delight when small, well-behaved waves chased them back to the shore. But it was the *other* beings that attracted Gerald's special sight.

Little grey and white creatures, that might have been mistaken for seagulls were it not for their tiny old-man heads, flew round and round and gave out mournful cries, that Gerald gradually translated into two drawn-out words.

'We're . . . lost . . .'

He wished Doctor Canfield had been present, for that clever person would doubtlessly have known what these creatures were. But his mother may have unwittingly revealed the truth when, at dinner that night, she said plaintively: 'What an awful noise those seagulls make. Really, they sound like lost souls.'

Gerald wondered how souls became lost and if they would ever find themselves again. But next day, when he was taken down to the beach and seated in a deck chair, it became apparent that they were not the only unusual phenomenon that existed in the land of sea and sunshine.

Sometimes a faint mist would rise up from the ocean and become a bright oval shape that took on all the colours of the rainbow. Then the lost souls – if that was what they were – tried to fly into the oval; became a mass of flapping wings and screaming faces, looking rather like a rush-hour crowd, all attempting to board a train at once.

And those that got in, never came out. After a short while, the oval shape dissolved back into mist, which sank into the sea, and the lost souls which had not made a successful entry, wailed their grief and flew round in ever-increasing circles, as though hoping it would reappear from a different place. But Gerald never saw it more than once a day.

Then clouds rolled a thick, grey blanket over the sun, and a cold wind transformed the gentle waves into roaring, foam-tipped monsters, that pounded the beach and tried to leap up on to the pier. Rain drove the erstwhile sunbathers into boarding house or hotel, and Mrs Brown was heard to remark: 'When it rains by the sea – it rains.'

Gerald's newly acquired strength waned with the dying summer, and he lay in bed and listened to the wailing wind, which sometimes was blended with the despairing cry of lost souls. That was not the only sound he heard. During the long night hours, when either his father or mother kept watch beside his bed, he would shiver when a banshee howled from just beyond his curtained window and murmur: 'Why doesn't the Gale-Wuggle come?'

His father, not believing, but wishing to comfort, said gently: 'It will come, son. Have no fear it will come.'

But would it find him here, in this house which was only two storeys high? Should one not be up on the roof of the world when the Gale-Wuggle sailed the stormy skies? 'Then he remembered that day when the banshees had perched on the parapet and they had been frightened away by the clap of thunder and the sudden roar of the wind. He had sent out an appeal for help, and the Gale-Wuggle must have heard, even though there wasn't a cloud in the sky. Suppose he tried again? Only not aloud, lest his mother become even more anxious, and his father send for the strange doctor, who was undoubtedly a no-nonsense person.

So Gerald sent out a silent message. He *thought*: 'Gale-Wuggle, I am very ill. Please come . . . please come,' and slipped into a dreamless sleep immediately afterwards.

He was awakened by the howling wind and lay quite still, trying to remember where he was. Then it all came back. He was in Mrs Brown's Guest House and he was ill, which was not unusual, only now he was much worse than ever before. He turned his head. Mrs Grantworthy was asleep in her chair. Head lowered, eyes closed, she was breathing heavily, worn out by three nights of continuous watching. Gerald supposed his father must be resting in the next room.

Then he heard the wind sink down to a loud whisper. 'Come . . . out . . . out . . .'

But how could he go out, when he scarcely had the strength to raise his head? He whispered: 'I can't. Honestly, I can't.'

The wind rose a little, and the whisper was transformed into an impatient growl.

'You . . . can . . . can . . .'

Gerald eased back the bedclothes and swung one leg down to the floor. Then he rested, taking deep breaths and watching his mother with great anxiety, for it was so important that she did not wake up. When he stood up, the room seemed to wobble from side to side, and the floor heaved in a most alarming fashion. Taking the first step was a perilous adventure, and the next a well-planned excercise. Then he reached the door where there was some difficulty, for he was obliged to cling to the doorpost with one hand, while turning the handle with the other.

Fortunately Mrs Brown left a light burning on the landing and in the hall, so Gerald could see quite clearly, as he clung to the banisters and went downstairs, one step at a time. Once down in the hall, he had to rest again and try to control his gasping breath and thumping heart, before tackling the double-bolted front door.

Easing each bolt from its socket was an awful job. They groaned so loudly, Gerald fully expected Mrs Brown to appear at any moment and demand to know what he was doing; and it was fully five minutes before he could turn the big brass handle and pull the door inwards. Then he staggered out into the wind-haunted night and held on to one of the pillars which supported the porch.

After a while he looked up.

The Gale-Wuggle was a scant three metres above the ground; the great bull-shaped mass a silhouette against the cloud-embattled moon, the head bent forward and the blue, luminous eyes looking downwards. Gerald knew they were watching him. The wind became a moaning sigh.

'Come . . . e . . . e . . . e . . . e . . .'

The Gale-Wuggle turned and glided towards the sea, and Gerald realised he must follow, even if it meant crawling across the road and on to the beach. But as he stepped down on to the pavement, it seemed as if the wind had formed a pair of strong arms that held him upright and, at the same time, propelled him forward. As Gerald lurched across the road, he heard a beautiful voice, that was sometimes just over his head, but at others was far away, singing the following words:

> It roams over land, air and sea.
> 'Tis whatever you wish it to be.
> To the evil its bad:
> To the mournful it's sad
> But those in distress
> Will find immediate redress,
> When they call upon the Gale-Wuggle.

Then he was lying on soft sand, and the night was suddenly without sound, save for the gentle murmur of tumbling waves that were rocking the sea to sleep. The moon came out from behind a cloud and turned the Gale-Wuggle into a glorious, silver-trimmed creature that had been created from the fabric of dreams, but would always be seen by those who have not been tainted by no-nonsense, I-don't-believe-it, it-stands-to-reason and other despicable terms. The large face looked down on Gerald and never before had he seen such an expression of compassion and love.

Slowly the gleaming body came lower – and lower – and Gerald was not in the least afraid, knowing that far from harming him, the Gale-Wuggle had the kindest intentions. Gradually he was enveloped in a warm mist, that seemed to seep into his lungs, pour along his bloodstream, do something wonderful to his liver and kidneys, and finally send him into a deep, health-giving sleep.

'An absolute miracle,' Mr Grantworthy exclaimed for the seventh time. 'There's no other word for it.'

'And I thought he was dead,' Mrs Grantworthy said, wiping her eyes on a lace handkerchief. 'Lying out there so still. And when I found his bed empty . . .'

'Never mind,' Mr Grantworthy consoled her. 'All's well that ends well.'

'Of course,' the strange doctor looked superciliously down his nose, 'these so-called miraculous cures always have a scientific explanation if one cares to investigate.'

Gerald had just finished eating an enormous breakfast and was looking forward to an entire day on the beach, where he would outrun, outswim and out-everything-else that little wretch Marcia. But it was necessary to at least try and convince these well-meaning, but so stupid adults of what really happened.

'It was the Gale-Wuggle. I called it last night and it made me go outside, then it came down on top of me and . . .'

'What a wonderful imagination,' Mr Grantworthy rudely interrupted. 'Takes after me, I shouldn't wonder.'

The strange, no-nonsense doctor nodded. 'Utter rot, of course, but quite amusing. Shouldn't be surprised if he becomes one of those writer chaps when he grows up.'

'But it's all true,' Gerald insisted. 'Please believe me.'

'Oh, look, there's a bright colour in his cheeks,' Mrs Grantworthy cried. 'Oh dear, I do believe I'm going to faint.'

She did – for the third time that morning. Gerald gave up. What was the use? None were so blind as those who had no eyes. He could have told the doctor about the tiny banshee that sat on his left shoulder, but this enlightening – if not encouraging – information would not have been received with the gravity it deserved. It would also be a waste of time to mention that a veritable army of tiny, transparent things was swarming over the bedside cabinet and trying to pull the lamp over.

'When I grow up,' he told himself, 'I will become a 'writer chap' and tell everyone about the Gale-Wuggle.'

And he did.

Afterword

Time Travel and Me

THE RUSSIANS HAVE JUST published a soul-shaking report that, in effect, states that the age of time travel is not so far distant. One rather gathers that if a man were shot into space at a speed above 180,000 miles per hour, and cruised at that speed for approximately seven days, when he landed again on Earth something like 560 years would have passed during his absence.

This is ancient history to the serious student of science fiction. Ever since H.G. Wells wrote *The Time Machine*, science phantasy writers have belaboured Professor Einstein's theory of relativity. I remember as a child reading such phrases as 'space-time continuum', and although I had but the slightest idea as to its meaning, I was suitably thrilled with the implied prospect.

A leading article in a national newspaper, commenting on the Russian announcement, expressed doubt that a volunteer would be found to take part in the experiment. The writer maintained that a twentieth-century man would be an outcast if marooned in the twenty-sixth century; within a week he would go mad.

I cannot agree. I believe he would have a wonderful time. In fact, if a volunteer is needed, I offer my services here and now. There are, however, one or two sensible precautions I would wish to be taken.

First, I insist a notice be served on the twenty-sixth century that I am on my way. I would suggest that a metal plaque be suitably engraved. Something like:

R. Chetwynd-Hayes. Launched 19—, expected arrival 26—. Feed three times a day on – then a carefully thought out diet – with a generous ration of pink gins between meals.

The plaque must be encased in a lead-lined casket and entrusted to the British Museum, with instructions to be opened around 2600.

Next, I would arrange my personal baggage:
1. To be on the safe side, I'll take along Mrs Beeton's cookery book. I understand there is a great danger that our descendants will exist on a weekly consumption of concentrated vitamins, and this kind of treatment to a person of my delicate, if healthy, appetite would be fatal.
2. Plenty of warm underclothes. I've got a nasty feeling they will be a pretty tough crowd six hundred years from now. I mean with all that space travel, and nudists becoming more popular every year.
3. A few hundred packets of throat pastilles. My tonsils are not all they should be, and if on my arrival I find that no one has caught a cold for two hundred years, it is more than likely that a down-to-earth sore throat will be beyond a joke.
4. *Items of historical interest.* I consider this idea to be little short of genius.
    (a) A genuine 1939 civilian gas mask. Even at this early date there are very few about. By 2600 and something, it should be a relic beyond price.
    (b) A cigar butt, tossed aside by Sir Winston Churchill. Always supposing I can lay hands on one.

(c) A button from Liberace's most fabulous suit.

(d) A ticket from a weighing machine on Margate pier, with a condensed version of my horoscope printed on the back.

5. A hot water bottle.

6. A goodly supply of cigarettes, and a few tobacco plants – just in case.

7. A pin-up picture of Bridget Bardot. No particular reason, except I would like to have her along.

8. My black tom cat. A feline ambassador from today to next week. He is not a very respectable animal. In fact he is rather a delinquent, but has a kind of natural dignity. In any case, he would refuse to be left behind.

9. Hundreds of tins of cat food.

10. Me.

I, of course, would be the most valued relic of all. A live, honest-to-goodness, twentieth-century barbarian. A thing from the dark ages. Thousands of twenty-sixth century super-civilized citizens would pay good money (always supposing they still use the stuff) to see me eat my savage fodder, shave the gross stubble from my bestial cheeks, and gaze in awe as I perform my early morning serenade whilst gargling my erring tonsils with Glycerine of Thymol.

Once a week I would gratify my now-adoring public by taking a bath. And to the select few, the intellectuals, I would confirm their worst suspicions of our age and render my raucous, but spirited version of 'Rock Around the Clock', accompanied by a few steps of my rather terrifying interpretation of the cha-cha.

By far and large, and all things being equal, I am sure I would be a worthy envoy from now to the future. I am fully aware that the chances are that, instead of finding an advanced form of civilization, I shall land my spaceship on a heap of atomic-infested rubble. But I have decided to take the risk.

So, gentlemen of Harwell – Cape Canaveral – what about it?

Footnote: On reflection – I don't insist, of course, but if you could think of some way I could come back – just in case – I'll be grateful.

R. Chetwynd-Hayes
Richmond, Surrey.